THE
QUARRY
WOOD

Anna (Nan) Shepherd was born in 1893 and died in 1981. Closely attached to Aberdeen and her native Deeside, she graduated from her home university in 1915 and for the next forty-one years worked as a lecturer in English. An enthusiastic gardener and hill-walker, she made many visits to the Cairngorms with students and friends. She also travelled further afield – to Norway, France, Italy, Greece and South Africa – but always returned to the house where she was raised and where she lived almost all of her adult life, in the village of West Cults, three miles from Aberdeen on North Deeside. Shepherd published just three novels, a single collection of poetry, and *The Living Mountain*, her masterpiece of nature writing, in her lifetime, but is remembered as one of the major authors of modern classic Scottish literature. To honour her legacy, in 2016, Nan Shepherd's face was added to the Royal Bank of Scotland five-pound note.

Also by Nan Shepherd

The Living Mountain

The Weatherhouse

A Pass in the Grampians

In the Cairngorms

THE
QUARRY
WOOD

NAN
SHEPHERD

Introduced by Roderick Watson

CANONGATE

For my Mother

This Canons edition published in 2018 by Canongate Books

First published in Great Britain in 1928 by Constable and Co. Ltd
First published in 1987 by Canongate Books Ltd,
14 High Street, Edinburgh EH1 1TE

canongate.co.uk

1

British Library Cataloguing-in-Publication Data
A catalogue record for this book is available on
request from the British Library

ISBN 978 1 78689 162 4

Typeset by Alan Sutton Publishing Ltd, Gloucester

Printed and bound in Great Britain by Clays Ltd, St Ives plc.

Contents

Introduction

Nan Shepherd once said that she didn't really like writing prose fiction and that she only wrote 'when I feel that there's something that simply must be written'. What *had* to be written amounted to three remarkable novels which appeared in the years between 1928 and 1933. These books, *The Quarry Wood*, *The Weatherhouse*, and *A Pass in the Grampians*, were published on both sides of the Atlantic to immediate critical acclaim. The *Times Literary Supplement* found 'a richness of expression astonishing in a first novel', while the *New York Times* Book Review commented on the 'vivid imagery' in her last book, '. . . sometimes as compact and condensed as poetry'. Miss Shepherd continued to write articles and poems for the rest of her long life, but these novels, produced in the five years before her fortieth birthday, mark a creative mastery which seems to have been attained, fulfilled, and then just as suddenly concluded. They have been most unfairly forgotten.

In her later years, Nan Shepherd edited the *Aberdeen University Review*, and I first came across her work with an essay she had written for it in 1938, on MacDiarmid's later poetry. This piece showed a fine insight into the poet's linguistic experiments at a time when many readers were merely puzzled or exasperated by them. It was too many years before I discovered that Nan Shepherd had also produced fiction of the first quality, or that her novels deserve a key place in that line which runs from *The House with the Green Shutters* to *A Scots Quair* and beyond.

Indeed, reading *The Quarry Wood* is to read what might have happened to Chris Guthrie, had she decided to go to university after all, for Martha Ironside makes the same difficult journey towards intellectual and emotional maturity at a time when such space was seldom freely given to women. An even greater gain, perhaps, is the unforced way in which Matty manages to bridge what Chris Guthrie felt to be the division between her 'English' and her 'Scottish' selves. Nan Shepherd's achievement is to make us feel this integrity, and to attain it herself in her narrative style. Her protagonist's home life is difficult, squalid and narrow, indeed her parents and neighbours would seem to be at home in any village between Barbie and Kinraddie. Yet Shepherd's wry and humane vision utterly eschews senti- mental naturalism, and she never once slips into Kailyard or polemical anti-Kailyard postures. This alone is a consider- able feat, and, for a first novel published only two years after *A Drunk Man* and four years before *Sunset Song*, it is a creative triumph.

Nan Shepherd's modest middle class upbringing was quite different from Martha's home circumstances; never- theless, like so many first books, *The Quarry Wood* is a 'development novel' clearly derived from the author's own life experience. The village of West Cults, King's College Library, the students' torchlight procession, the lectures of J. Arthur Thompson on Natural History and those of Herbert Grierson on Literature ('Professor Gregory'), all these are recognizably part of the Aberdeen scene that Shepherd knew. Indeed, 'the Quarry Wood' itself (now no longer there) rose towards the Black Top hill behind the houses where she lived almost all her life. In later years she was to recall its beauty on misty dawns when she used to walk through the trees to fetch milk from a nearby farm, before travelling to town and university classes each day. Yet *The Quarry Wood* is not a naive nor a 'student life' produc- tion, for it displays a striking maturity of style and insight.

Shepherd has an acute and unsentimental grasp of cha- racter and motivation—witness her account of Stoddart Semple, for example, in chapter four, or her very sharp eye for the intolerable social and sexual complacencies of young men—yet she never loses compassion. When such insight is matched to the reserve and dry humour of her prose, Nan Shepherd's writing has all the grace of Chekhov, not least in its delight at how revealing the casual juxtapositions of everyday speech and action can be made to be. The most ordinary domestic events come alive under this subtle touch, made even more dynamic by a splendid ear for the vigour of common North East speech. In this respect the novelist honours the community she depicts—notwithstanding the often hilarious direness which she finds there—as for example in the plight of the Leggatt sisters, led by the dreadful Jeannie who learned from an early age to use religion and respectability like a two-handed engine for subduing her timorous mother and the rest of her dust-free household.

The limitations of Martha's point of view are dealt with equally fairly. Matty is an intellectual being who has yet to find that one 'does not learn from books alone', and indeed for a time in the novel she remains unaware of her own emotions and her own passionate and jealous nature. She resists and resents the coarseness of home life around her— and it's coarse enough—yet Shepherd's skill lets us see that there's more there than her protagonist has yet realized despite the scandals that are told against her. Then, too, Martha has to learn that the claims of the ideal can turn into a burden or a kind of exploitation, if they are divorced from physical expression and common life. Her own infatuation with Luke and the unfairness of his spiritualization of her, teaches Matty this.

Such wisdom is not to be found in lectures, and its spokesperson is Great Aunt Josephine, whose formidable and friendly influence opens and closes the tale. Josephine possesses 'the same sure capable grasp of life' that Matty finds in one of her most gifted professors, and that she herself will eventually inherit. Thus it is Josephine who will restore to Matty what is best in her roots, without denying the possibilities of a wider intellectual life beyond them. Paradoxically, perhaps, she does this by the manner of her death, which is where the novel ends.

In re-reading *The Quarry Wood* it becomes clear that an apparently episodic unfolding has been rather carefully controlled from the start, for its delightful opening paragraph has given us what amounts to a summary of the book's central theme and evolution. When Josephine Leggatt dies, 'aged seventy-nine and reluctant', it is after an agonizing

and extended struggle against cancer, a grim vigil which
Matty (and the reader with her) has assumed responsibility
for and has had to undergo. It is a harrowing sequence, and
yet Josephine's end comes as a triumph of affirmation,
linked as it is to the turning of the seasons, and to the
evocation of the dour and delicate moods of the weather at
which Nan Shepherd particularly excels. There is no melo-
dramatic heightening here, such as the Gothic crescendo
which makes a 'clean sweep o the Gourlays' at the end of
George Douglas Brown's novel; nor does the narrative
conclude with the sweet fatalism of Chris's ebbing away at
the end of *Grey Granite*. Nan Shepherd's vision is not
without its own wry ironies, but she speaks positively and
wholly on behalf of life. Like Josephine Legatt, she has an
eye that sees everything, 'a serene unclouded eye', but 'an
eye, moreover, that never saw too much'.

In the last chapter, Matty's father helps her to wring a
hen's neck for the family meal:

> Geordie stood with an admirer's eye upon the fat breast
> of the fowl, holding her out from him until her spasms
> of involuntary twitching were over. Martha watched,
> breathing the clean sweet air of a July morning. When
> she raised her head she saw the wet fields and the soft
> gleam of the river. 'How fresh it is,' she said.
>
> 'Ay, ay,' answered her father, still holding the hen.
> 'It's a grand thing to get leave to live.'

Roderick Watson

ONE

Aunt Josephine Leggatt

Martha Ironside was nine years old when she kicked her grand-aunt Josephine. At nineteen she loved the old lady, idly perhaps, in her natural humour, as she loved the sky and space. At twenty-four, when Miss Josephine Leggatt died, aged seventy-nine and reluctant, Martha knew that it was she who had taught her wisdom; thereby proving – she reflected – that man does not learn from books alone; because Martha had kicked Aunt Josephine (at the age of nine) for taking her from her books.

Mrs. Ironside would have grumbled on for long enough and Aunt Josephine knew it.

'Ye'll just tak the craitur awa fae the school Emmeline,' the old lady said. 'Ye'll never haud book-larnin' in a wizened cask. Stap it in, it'll aye rin oot the faister. The bairn's fair wizened.'

'Oh, I ken she's nae bonny, Aunt Josephine—'

'O ay, ye were aye the beauty yersel, Emmeline, I'se nae deny it. But ye've nane to blame but yersel that the bairn's as she is. "There's Emmeline, noo," I says to Leebie, "throwin' hersel awa on yon Geordie Ironside, and the bairn's as ugly a little sinner as you'd clap e'en on in a month o' Sabbaths." "Dinna mention the wean," says Leebie, "nor Emmeline neither. If she hadna the wit to pit a plooman by the door, nor the grace to mind on fat was due to her fowk and their position, she can just bide the consequences. Dinna speak o' Emmeline to me," says Leebie. "She's never lookit richt upon her man if she's gotten a surprise that the bairn's nae a beauty."'

'Geordie's nae that ill-looking, Aunt Josephine.'

'Na, mebbe no. But look at his sister Sally – as grim's an auld horse wi' a pain in its belly. Matty's an Ironside, ma

dear, and ye've gotten fat ye hae gotten by mairryin' aneath
ye.'

Aunt Josephine said it calmly, without passion or malice,
as one delivers an impersonal truth. She alone of the Leggatt
family had recognised Emmeline since her marriage; but she
would never have dreamed of denying that the marriage was
a folly. She had even, in the early years, attempted on her
sisters the thankless task of persuasion in Emmeline's
behalf. After all, she was the only bairn of their own brother
– 'blood's thicker nor water,' Aunt Josephine had the
audacity to remind Aunt Jean, even after that lady had
delivered her ultimatum with regard to Emmeline.

'But it's nae sae easy to get aff yer hands,' said Jean.

That made the matter conclusive. To have Emmeline on
their hands would have been an impossible disaster for the
respectable Leggatts.

Emmeline tossed her head at their opinion. With base
effrontery she married the man she loved, and after twelve
pinched and muddled years, with her trim beauty slack, two
dead bairns and a living one mostly nerves and temper, she
stood in her disordered kitchen and fretted that she could
not offer her aunt a decent cup of tea.

'Beautiful, my dear, just beautiful,' said Aunt Josephine,
sipping the tea; and she returned to the question of Martha's
schooling. Emmeline, to be sure, had a dozen reasons
against taking the child away. Reasoning to Miss Leggatt
was so much moonshine. Fretful little girls are solid real-
ities (if not so solid as their grand-aunts might wish):
reasons, merely breath. It was not to be expected that a
vapour would impede Aunt Josephine. She announced
calmly and conclusively that she was taking the child back
with her to Crannochie.

'We'll just cry on the craitur,' she said, 'and lat her know.'

The *craitur* all this while, serenely unaware of the
conspiracy against her peace, was dwelling on a planet of her
own. A field's breadth from the cottage, where two dykes
intersected, there was piled a great cairn of stones. They had
lain there so long that no one troubled to remember their
purpose or their origin. Gathered from the surrounding soil,
they had resumed a sort of unity with it. The cairn had

settled back into the landscape, like a dark outcrop of rock. There Martha played. The stones summed up existence.

Aunt Josephine walked at her easy pace across the field. Mrs. Ironside followed for a couple of steps; then stood where she was and bawled across Aunt Josephine's head.

Aunt Josephine paid no attention: nor did Martha. The one plodded steadily on through the grass, the other made a planet with her dozen stones; both thirled to a purpose: while Mrs. Ironside behind them shrilled and gesticulated to no purpose whatsoever.

As her mother acknowledged, the child was no beauty: though impartial opinion, at sight of her, might well have decided that the mother was; intensifying the description by aid of the sturdiest little helot of the local speech – 'a gey beauty': inasmuch as the bairn's frock was glazed with dirt and drawn up in a pucker where it had been torn; and of her two clumsy boots, one gaped and the other was fastened with half a bootlace and a knotted bit of string, and both were grey. Her hair was a good sensible drab, not too conspicuous when badly groomed; and she had a wicked habit of sucking one or another of its stribbly ends.

'She's just a skin,' said Miss Leggatt, pausing at the foot of the cairn, while Mrs. Ironside's voice came spattering past her in little bursts:

'Tak yer hair ooten yer mou', Matty . . . and say how-do-you-do . . . to yer aunt. Mumblin' yer hair . . . like that . . . I never saw the like.'

'She's hungry, that's fat she is, the littlin,' said Aunt Josephine. 'Ye're fair hungerin' her, Emmeline.' And she put out her hands and drew Martha towards her by the shoulders. 'Now, my dear,' she said. It was a finished action and a finished phrase. Miss Leggatt's simplest word had a way of suggesting completion, as though it conveyed her own abounding certainty in the rightness of everything.

Emmeline told her daughter what was in store for her.

'Wunna that be fine?' said Aunt Josephine.

Martha firmly held by the shoulders in Aunt Josephine's grasp, answered by the action and not by word. Words came slowly to her need; and her present need was the most unmanageable she had ever experienced; for school to

Martha was escape into a magic world where people knew
things. Already she dreamed passionately of knowing all
there was to know in the universe: not that she expressed it
so, even to herself. She had no idea of the spaciousness of her
own desires; but she knew very fervently that she was in love
with school. Her reaction to the news she had just heard,
therefore, was in the nature of protest – swift and thorough.
She simply kicked out with all her strength of limb.

'I wunna be ta'en awa fae the school,' she screamed. 'I
wunna. I wunna.'

'Did ever ye see the likes o' that?' panted her mother. 'Be
quaet, will ye, Matty? I'm black affronted at ye. Kickin' yer
aunt like that. Gin I cud get ye still a meenute, my lady, I'd
gar yer lugs hotter for ye.'

Martha kicked and screamed the more.

Aunt Josephine let them bicker. Troubling not even to
bend and brush the dust of Martha's footmarks from her
skirt, she walked back calmly to the cottage.

Aunt Josephine Leggatt was a fine figure of a woman. She
carried her four-and-sixty years with a straight back and a
steady foot. She would tramp you her ten miles still, at her
own pace and on her own occasions. Miss Leggatt made
haste for no man, no, nor woman neither: though she had
been known to lift her skirts and run to pick a sprawling
child from the road or shoo the chickens off her seedlings.

'We'll need to put a fencie up,' she said.

It was just a saying of Aunt Josephine's, that – a remark
current for any season. She said it as one says, 'It's a bonny
day,' or, 'I dinna ken fat's ta'en the weather the year.'

'Josephine'll mebbe hae her fencie ready for her funeral,'
said Sandy Corbett, Aunt Jean's gristly husband.

The fence was not neglected from carelessness, or procras-
tination, or a distaste for work. Still less, of course, from
indifference. Miss Leggatt had a tender concern for her
seedlings, and would interrupt even a game of cards at the
advent of a scraping hen. But deep within herself she felt
obscurely the contrast between the lifeless propriety of a
fence and the lively interest of shooing a hen; and Aunt
Josephine at every turn chose instinctively the way of life.
The flame of life burned visibly in her with an even glow. A

miracle to turn aside and see – the bush burning and not consumed. One could read it in her eye, a serene unclouded eye, that never blazed and was never dimmed. An eye, moreover, that never saw too much.

But pleasant as one found her eye, it was the nose that was the feature of Aunt Josephine Leggatt's countenance. It was as straight as her back. A fine sharp sculptured nose that together with her lofty brow gave her profile a magnificence she had height enough to carry. A good chin too: though Jean, as Josephine herself was the first to acknowledge, had the chin of the family. Jean's chin spoke.

To look in Aunt Josephine's face, one felt that life was a simple matter, irrationally happy. Temper could not dwell with her. On this June day, hot and airless, with the spattered dents of early morning thunder-drops still uneffaced in the dust, not even Emmeline could withstand her serenity.

'She's ta'en a grip o' ill-natur,' Emmeline grumbled, shaking the child. 'She's aye girnin', an' whan she's nae she's up in a flist that wad fleg ye. An ill-conditioned monkey.'

'Leave the bairn's temper alane,' said Miss Leggatt. 'The inside'll clear o' itsel, but the ootside wunna. A sup water and some soap wad set ye better'n a grumble.'

Martha was accordingly washed, and another frock put on her. She possessed no second pair of boots, and therefore the existing pair remained as they were. A bundle that went under Aunt Josephine's arm, and a hat pulled over Martha's tangled wisps of hair, completed these preparations for the child's first sojourn from home: a sojourn upon which she started in wrath.

TWO

Crannochie

Aunt Josephine made no overtures. She trudged leisurely
on through the soft dust, her skirt trailing a little and
worrying the powder of dust into fantastic patterns. If she
spoke it was to herself as much as to Martha – a trickle of
commentary on the drought and the heat, sublime useless
ends of talk that required no answer. Martha heard them
all. They settled slowly over her, and she neither acknowledged them nor shook them off. She ploughed her way
stubbornly along a cart-rut, where the dust was thickest and
softest and rose in fascinating puffs and clouds at the shuffle
of her heavy boots. She bent her head forward and watched
it smoke and seethe; and ignored everything else in the
world but that and her own indignation.

But in the wood there were powers in wait for her: the
troubled hush of a thousand fir-trees; a light so changed, so
subdued from its own lively ardour to the dark solemnity of
that which it had entered, that the child's spirit, brooding
and responsive, went out from her and was liberated. In
that hour was born her perception of the world's beauty.
The quiet generosity of the visible and tangible world sank
into her mind, and with every step through the wood she
felt it more closely concentrated and expressed in the
gracious figure of old Miss Leggatt. She therefore drew
closer to her aunt, looking sidelong now and then into her
face.

Beyond the wood they were again on dusty road, and
curious little tufts of wind came *fichering* with the dust; and
suddenly a steady blast was up and about, roaring out of the
south-east, and the long blue west closed in on them, nearer
and denser and darker, inky, then ashen, discoloured with
yellow like a bruise.

'It's comin' on rainin',' said Martha; and as the first deliberate drops thumped down, she came close up to Aunt Josephine and clutched her skirt.

'We're nearly hame, ma dear, we're nearly hame,' said Aunt Josephine; and she took the child's hand firmly in hers and held back her eager pace. Thunder growled far up by the Hill o' Fare, then rumbled fiercely down-country like a loosened rock; and in a moment a frantic rain belaboured the earth. Martha tugged and ran, but Aunt Josephine had her fast and held her to the same sober step.

'It's a sair brae this,' she said. 'We'll be weet whatever, an' we needna lose breath an' bravery baith. We're in nae hurry – tak yer time, tak yer time.'

They took their time. The rain was pouring from Martha's shapeless hat, her sodden frock clung to her limbs, her boots were in pulp. But Aunt Josephine had her stripped and rolled in a shawl, the fire blazing and the kettle on, before she troubled to remove her own dripping garments or noticed the puddles that spread and gathered on the kitchen floor.

Martha was already munching cake and Aunt Josephine was on her knees drying up the waters, when the sound of a voice made the child glance up to see a face thrust in and peering. A singular distorted monkey face, incredibly lined.

'It's Mary Annie,' said Miss Josephine. 'Come awa ben.'

A shrivelled little old woman came in.

She came apologetic. She had brought Miss Josephine a birthday cake and discovered too late that she had mistaken the day; and on the very birthday she had made her own uses of the cake. She had set it on the table when she had visitors to tea, for ornament merely. Now, in face of the wrong date, her conscience troubled her; and what if Jeannie should know? Jeannie was her daughter and terrible in rectitude; and Jeannie had been from home when Mrs. Mortimer had held her tea-party.

'Ye wunna tell Jeannie, Miss Josephine. Ye ken Jeannie, she's that gweed – ower gweed for the likes o' me.'

'Hoots,' said Aunt Josephine, 'fat wad I dae tellin' Jeannie? Jeannie kens ower muckle as it is. There's nae harm dane to the cake, I'm sure, by bein' lookit at.'

Her heartiness restored Mary Annie's sense of pleasure; but she went away with no lightening of the anxiety that sat on her countenance.

Aunt Josephine had a curious belief that it was good for people to be happy in their own way: and a curious disbelief in the goodness of Jeannie.

'She's a – ay is she – ' she said, and said no more.

'An' noo,' she added, looking at Martha, 'we'll just cut the new cake, for that ye're eatin's ower hard to be gweed. It's as hard's Hen'erson, an' he was that hard he reeshled whan he ran.'

She plunged a knife through the gleaming top of the cake, and served Martha with a goodly slice and some of the broken sugar.

'Yes, ma dear, he reeshled whan he ran. Did ye ken that? An' the birdies'll be nane the waur o' a nimsch of cake.'

She moved about the room all the while she spoke, crumbling the old cake out at the window, sweeping the crumbs of the new together with her hand and tasting them, and breaking an end of the sugar to put in her mouth – with such a quiet serenity, so settled and debonair a mien, that the last puffs of Martha's perturbation melted away on the air.

But even in the excitement of eating iced cake, following as it did on her struggle and the long hot walk through the dust, was not prickly enough to keep her waking. Half the cake still clutched in her messy fingers, she fell asleep against Aunt Josephine's table; and Aunt Josephine, muttering, 'She's clean forfoch'en, the littlin – clean forfoch'en, that's fat she is,' put her to bed, sticky fingers and all, without more ado.

Martha awoke next morning with a sense of security. Like Mary Annie, she proceeded to be happy in her own way. That consisted at first in following Aunt Josephine everywhere about, dumbly, with grave and enquiring eyes. By and by she followed her to the open space before the door, and plucked her sleeve.

'Will I dance to you now?'

'Surely, ma dear, surely.'

She had never been taught to dance. Frock, boots, big-boned hands and limbs were clumsy, and her dancing was little more than a solemn series of ungainly hops. An intelligent observer might have been hard put to it to discover the rhythm to which she moved. A loving observer would have understood that even the worlds in their treading of the sky may sometimes move ungracefully. A young undisciplined star or so, with too much spirit for all its mastery of form . . . Aunt Josephine was a loving observer. She had never heard of cosmic measures, but she knew quite well that the force that urged the child to dance was the same that moved the sun in heaven and all the stars.

So she let her work alone and stood watching, as grave as Martha herself, and as happy.

'Lovely, ma dear, just lovely,' she said: and forgot about the tatties to pare and the dishtowels to wash before another thunder-plump came down. For be it understood that nothing so adaptable as work was allowed to put Aunt Josephine about. She was never harassed with it. She performed the meanest household task with a quiet gusto that made it seem the most desirable occupation in the world. But as soon as anything more interesting offered, she dropped the work where it was, and returned to it, if there was reason in returning to it when she was again at leisure, with the same quiet gusto. If there was no longer any reason in completing the work, why, it was so much labour saved.

'Josephine sweeps the day an' dusts the morn,' Leebie once said with her chilliest snort.

But Leebie's attitude to labour had been subtly deranged by her many years' sojourn in Jean's immaculate household. Early left a widow, and childless, Leebie had lived for nearly thirty years with Mr. and Mrs. Corbett. To the discipline of Jean's establishment she owed her superb belief in labour as an end in itself. To rise on Tuesdays for any other reason than to turn out the bedrooms, or on Fridays for a purpose beyond baking, would have seemed to both sisters an idle attempt to tamper with an immutable law of life. Indeed it is to be doubted, had Mrs. Corbett not been too much engrossed with the immediate concerns of this world to have any attention for a world beyond, whether she could possibly have envisaged a Tuesday spent in singing hymns. Bedroom day in heaven . . . the days in their courses, splendid and unshakable as the stars. . . .

Aunt Josephine, on the other hand, had time to spare for
the clumsy young stars, not at all splendid and still rather
shaky as to their courses. She stood in great contentment and
watched the one that was dancing on her path. Peter Mennie
the postie, coming up the path, was drawn also into the
vortex of the clumsy star.

'See to the littlin,' said Aunt Josephine.

'She'll need a ride for that,' answered Peter.

He was an ugly man – six foot of honest ugliness. He could
never be ugly to Martha. She stopped dancing at sight of
him, too shy even to run and hide. He hoisted her on to his
shoulder and she went riding off in terror that soon became a
fearful joy.

Next day she watched for Peter and went with him again;
and the next day too. At Drochety – the farm west from Aunt
Josephine's where they delivered the newspaper – Clemmie
had always heard them coming and was there at the door,
waiting. A raw country lass, high-cheeked, with crude red
features and sucked and swollen hands, she managed Drochety and his household to the manner born. Mrs. Glennie,
Drochety's feeble wife, lay upstairs in her bed and *worritted* –
Aunt Josephine told Martha all about it as though she were a
grown-up and Martha listened with grave attention. But she
need not have *worritted*, for Clemmie, though she came only
at last November term, had the whole establishment, master
and mistress, kitchen and byre and *chau'mer*, securely under
her *chappit* thumb.

Clemmie had a soft side to Peter, and for his sake was kind
to Matty: though she would not of her own accord have
made much of a lassie. 'It's aye the men-fowk I tak a fancy
to,' she said with perfect frankness. Martha could hear her
skellochin' with the cattleman in the evenings, 'an' him,' said
Aunt Josephine, 'a merriet man.'

The rest of the day Martha trotted after Aunt Josephine or
played among the broom brushes above the house. And each
day was as sweet smelling and wholesome to the taste as its
neighbour.

On the tenth of these days Miss Leggatt straightened
herself from the rhubarb bed, where she had been pulling

the red stalks for Martha's dinner, and saw young Willie
Patterson come cycling down the road. And when young
Willie Patterson visited Miss Leggatt, three things always
happened: they played a game of cards; they talked of old
Willie and the crony of his young days, Rory Foubister; and
Miss Josephine forgot the passage of time.

She forgot Martha also. The child stood gravely by,
watching; and heard for the first time the name of Rory
Foubister. Willie and Miss Josephine took him through
hand – a likely lad he had been, 'the warld fair made for him,'
said Miss Leggatt. 'But he wasna a gweed guide o' himsel.
Never will I forget the day he cam to say fareweel. "I've been
a sorrowfu' loon to my parents, Josephine, an' mebbe I'll
never come back."'

'Well, well, now,' said Willie, 'it's just as well you spoke of
Rory' (as though Miss Josephine ever neglected so to do),
'for didna I just look in on his cousin, old Miss Foubister at
Birleybeg. "Tell Miss Josephine," said she, "that Mrs.
Williamson and Bella will be here in an hour's time, and
we'll be looking for her to make the fourth, and stay as lang's
she can," she says.'

'Weel, weel, noo,' said Miss Josephine.

The good humour shone in her. She was burnished with
it. When Mrs. Williamson and Bella came to Birelybeg, the
summoning of Aunt Josephine followed as a matter of
course. So did whist: and it was no idle game.

Aunt Josephine was in a delightful bustle. There was her
best black silk *boady* to fetch and air, her boots to polish, her
clean handkerchief to lay in readiness beside the bonnet with
the velvet pansies. One thing Aunt Josephine forgot was the
dinner. The beheaded stalks of rhubarb lay in a heap in the
garden where she had left them when Willie Patterson
appeared. Their skin had tightened and toughened in the
sun and shreds of it were curling up like tendrils. The mince
was still upon the shelf.

'We canna wait noo or it's cookit,' said Aunt Josephine
when she remembered. She was standing in her petticoat and
slip-body in the middle of the kitchen floor. 'We'll just hae a
cup of tea an' an egg, an' you'll carry hame the mince to yer
mither in yer bundle.'

On the strength of the cup of tea and the egg Aunt Josephine locked her house door and pocketed the ponderous key. On the strength of the cup of tea and the egg Martha watched her go and turned to face her first revisitation of her home.

Family Affairs

When Aunt Josephine had walked off westward in her best silk *boady*, Martha turned back alone to Wester Cairns. Life was a queer disappointment. Its Aunt Josephines had incomprehensible transactions with the world. Its very woods were dumb. She crawled in among the bracken to rest. Its great tops swayed above her, smelling good. The earth smelt good too; and she fell asleep.

When she awoke the shadows had altered. Thin blades of sunshine had stolen into the wood, shadow had stolen over great patches of the sunny land. She had slept till evening. But Martha was as yet unskilled to read the light and did not know that she had slept so long. She rose and left the wood.

The iron gate to the field was open and two small boys lay on their stomachs beside the puddle. Beyond, a black-eyed girl was strutting, an old cloak tied round her middle.

'Ye micht lat me by, Andy,' said Martha.

Neither of the boys budged.

The lady in the cloak here intervened. Martha had never seen her before; and suddenly she noted that it was her own mother's cloak that dangled from the stranger's waist.

'You can't get this way,' said Blackeyes. 'It's to my house.'

'It's nae to your hoose,' cried Martha. 'It's to my hoose and it's my mither's cloak ye've got on.'

'It's her hoose richt eneugh,' said Andy. 'She bides there.'

'She disna bide there,' said Martha. 'It's nae her hoose and it's nae her cloak. Ye've stealed that cloak. It's my mither's cloak.'

And with that Martha sprang at the puddle, leaped short, and fell in the mire on the farther side.

'Sic a mucky mess ye're in, Matty,' said Andy with deep satisfaction. '*You*'ll get yer hi-ma-nanny when ye win hame. Yer mither's in an awfu' ill teen the day. Isna she, Peter?'

'Ay,' said Peter, without looking up from his mud-grubbing. 'She's terrible short i' the cut.'

'Ye'll fair get it, Matty. I wadna hae a mither like yon. She's a tongue, yon woman, an' nae name feart to use it,' went on Andy, repeating lusciously the judgements current in his home on Mrs. Ironside. 'Hisna she, Peter?'

'Ay,' said Peter, intoning his portion of the antiphon from the mud. 'She's a tongue that wad clip cloots.'

'An' a gey heavy han' as weel,' chanted Andy. 'She fair gied it to Peter the day as she gaed by. She fair laid till him. Didna she, Peter?'

'I dinna care a doit,' said Peter, altering the antiphon abruptly under stress of recollection.

Martha attended to neither. She was now on the black-browed stranger's side of the puddle and promptly laid violent hands on the cloak. Blackeyes wrenched herself free, pirouetted out of reach, and over one shoulder, with the most mischievous little sparkle in the world, thrust out her tongue at Martha.

Martha flew upon her, her limbs dancing of themselves with indignation. The black-burnished lady raised a pair of active sun-browned arms in readiness for the onslaught, and as soon as Martha was near enough, flung them tempestuously round her neck and smacked down a slobbery kiss upon her mouth. Martha had no time to adjust herself to the astonishment of a kiss. Her lifted hand came against the stranger's cheek with a sounding slap, and turning she ran until she reached the cottage.

On the flag by the door she paused and stared for a minute or two at the untidy thatch, the jagged break at the bottom of the door, the litter of cans and leaky pots and potato parings beside the pump. When she went in, her father was alone by the fire, in shirt sleeves, his sweaty socks thrust up against the mantel.

'Ye're there, are ye?' he said to his daughter.

Martha said, 'Imphm,' and climbed into the chair opposite her father.

Not a word from either for a while.

Then: 'Faither.'

'Weel?'

'Fa's the lassie wi' the black pow?'

'It's a lassie come to bide,' said Geordie slowly, 'Yer mither brocht her.'

Silence again, through which Martha's thoughts were busy with the queerness of family relationships. Other people's families were more or less stationary. Martha's fluctuated. It was past her comprehension.

'Faur's mither?' she asked.

'She's awa oot.'

Geordie did not think it necessary to add that she was out in search of more family. His wife's preoccupation with other people's babies was a matter for much slow rumination on the part of Geordie. He knew well enough that she did not make it pay. But Emmeline would undertake any expedition to mother a child for gain. She liked the fuss and the pack in her two-roomed stone-floored cottage. The stress of numbers excused her huddery ways. Some of the babies died, some were reclaimed, some taken to other homes. Martha accepted them as dumbly as her father, brooding a little – but only a little – on the peculiarities of a changing population.

Geordie himself interrupted her thoughts this evening. It had occurred to him to wonder why she had come home.

Martha explained. Roused from her brooding, she realized that she was hungry.

'Is't nae near tea-time, faither?' she asked.

Geordie took his pipe from his mouth and surveyed his daughter with trouble in his eyes.

'The tea's by lang syne,' he said. 'Did ye nae get ony fae yer aunt?'

'Nuh . . . Ay . . . I some think I had ma tea, but it was at dinner-time. I hadna ony dinner. She was ower busy wi' the cairds to mak' ony, an' syne whan she heard she bude to ging to Birleybeg there wasna time.'

This preposterous situation slowly made itself clear to Geordie's intelligence. Aunt Josephine had neglected for a new-fangled triviality like cards the great primordial busi-

ness of a meal. It was a ludicrous disproportion. Geordie
flung back his head against the chair and roared with
laughter.

There was something elemental about Geordie's laughter.
It flooded up out of the depths of him – not gurgling, or
spouting, or splashing up, but rising full-tide with a steady
roaring boom. It had subterranean reserves of force, that no
common joke was able to exhaust. Long after other people
had fatigued their petty powers of laughter at some easy joke,
the vast concourses of Geordie's merriment were gathering
within him and crashing out in mightily renewed eruptions
of unwearied vigour. He found a joke wholesome until
seventy times seven.

So he laughed, not once, but half a dozen times, over Miss
Leggatt's departure from the common sanities. But after his
seventh wind or so, he put his pipe back in his mouth and
drew at it awhile in silence. Then he hitched himself out of
his chair, with the resolution of a man who has viewed the
situation impartially and made up his mind.

'Yer mither disna like me touchin' her thingies,' he said,
'but we'll need to get a bit piece till ye.'

Martha did not budge. She lay back in her chair with her
legs dangling, and awaited the pleasure of her Ganymede.

'Here's a sup milk an' a saft biscuit,' said Ganymede,
returning (silent-footed as became a banquet). 'That'll suit
ye better'n the cakes.'

Martha nodded and bit deep into the floury cushion of the
biscuit. She loved soft biscuits.

She lay still in the chair and nibbled luxuriously, her
thoughts drifting.

Ganymede resumed his leisure. He sprawled, his stock-
inged feet upon the arm of Martha's chair. They gave her a
happy, companionable feeling. She moved the least thing in
her corner so as to nudge them gently. Ganymede gave her in
response the tenderest, most tranquil, subjovial little kick.
Father and daughter shared a silence of the gods, in which all
is said that need be said.

The clatter of a distracted earth broke by and by upon
Olympus. Noisy voices, with anger in the flying rumours
they sent ahead.

'Here's yer mither comin' in aboot,' said Geordie, disposing of his legs, 'an' I some doot she's in ane o' her ill teens.'

Geordie's diagnosis of his wife's spiritual condition was correct. Mrs. Ironside appeared, herding in Blackeyes. Her very skirts were irate. The three-year old bairn who hung in the wind of them was in some danger of blowing off. A baby kept her arms steadier than they might otherwise have been. Mrs. Ironside had multiplied her family by two.

Her wrath against Blackeyes was checked by the sight of Martha, motionless in the depths of her chair.

The situation was explained.

'Ye maun jist ging back to the school, than,' said Mrs. Ironside, eyeing her daughter.

Passionate tears broke over Martha's cheeks.

To make herself conspicuous by marching back to school when Aunt Josephine herself had made arrangement for her absence, publicly to give report of the drab conclusion to her travels, was more than Martha's equanimity could face. She went hot with shame at the very thought.

She battered the arm of the chair with her fists.

'I canna ging back,' she sobbed. 'I canna ging back.'

'You're a queer ane,' said her mother. 'Ye hinna a please. Temper whan we tak ye fae the school an' temper whan we pit ye back.'

'She can bide aboot the doors, surely,' said Geordie.

'I canna hae her trallopin' at my tails a' day lang. An' look at the mess she wad be in. She's a gey lookin' objeck as it is,' said Emmeline, whose appreciation of cleanliness varied inversely with the godliness of her calm. The more serene she was, the more she tolerated dirt.

'I gaed dunt intil the puddle,' said Martha miserably.

'Fit way cud she help it, whan she hadna had ony dinner?' said her father: a notable man for logic of a strictly informal variety.

Blackeyes was crying, 'It was me that made her do it,' and Martha, suddenly remembering her parcel, jumped up and said,

'But I got the mince.'

A pound of mince may not go far to counterbalance an

increase in family, but it helps. It abated Emmeline's
aggressiveness. Mollified with mince, she put her family to
rights. Martha was *beddit* side by side with Blackeyes, who
fell asleep with one swarthy arm curved round her middle.

The newcomers were Dussie, Madge, and Jim. In August
the elder children went to school again. Soon it was dark by
supper-time, then by the closing of afternoon school. Winds
were up. Mornings of naked frost changed to afternoons of
black and sullen rain. There were nights when the darkness
blared and eddied round the thatch and sang in the
chimney; white nights, all sky, with the moon riding
overhead and round her half the heaven swirling in an
enormous *broch*; moonless nights when Orion strode up-
valley and the furred and fallen leaves glistered on the silken
roads.

The children saw nothing of these night festivities. They
were jammed together in the huddled kitchen, under the
smoky and flaring lamp. But one evening Geordie, from the
open house-door, whence a guff of caller air flapped through
the stifling kitchen, called the girls out to the night.

At Geordie's call, Dussie was up on the instant. Martha
came reluctantly, stooping back over the table to add
another stroke to her map.

Outside, after the flare of the lamp and the burnish of
firelight, they stepped into a bewildering January dark.
Bewildering, because not really dark. Their eyes accustomed to it, they found it was a dark that glowed. No moon;
infrequent stars; but when Geordie led them round the end
of the house they saw the north on fire. Tongues of flame ran
up the sky, flickered, fell back in the unstable pools of flame
that gathered on the horizon, rose to crests again and broke
into flying jets. The vast north was sheeted in light; low
down and black, twisted firs, gnarled, shrunken, edged the
enormous heaven. The Merry Dancers were out.

A shudder ran over Martha. Something inside her grew
and grew till she felt as enormous as the sky. She gulped the
night air; and at the same time made a convulsive little
movement against her father. She was not afraid ; but she
felt so out of size and knowledge of herself that she wanted
to touch something ordinary.

'Some feart kind, are ye?' said the ploughman, taking her hand tight in his own. Dussie clung to his other hand, rapping his knuckles, waggling his fingers, stroking his leg, sneaking a supple hand in his trouser pocket, all the while that she made lively comment on the sky. Geordie and Dussie had half a dozen private finger games before Martha had had enough of gazing upon the light.

It was Dussie who put the eager questions Geordie could not answer.

'Weel, I dinna richtly ken fat they micht be. They ca' them the Northern Lichts. Fireflaughts.' Then an ancient memory stirring (a rare occurrence with Geordie), 'I min' fan I was a laddie there was a bit screed I used to ken. It was some like the geography, Matty, gin I could get a haud o't. Arory . . . arory . . . bory . . . syne there was a lassie's name on till't. Fat div ye ca' yon reid-heided craiturie o' Sandy Burnett's?'

'Alice,' said Matty.

'Ay, ay, that's the very dunt. Arory-bory-Alice. Weel. Noo, Matty, fat is there a' roun' Scotland, lassie?'

'The sea,' said Matty, 'a' the way roun', except faur there's England.'

Geordie stood so long considering it that Martha grew impatient. She was jumping up and down against his hand in her excitement.

'An' fat aboot the Arory-bory-Alices, faither?'

'Weel, I canna get a richt haud o't,' said Geordie deliberately, 'but it gaed some gait like this: On the sooth o' Scotland there's England, on the north the Arory-bory – Burnett's lassie, the reid-heided ane – Alice; on the east – fat's east o't?'

'The sea,' said Martha, turning eastward, where a span of sea, too dull a glint under the Dancer's light to catch an ignorant eye, notched their eastern view.

'Weel, aye, but it wisna the sea. It was something there was a hantle mair o' than that.' Geordie's thoughts, like Martha's, glanced upon their private notch of sea. 'I some think it was the sun – the risin' sun. Ay, fairly. That's fat it was. Noo, the wast. Fat's wast o' Scotland, Matty?'

'The sea,' said Martha again.

'It's nae that, though, i' the bit rhyme. It was a bigger word nor that.'

'Ye cud ca't the ocean – that's a bigger word,' suggested Dussie.

'It's the Atlantic Ocean,' Martha said.

Geordie -could get no further with the boundaries of Scotland: but his assertion of the northward edge was too obvious at the moment to be doubted. They stood on Scotland and there was nothing north of them but light. It was Dussie who wondered what bounded Scotland when the Aurora was not there. Neither Martha nor Geordie had an answer.

Some weeks later Geordie had a shaking and shuffle of excitement in the middle of the kirk. He nudged Martha with signs and whispers she could not understand. She held her eyes straight forward and a prim little mouth, pretending not to see or hear. It was dreadful of her father to behave like that in church. Once out on the road again,

'Yon's the wordie, Matty – fat's the meenister was readin' aboot. Eternity. That's fat wast o' Scotland. I mind it noo.'

Martha said it over and over to herself: *Scotland is bounded on the south by England, on the east by the rising sun, on the north by the Arory-bory-Alice, and on the west by Eternity.*

Eternity did not seem to be in any of her maps: but neither was the Aurora. She accepted that negligence of the map-makers as she accepted so much else in life. She had enough to occupy her meanwhile in discovering what life held, without concerning herself as to what it lacked.

She repeated the boundaries of Scotland with the same satisfaction as she repeated the rivers in Spain. Up to her University days she carried the conviction that there was something about Scotland in the Bible.

The Merry Dancers danced in storm.

Huge galleons of cloud bore down upon the earth, their white sails billowing on the north horizon. Swiftly their glitter and their pride foundered in a swirl of falling snow. The air was darkened. The sun crept doubtfully back to silence. Shifty winds blew the road bare and piled great wreaths at corners and against the dykes. An unvarying wind chiselled knife-edged cornices along the wreaths.

Thaw blunted them, and filled the roads with slush. Rain pitted the slush and bogged the pathways.

The children went to school through mire. There was no scolding now for mucky garments; boots were clorted and coats sodden and splashed. Their ungloved hands were blue and swollen with chilblains.

There was east in the spring. Summer winds tumbled the sky. Dykesides smelt of myrrh and wild rose petals were transparent in the July rain.

Dussie and Martha were each a year older. So was Madge. She was not communicative. Her conversation was yea and nay – except to Geordie, and her own small brother Jim, to both of whom she would occasionally impart much astonishing information. Geordie received it with composure, Jim with fists or chuckles according to the edge of his appetite.

In August Mrs. Ironside brought home another baby boy.

One result of this was that Madge, who because she took frequent colds had hitherto slept in the unfreshened kitchen, was sent to share the west room with the other girls. Dussie and Martha found her inconvenient. She interrupted their disclosures to each other regarding the general queerness of life. Not that she seemed to be paying any attention; but one day Martha overheard her solemn and detailed recital to baby Jim of one of their dearest secrets. Martha had shaken her till her yells resounded from the Quarry Wood; and Emmeline had shaken Martha till she was sick and had to have castor oil.

It was some consolation for the castor oil that Dussie heartily approved her action. Dussie also commandeered two sweeties from Andy Macpherson and raced home with them triumphantly to Martha as an aid to the castor oil in its kindly office.

Dussie and Martha had things to tell each other that were not for the ear of infants.

FOUR

In Which a Latin Version Is Spoilt

On a February evening, when sleet lashed the window in tides of deepening violence, and spat upon the flames, and sluiced under the ill-fitting outer door, was debated with pomp and circumstance the question of whether or not Martha should go to the University. For days the wind had streamed up-valley; a dull, grey wind, rude and stubborn, that subdued the whole landscape to its own east temper. The howl of it was in the ear at night, long after dark had hid its bleakness from the eye. Gulls screamed and circled overhead – a wild skirl against the drone of the firwood. Spring was late. Hardly a peewit, not a lark, to hear. A drab disconsolate world.

Martha had pushed against the sodden wind four miles and a half that morning, her heavy bundle of books tied on behind her cycle. She was eighteen now and in the highest class at school; but the bursaries on which she had carried herself so far ran to no unnecessary railway fares – not in the Ironside family, where a penny saved had a trick of turning to a penny squandered – and in most weathers she cycled back and fore to town night and morning.

That morning Emmeline had said:

'Ye'll nae get in dry. It'll be a doonpour. Yon win's nae for naething. Hae. There's yer coppers.'

She gave her daughter the pence for her return fare to town. Martha had never had money of her own. She handed over all her bursary money to her mother and had to ask back what she needed. She very seldom asked back. It was too unpleasant being made to feel an undue drag upon the house. Not an exercise-book was purchased but it was audibly grudged. Martha felt a felon when her teachers ordered her to buy a pencil. Her journey home at night was sometimes spent devising ways and words to approach the theme of another new text-book; she would sit all through supper-time with a sickening twinge pulling and twisting inside her body; her back would not hold up; when she washed the supper dishes her knees were sagging. Emmeline had no understanding of her own tyranny. She objected for the sake of objecting.

Martha put the train fare in her pocket and looked at the sombre sky. It had been just as heavy for days and she had escaped a wetting. She pulled her cycle from the shed and raced along the beaten path that crossed the field. The field was lately ploughed. At every dozen steps she stumbled off the narrow path (moist enough itself in the sodden weather) into the heavy upturned earth. Clods hung upon her boots. She raced on, to gain the road before her mother saw her go. The pennies in her pocket jigged to a dance tune. They meant a candle (if the candles could be bought before her mother knew the pence were saved), and a candle meant peace to work at night in her own chill room.

She dared not buy the candles in town lest at the last minute the storm broke and she had to return after all by train. At half-past four the wind still screamed up-country; no change since morning, and Martha set off to cycle home. She intended to dismount and buy her candles in the last shop on the outskirts of the city; but the wind, and her own fear of being caught in rain and her mother's anger, drove her at such a frantic speed that she was already past the shop before her mind snatched at the necessity for dismounting. It would have been foolish to turn back and fight the wind – the candles could be bought at Cairns. The shop was far behind her by the time her mind had worked itself to that resolve, so irresistible a vigour was in the wind that pushed her on. She let herself go to its power, pedalling furiously on her old machine that had no free-wheel and one inefficient brake.

A long stretch of unsheltered road lay ahead, running beneath a low sky that sank farther and farther as she advanced. Suddenly the grey wind turned dirty-white, drove upon her in a blast of sleet. It chilled her neck, soaked her hair, dribbled along her spine, smothered her ears; the backs of her legs and arms were battered numb; her boots filled slowly with the down-drip from her skirt and stockings; once or twice she looked at the handle-bars to make sure that her hands were there. She had dismounted when the sleet began, to unfasten her books from behind the bicycle; her person might be soaked, but not her precious books. She rammed them in the bosom of her coat, that gaped and would not fasten over the unwieldly bundle. When she mounted again she had to pedal furiously in spite of her hampered and clammy limbs, because to pedal furiously was easier than to hold back against the sweep of the wind; but as the sleet continued to fall and filled the road with slush and semi-liquid mud, her pace slackened, till at last she was pushing with effort over the pasty ground, her front wheel bumping, splashing, squirming by reason of her inability to guide it. Darkness had come down too soon. She had a lamp but no means of lighting it, nor could it easily have been lit in the violence of the weather. A passing cart filled her with nameless dread; a chance pedestrian loomed horribly distorted through the sleet; there were no recognizable sounds. The beat of the storm upon her back had plastered her shoddy clothing to her skin. By the time she rode through Cairns, its early lights diffused and smudgy in the thickened air, she was too numb to think, even to picture the possession of a candle, much less procure it. She rode like an automaton.

At the foot of the long brae to the cottage she stumbled from her machine. Light had gone from the earth. The sleet drove now upon her side as she battled uphill pushing her bicycle. Thought began to stir again when she reached the puddle at the gateway of the field. She went straight ahead through the puddle because it mattered little now how much wetter she became; and with that she began to wonder what reproach her mother would have ready. She had not even candles for consolation; and Emmeline would say next morning, 'Ye've got yer money for the train.' She tumbled her cycle into the shed and pushed open the house-door, standing dazed a moment on the threshold.

Emmeline's back was towards the door, as she bent over the fire and stirred the sowens for supper. Without turning, when one of the children said, 'Here's Matty come,' she complained to her daughter.

'Ye've ta'en a terrible like time to come up fae the station.'

Martha's heart fluttered and thumped, and pulses beat hot and hurried in the chill of her temples. So her mother had not been in the shed and did not even know that the cycle had been taken out!

'It's a terrible night. I'm wet through,' she said. But the wetting had suddenly become of no importance. Her mind did not even run forward to the pennies she had gained; the mere relief from an immediate onslaught by her mother's tongue was joy enough. She went in a sort of stupid excitement to remove her dangling clothes; but she had to call Madge through from her Pansy Novelette to help her strip.

Geordie came in, soaked too. The fireplace was hung with dripping garments and the iron kettles perched with sopping boots. The steam of them eddied about the room, mingling with the wood-smoke blown back from the chimney. Emmeline worked herself into a lather of vituperation at the weather and the folk, but gave the latter none the less their sowens in ample measure, smeared with syrup and piping hot. She set the boys to feed the fire with branches and logs of pine. Every now and then a resinous knot spluttered and sang, flared out in blobs and fans of flame. Emmeline made no economies with fire. She loved heat. The little kitchen was shortly stuffed with a hot reek – the reek of wood and folk and sowens, wet clothes, steaming dishwater and Bogie Roll.

For once Martha did not regret her lack of candles. She was shivering violently from her exposure and glad of the heavy heat of the kitchen. She sat at the deal table, catching her share of light from the lamp upon her open school-books. Geordie was playing Snakes-and-Ladders with the bairns – Madge and the eight- and nine-year-old boys. There was no Dussie now. Something less than three years after her arrival, Mrs. Ironside had polished her one day according to her lights and taken her away. Her folk reclaimed her. Dussie was in a whirl of excitement. She had tangled the processes of washing and dressing with fifty plans for interminable futures, and Martha was to share her fortune and her favour. They had not seen her since.

A three-year-old girl was asleep in the kitchen bed, to be carried *ben the hoose* in Madge's ruddy arms when she herself retired. Madge was twelve, a strong-built girl, not tall, no great talker, knowing and not sharing her own mind.

In spite of the driving sleet, which had sting enough to keep most folk by their own firesides, Stoddart Semple lounged in the ingle nook and smoked his filthy cutty. He was a grey cadaverous man in the middle fifties, who did for himself and doggedly invaded his neighbours' homes. 'Stoddart's takin' a bide,' folk said. They growled at him but seldom put him out. He was good to laugh at.

Emmeline, still standing, a dish-towel lumped beneath one arm, and her elbows dug into the back of her husband's chair, was having her turn of the Pansy Novelette.

Geordie could rattle the dice with the best when it was a matter of Snakes-and-Ladders or so, and was unaffectedly happy in his slow deliberate play with the bairns; but jerking back his chair he chanced to dislodge Emmeline's elbows, and drove her fists against her chin, her teeth closing upon her tongue.

'Tak care, will ye?' said she. 'Garrin' a body bite their tongue. . . .'

'Haud oot ower a bit, than,' said Geordie, and he slapped his knee and roared with laughter. The game was upset, and the boys began a monkey-chase about the room. Madge climbed on a creepie to see over Emmeline's shoulder on to the jewelled-and-ermined pages of the Pansy Novelette, which Emmeline was still reading voraciously, bending as often as the boys scuttled within her reach to flick them with the dish-towel.

Martha all this while sat at another board, playing a different game: a game of shifting and shuffling and giving in exchange. Its most fascinating move consisted in fitting four flighty little English sentences into one rolling Latin period. Martha bent her energies upon it, too absorbed to heed the racket around her. Even when a bear beneath the table worried her knees, she only moved aside a little impatiently, saying nothing.

Martha had grown up quiet. After all the flaring disquietudes of her childhood, she had settled into a uniform calmness of demeanour that was rarely broken. Her silences, however, were deceptive. She was not placid, but controlled. She had the control that comes of purpose; and her purpose was the getting of knowledge. There was no end to the things that one could know.

Goerdie was still in his cups, metaphorically speaking, an honest joke suiting him as well as a dram; and Mrs. Ironside was grumbling still: 'Garrin' a body bite their tongue . . . I never heard . . .'; when Willie sprang on the top of the table and upset the bottle of ink upon Martha's Latin version. She had written half of it in fair copy, in a burst of exasperation at the refusal of the second half to take coherent form. Now she sprang to her feet and watched the black ruin, staring at the meandering of the ink.

'Ye micht dicht it up,' said Emmeline.

Emmeline had stuffed the novelette under her chin, pressing it there, head forward, to keep it in position, and had lunged out after Willie, flicking at his ear with the dish-towel. The lurch she gave as he dodged jerked the book on to the floor and Emmeline herself against the table; and the dish-towel flicked the ink.

'Blaudin' ma towel an' a',' she grumbled; and then,

'Ye micht dicht it up,' she said to Martha.

Martha gulped. She suddenly wanted to scream, to cry out at the pitch of her voice, 'I haven't time, I haven't time, I haven't time! What's a kitchen table in comparison with my Latin, with knowing things, with catching up on the interminable past! There isn't *time!*'

She set to work cleaning up the mess.

Then tears scalded her. Through them, blurred, ridiculous, all out of shape, fantastically reduplicated, she was watching her mother pick up the Pansy Novelette, bunch the towel beneath her arm again, and read.

Martha felt her mouth twist. The reeking air of the kitchen choked her. Its noises hammered and sang through her brain. The room was insufferably tight. She pushed viciously with both hands at the wet cloth she was using, smearing the table still further with pale blue stains. She licked a tear from her upper lip. Quite salt. Another – she licked that too. Her eyes and cheeks were fired where they had run. . . . And the intolerable waste of mood! She had been saturated with the spirit of Latin prose – it had soaked in. Words, phrases, turns of speech, alert and eager in her brain, drumming at her ears, clamouring in an exultant chaos. And that last triumphant mastery, forcing on the chaos order and a purpose – the god's security. Gone now. Spilt like the ink, as irretrievably. A worse waste even than the time.

'Ye're skirpin' a' ower the place,' said Emmeline.

Martha flung the cloth into the basin of water.

'Oh why can't you do it yourself!' she cried. '*Mother*! You've more time than I have. You're just reading. Just rubbish. – Oh, it doesn't matter – I didn't mean – you needn't be angry anyway. It *is* just rubbish. And I've all my Latin to do for tomorrow.'

'Latin?' said her mother.

'I'll never get it done tonight now.'

'Latin,' said Emmeline again. 'Fat sorra div ye need wi' Latin for a teacher? Ye're nae to larn the geets Latin, I'm hopefu', an' them disna ken ae year's en' fae the t'ither.'

Martha moistened her lips. The hot salt tears had shrivelled them.

'I need it to get a bursary,' she said.

'Oh, that's something new,' said her mother. 'It's the first I've heard o't.'

Stoddart Semple glowered at Martha. He was a long loose man, *ill-shakken thegither*. Useless laps of skin sagged round his mouth. '*Nos et mut . . . ,*' he mumbled, forgetting the conclusion. Then he broke into a tirade against learning. Abject the people who value what we valued once and today despise. Stoddart had hankered once after knowledge; once he too had stormed the fastnesses of understanding. The fastnesses unfortunately had stood fast. His father, who had jogged for a lifetime behind his *shaltie* selling smokies and finnan haddies to the country wives, and had jogged more pence into his pocket than wisdom into his head, satisfied the boy's ambition and sent him to college. Strangely, not a professor among them could be found to endorse young Stoddart's opinion of his brains. Old Semple would have bribed them cheerfully, the whole Senatus, Sacrist and all, to

let the laddie through: but he died before it became plain
that the laddie had stuck; and the old man's transactions
began and ended with fish. Stoddart sold the fish-cart and
the decrepit horse, counted (in an evil day) his father's
savings, and from that day onward never did a stroke of
honest labour. He lived alone in his father's cottage,
meditating projects to astonish the earth: soon he would
have been glad to astonish even the parish. The parish had
little use for a fine phrase, and did not know what to do with
learning authenticated by no official stamp. Had he passed
his examinations they might have listened to him, even
without understanding; once he had been ploughed, they
were at liberty to laugh. He let them laugh, but in a fury of
contempt. He grew increasingly morose, striding by in a
sort of bickering speechlessness. He shunned society: then
mooned; then slouched, body and mind settling to a habit
of slackness; his features coarsened; he seeded and grew
stringy. His grudge against ungrateful man blackened and
rotted his powers. The devotee's indignation at the
disdaining of his god had turned to a black and brooding
madness on this one subject of himself.

With the passage of years he ceased himself to believe in
his discredited dignity.

The neighbours saw the deterioration of face and figure,
the hanging jaw, the rag-nailed thumbs, the sloven countenance; they saw refuse encumber his doors; the smell of
his body *scunnered* them; they cackled at his clothing,
sodden from exposure to every weather, matted and split.
He trailed through any *dubs*, under any sky. A night
prowler too, haunting the deep of the wood by midnight.
His neighbours' premises, perhaps, as well: who could
know? Labouring folk sleep early and sleep sound. But
there were suspicions anent him – queer ends of talk. A
dark bulk – an indeterminate shadow – a malignant *reeshle*
of the leaves without wind – sorry matters, but from them
grew half-broken tales. A troubler of men's imaginations,
generating legend . . . a queer rôle for the *stickit* graduate.
A looking-glass progression towards the object of his old
ambitious desires . . . troubling men's imaginations . . . .

The neighbours saw the change in him – his rotting look:

it was not for them to know that under the external squalor
seethed horribly a spiritual regeneration.

Stoddart had need of his kind.

He blundered his way back into society by virtue of an
inlaid dambrod. Old Semple had been a craftsman of sorts
and had begun to fashion a dambrod of two varieties of
wood, each square inset with patient skill. Death made a
move on his board before the man's board was completed. It
lay where chance had tossed it, till Stoddart unearthed it one
morning and set to work to finish it. No craftsman, he made
a sorry enough job: but the board was ready for the game and
Jamie Lowden liked a game fine of a blank and blustery
winter evening. Stoddart carried the dambrod to Jamie
Lowden's.

By what processes of pity, curiosity, persuasion, the
dambrod gave him entry to other houses, would be hard to
say: but in course of time, shambling, apologetic, he slunk
his way wherever he desired: accompanied always by the
board. He loved the bit of wood. He would shuffle round
with it under his arm, 'oxterin' at it as though it were a
body.' Humbly at first, he ventured the piece of work-
manship into view, claiming praise for his father's handi-
work; but careful to add that it was he who had finished it.
By and by the squares that he had fashioned subtly shifted
their position on the board. He was not oversure himself
which he had made; and at the thought that he might really
be the framer of this dark beauty or of that, he regained
something of the belief in himself that he had lost. In
consequence he tidied his homestead a little and cleaned his
person; and became a more decent member of human
society. With the passage of another year or two he was very
comfortably convinced once more of his own dignity and
importance: with this difference, that he had ceased to
trouble very much whether others believed in them or not.

One house to which he did not carry the dambrod was the
Ironsides'. Emmeline could not abide him, in his days of
grandiloquence. 'He's fair clorted wi' conceit,' she said
impatiently to Geordie. 'Ye cud tak a rake an' rake it aff'n
him.' Emmeline's own conceit, in those early days of marriage, was at too low an ebb to allow her to enjoy the quality

in others: hence perhaps her ineradicable grudge against Stoddart. When he rose out of the nadir of his degradation and Geordie brought him *in aboot* of an evening, she suffered his presence but gave short shrift to the dambrod. Geordie indeed, in the natural complaisance of his soul, sat to study the play: but it exacted too much of a man wearied out and sodden still with the heavy sense of wet fields and claggy soil. Geordie carried back with him to his own fireside, stored up in his own body – his stiff and aching muscles, his numbed brain, his slow and inattentive nerves – the memory of a thousand generations wearing down the long resistances of the earth. A desperate task, to shake oneself quickly free from memory that had worked itself in. Geordie was not altogether sorry when Emmeline's tongue banished the dambrod from her kitchen.

'Sic a cairry-on he hauds wi' himsel an' yon boardie,' she said contemptuously. – 'Wheesht, wheesht, he's hearin' ye,' from Geordie. – 'I named nae names,' said Emmeline. 'Them that has lang noses can tak tae them.' Stoddart was touchy. The dambrod was effectively dismissed.

The man, however, kept coming, in spite of abuse. He was stingy with his own fuel and liked Emmeline's lavishness with hers: especially on a night of driving bitter sleet, like the one in question.

So he slouched in the heat and, diving among recollections that had gone sour, miscalled knowledge.

Martha listening did not divine the man.

Our acquaintances have no past for us until we have a past ourselves.

She was merely irritated at his opposition. Rashly, she had precipitated her fight, and the fortune of war was against her. This henchman of darkness, sunken-eyed, slack-mouthed, betrayed her to the enemy. The wastrel forces of ignorance were in power.

For Martha was set upon a purpose not yet divulged. It was understood that she was to be a teacher, after a two years' course at a Training Centre; but Martha herself was working secretly for more. She had learned as yet to be passionate on behalf of one thing only – knowledge: but for that she could intrigue like any lover. She had made her own plans for going, not to the Training Centre but to the University. So, quite unnecessarily, she was learning Latin. When her bursary was gained, it was time enough to tell.

And now, fool that she was, she had given her position away.

And to let Stoddart Semple, whom she hated, see her cry! She swallowed hot tears and listened, craning for every word, to her mother and Stoddart, disputatious, grumblers both, using Martha's preposterous ambition to justify their own particular grievance.

'Fat ails ye at bein' a teacher?' demanded Emmeline.

'Nothing ails me. – I'm going to be a teacher. But I want to go to the University.'

'An' how muckle langer'll that tak ye?'

'Two years,' Martha said.

Emmeline's exasperation had a deeper basis than Martha understood; than Martha indeed was capable of understanding, for she had never breathed a Leggatt atmosphere nor been nurtured in the *pietas* of Leggatt respectability: except, and that dubiously, at Crannochie; for Aunt Josephine was not a thoroughbred. Her social status did not exist for Martha. She had never thought about it. But Emmeline had dreamed with undiminished ardour for twenty years of being respectable again. She had consented to let Martha be a teacher for no other end than this. And after twenty years you ask an Emmeline to wait another four instead of two to see her dream fulfilled! How could a Martha, hungry for the tartness and savour of knowledge, be expected to understand? Martha saw only a slovenly and inefficient woman, given to uncertainties of temper and meaningless indulgences, and with a cankering aptitude for objection. She had never even known that her mother was beautiful; nor that men have decreed rights to beauty that reason need not approve. Dumbly, fitfully, Emmeline was aware of a trouble within her consciousness. She had been somehow foiled – blame it on any wind you will, not on Emmeline – of the right of loveliness to queen it over the imaginations of men. Ill-trickit rascal, that godling with the bow, at whose caprice she had given her love, and been thrust away in consequence to the middle of this dull ploughed field!

Emmeline hankered still after the respect men pay to beauty, though what she dreamed she wanted was the respect they pay to the respectable. She had built herself a formidable conviction of the automatic increase in reputation that would come to the family when Matty was a finished teacher. Add two years to that! – Two and two in this case made an eternity.

Mother and daughter fronted each other, antagonistic, weighing the years in a balance, but with what differing weights!

Stoddart Semple grumbled on. 'She wants to mak hersel oot somebody,' he said. All the rasping irritation of his own discomfiture was in the sneer.

'Some folks are grand at that,' said Emmeline sharply. But he took her up, not heeding the home-thrust.

'Deed they are. You cud dae fine to be somebody yersel, Mrs. Ironside, an' Matty's nae far ahin ye.'

'She wunna be't, then,' said Emmeline with tart decisiveness, furious that Stoddart should read her secret desires. 'My lassie wunna ging like Maggie Findlater, terrible goodwillie to yer face an' despisin' the hale rick-ma-tick o' her fowk ahin their backs.'

'Maggie!' said Stoddart. 'Maggie's nae that ill.'

'A muckle easy-osy lump,' snorted Mrs. Ironside. 'If she'd keep her mou' shut an' her feet in she'd be a' richt. She taks a gweed grip o' the grun' yet an' a grand mou'fu' o' her words for a' her finery.'

'Yon's a terrible pit-on.' Mrs. Ironside's voice expressed the loftiest contempt that a woman who has married ill can possibly bestow on one who has married gorgeously. 'An' a' the men maun be like her man to be men ava'. "Do you play golf, Mr. Ironside?" she says, most gracious-like. Imagine asking Geordie wi' his sharny sheen if he played golf!'

Geordie came to the suface again. He had been out of depth, uneasy at every quirk in the conversation that his slow mind could not follow.

'I dinna haud wi' that cleverness masel,' he had said.

Nobody was listening to him. He tried in vain himself to listen to his own thoughts pounding within him. They said nothing intelligible. Now at the relief of a tried and accepted

joke he let himself go, laughing immoderately. His eye on
his miry boots flung sidelong in the corner – to focus the
idea – he pictured their befouled and clumsy strength
companioning the natty smartness of the golfers.

Sane man, seeing always in relation such things as he did
see.

Martha meanwhile burned in an agony of impatience.
What did they mean, chattering of these indifferent occasions while she waited for her doom? If they would only let
her back to work. . . . Wasted time! She stood and fretted,
not daring to interrupt, able hardly to endure. And why
should her father laugh like that and she in mortal stress?

Geordie came out of the absorption of his joke and heard
his wife and his neighbour dispose of Martha's pretensions
to a University education. He ruminated soberly. In the
cramped kitchen prodigious horizons lengthened out.
There were vast unenclosed tracts within him where his
thoughts lost themselves and disappeared. He pursued
them deep within himself, past his land marks.

The noise of tongues went on.

'Ye're gey forcey, though,' said Geordie.

He said it very loud, with a sharp resonance that startled
Emmeline and Stoddart into silence. He jerked forward on
his chair, sitting unusually upright, and spoke unusually
loud all through his disquisition. The voice of a man who
knew the disabilities of Providence – 'deaf in the ae lug an'
disna hear wi' the ither.' . . . Providence against Emmeline
– it needed that.

'We'll nae be nane waur aff wi' Matty at the college than
we are e'noo whan she's at the school, will we?' He boomed
the question at them as though they too were a little deaf.

'But we'll be a hantle better off, it's to be hopit, whan
she's a finished teacher.'

'Weel, but that's nae the pint. We are as we are an' we're
nae that ill – we micht be a hantle waur. But we wunna be a
hantle waur wi' Matty at the college. It wunna mak nae
differ.'

Emmeline felt a little giddy. Geordie argumentative! A
new departure.

Being set on concealment of the true reason for her

obstructionist policy, she could not immediately find another plausible enough to check him with.

'We've gotten a' we need,' he was saying. 'We've aye a tattie till wer dinner.'

'O ay, it's aye the meat you look till. Ye're a grand hand at yer meat, I will say that for ye. But there's mair things nor meat in *this* world.'

Emmeline laid a violent emphasis upon *this*, as though she were quite willing for her husband to circumscribe his activities at eating in a world to come.

'Ye wunna beat a tattie,' said Geordie, 'an' ye wunna ging far wantin' ane. – Nae in this warld,' he added, as though he were willing in his turn for his wife in her next existence to be freed from the encumbrance of food.

Martha crushed the ruined sheet of paper suddenly in her fists and began plucking it to pieces with a series of savage staccato rents.

'Jist you write it ower again, lassie,' said her father. 'There'll aye be a tattie for ye or ye're dane.'

Emmeline broke into abuse. She was defeated by one of the few loyalties she retained. Queer, she never taunted Geordie with her loss of status, nor *deaved* him with her dreams of respectability to come. Queerer still, she had no motive but her love for him. Her fury against Stoddart Semple increased. He had her inner argument pat. She tongued him therefore with virulence, cutting across his rumbling sentences.

'It's a mou'bag that you wad need. A body canna hear themsel's speak in their ain hoose.'

At that moment the wind flared in the chimney, driving the smoke down gustily into the room. Emmeline snatched noisily at the interruption.

'See to yon flan,' she cried, seizing the poker and beating at the fuel as though she would batter the smoke back up the chimney. 'We'll be smokit ooten existence. Haud back yer chairs a bit.' And she swung the poker with a virago brandish that made both Geordie and Stoddart scrape back their chairs. The feathery ash from the charred wood blew in their faces.

Balked of serenity, Emmeline took refuge in cleanliness.

The kitchen was certainly not out of the need of it. Slush and smoke together – smuts and soot and dribbled snow – clods of earth tumbled from drying boots – *dubs* and dung and crumbs and ink and dishwater not yet emptied out, tea-leaves swimming in it, and the rind of bacon flung on the hearth and dissolving in greasy dirtiness among the ashes – a very slattern among kitchens. Emmeline flung herself upon the dirt like a tornado.

'As black's the Earl o' Hell's waistcoat,' she grumbled, sousing the floor.

She splashed and soaped and scrubbed. The steam from her soap suds thickened the air. She lunged with her scrubbing-brush towards Geordie's seat and he moved farther and farther back before the soapy flood; she dived towards Stoddart and he retired with an edgy and raucous creak from the legs of his retreating chair.

By the time the chair was marooned against the wall Stoddart bethought himself and took his leave. Geordie tip-toed across the dripping floor and reached for his boots. Hospitality hardly requires of a man that he conduct his neighbour home (if the neighbour be so ill-advised as to visit him in such conditions) through pitch-black ploughland, an edged south-easter and a barricade of sleet. But Geordie pulled to the outer door with a terrific bang, settling the business of that impudent baggage the wind that threatened to wrench his own door-handle out of his hand with its blufferts, and steered Stoddart across the field by the elbow, roaring at him in gusts between the palavers of the gale.

'They tell me she's byordinar clever. . . . Faith, it beats me a' thegither fat way a bairn o' mine can 'a gotten brains. . . . Man, it's a sort o' judgement on a body. There ye ging, a' yer life long, rale pleased an' comfortable. Naething to gie ye a shog ooten yer ain road. An' then yer ain lassie, that's the fruit o' yer ain loins. . . . Man, it beats a'.'

In the kitchen Martha fumed miserably. She was troubled with a raging conscience. She was wrong. Of course she was wrong to burden the family for two extra years. – But might her father's authority be considered final? Was her fight really won? – She had not fought at all, then! – stood mute and foolish. She underwent a rush of self-contempt. And in spite of conscience and contempt together she was throbbing with exultation. Back to work, quick – master the throb before it mastered her; though how could she work with her mother *nyattering* like that?

'That's jist yer faither a' ower,' Emmeline was grumbling. She had already raised Geordie's aberration into a universal law governing his being. 'That thrawn there's nae livin' wi' him. Aince he taks a notion intil his heid, naething'll move him. He wad argy-bargy ye intil the middle o' next week. Ye micht as weel ging doon on yer knees an' speak to a mole that was crawlin' on the grun'. He taks a bit o' understandin'.'

Martha bent grimly to her Latin. But inspiration had fled. The four shabby sentences declined to be made less than four. The prose was completed, with much searching of the heart and the vocabulary.

Geordie came in again. Wind, water, earth, came with him, spluttered in his tracks. Emmeline dabbed at the filthy runlets – 'as muckle dirt's wad fill a kirk. I never saw. . . .'

The boys were *beddit*. They slept in the middle place, a sort of box between the rooms. Madge was sent packing. Martha pulled her books together and went too.

Emmeline's resentments were messy, but brief.

Next day Martha went to town – in a bitter downpour – by train. Her mother gave her the fare without demur: but she missed the early train home and it was already past the family meal-hour when she returned. There was sign of neither family nor meal. Emmeline on her knees, in splendid isolation, scoured the floor as though it had not felt water for a twelvemonth.

'Where's father?'

'Awa' to the wall for peats.'

Finality in that reply. Martha's heart sagged. She went through to the bedroom.

There she found Madge, curled on the bed, her shoulders hunched, devouring her penny trash. Her grunt was inarticulate; she did not lift her eyes from the page. She had an end of candle stuck in Martha's candlestick.

'Where did you get the candle?' cried Martha sharply. Was it hers? Had Madge stolen it? secreted it?

Madge smirked: not audible enough for one to say, giggled.

'It's nae yours, onyway. – Ye needna stand there and
glower,' she added, raising her head. 'I've tell't you, it's nae
yours. I suppose I can hide things as well's you.'

But where did she get it? Martha continued to ponder,
still glowering at the child. One fragment of her brain said
reasonably: Of course she can; and another cried in fever:
She mustn't criticize me – she's much too young. The voices
in her head circled and intersected; shortly she became
aware that they were laced by actual voices, coming through
the shoddy wall. She listened – noises too: the stir of
industry. Her father and the boys must be in the lean-to
against the house-end. She dashed out through the rain and
pushed the door. Inside was a reeking, buzzing warmth – an
oily lantern, unwashed and sweaty skins, stale air, anim-
ation, laughter. Geordie was cleaning Martha's neglected
bicycle. The boys were also engaged on the bicycle; wreath-
ing a towsled bit of rope through the spokes of the front
wheel and ripping it smartly out again. A terrific display of
industry. The flaring and smoky light from the open lantern,
shifting, smearing, exaggerating what a moment ago it had
suppressed, suppressing what it had exaggerated, gave their
actions a fantastic air of unreality. Baby Flossie, hoisted aloft
on a barrel and some boxes, a little insecure but in great
content, presided over the scene like some genius of the place
– an immature deity whose effort at creation had resulted in
grotesquerie. She was like a grotesque herself – a very tiny
baby, 'an image' Emmeline contemptuously called her: and
there she squatted on her barrel, preternaturally solemn, a
little above the level of the lantern, that juggled her features
all askew so that she seemed to wink and leer upon the
workers. But then of course the workers (Geordie excepted)
were labouring a little askew.

'She'll kick up a waup for a whilie,' Geordie said when he
saw his daughter, 'but it'll wear by. She'll keep's ooten
languor an' inen anger.'

He wiped his oily hands on his buttocks, picked up Flossie
and happed her in his coat, and extinguishing the lantern
made for supper.

'Ay, ay, it'll wear by,' he said.

In spite of a sore throat and aching limbs, Martha did her lessons that night in the cold. She held an illumination, lighting two candles to elucidate *the sine of A + B*. Madge's candle-end was gone: she must have secreted the stump for future use. Martha pushed one of her candles into the candlestick and fixed the other by its own melted end to a broken saucer.

Madge poked her head in.

'You've got to come ben. You'll be perished.'

'I'm not coming. I'm quite warm.'

'A' richt, then, dinna.'

She remained staring for a minute at the twin candles, but said nothing and went away. She could keep her own counsel and was quite willing to keep Martha's also.

Martha was glad of the feeble heat the candles gave. There was warmth also in the recollection of her father's words, 'Ay, ay, it'll wear by.'

It wore by. In very short time Emmeline had comfortably persuaded herself that a daughter with a University degree was a grandiloquence worth the waiting for. She took care, however, to hide her persuasion: in case of need still protestant.

When some months later Martha's examination was over and she had gained her bursary, Geordie sat a long while in his shirt sleeves, unbraced after supper, gripping the newspaper that had published the results, 'aye takin' the t'ither keek at her name.' Emmeline too was moved by the sight of her daughter's name in print. They would see it at Muckle Arlo! She pictured Uncle Sandy Corbett spreading out the paper and reading it aloud. Aunt Leebie would sniff, no doubt, and Aunt Jean receive it in silence: but they would know!

'Ye can jist snifter awa' there' – she addressed an imaginary Aunt Leebie – 'but ye canna say ye hinna seen't.'

'She's got ma sister Sally's gump.' Geordie's voice broke across her pleasant reverie. 'She's rale like Sally whiles.'

'Sally!' screamed Mrs. Ironside, her fancies scattering like a pack of cards. 'Her that disna richt ken gin she's merriet or no.'

'Merriet or nae merriet,' said Geordie, 'she had a sicht

mair gumption nor ony ither o' my fowk.'

Sally Ironside's life, indeed, had demanded, or perhaps developed, gumption. For nine brief days she had been the speak of the place. She had left home at the age of thirty, with neither wealth nor looks to commend her, and gone through a marriage with the man whose taste in womankind had roused the astonishment of all Peterkirk and Corbieshaw and Crannochie.

'If Sally Ironside's gotten a man, an' her thirty an' nae a stitch o' providin', there's hope for me yet,' said one old crone to another.

'There's queerer things happened,' answered she. 'But fat's the notion in nae settin' aboot it the proper gait, tell me that, will ye? A gey heelster-gowdie business, this rinnin' awa' to get yer man.'

Eighteen months later, the sole addition to her worldly gear the bairn in her arms, Sally found herself on the street, her husband having given her to understand that their marriage was a form only, and invalid. Sally disputed nothing; nor did she offer any interference – legal or moral – with his subsequent marriage to a lassie with siller. Ten years later she paid a brief visit to her old home at Peterkirk, in the garb of the Salvation Army. She was well-doing and self-respecting, but what sieges and stratagems she had carried on in the interval against a callous world only Sally herself could tell. She did not choose to tell too much. The bairn had died. 'Good thing,' said Sally briefly.

Questioned as to her marriage, she acknowledged her private suspicion that the ceremony had been valid enough but that the man had taken advantage of her ignorance to get rid of her. She had no marriage lines and did not even know the name of the place where the marriage took place.

'He had a perfect right to tire of me,' she said.

Urged to set enquiries afoot, to seize what chance there was of being proved an honest woman,

'Honest fiddleyorum!' said Sally. 'I'm honest enough in myself, I hope, and a name won't make me any honester that I can see. I'm best quit of him – to start speirin' might only raise the stew. Besides if it turned out I was his true wife, it would be a gey-like pliskey on the lassie wi' the siller.'

'Like Sally!' screamed Mrs. Ironside. . . .

She added, by and by,

'It's fae the Leggatts, onyway, she gets the brains. Your fowk's a' feel.'

Which was a proposition Geordie did not take upon himself to contradict.

FIVE

Luke Comes In

Luke came in upon a day in August.

Martha was wandering in the wood.

'It's a queer like thing that ye canna bide at hame,' Emmeline would say querulously, 'an' nae a stockin' fit to ging on to the bairns the morn's mornin'. Faur hae ye been?'

'In the wood,' Martha would answer, with the same miserable sense of disaster wherewith she had confessed to tumbling in the mire on her return from Crannochie.

'That's richt, ma dear,' said Aunt Josephine, if she happened to be by: and her voice had the quiet decisiveness that suggested something absolute and took the wind from the best-sailing of squabbles. 'They say trees is awfu' gweed for ye.'

She was wandering then in the firwood on the August afternoon when Dussie reappeared: Dussie come back, true to her old fore-visioning, with fortune at heel! – If this were indeed the guise wherewith she ushered fortune in, lanky and sober-suited, a plain unsmiling youth.

Fortunate, by tale of her own appearance. Dussie had a costly look. A silken shimmer on her gown, like the play of flame when she moved and every detail exquisite, from the burnished mass of her hair to the burnished buckles of her pretty shoes: for Luke Cromar had cobbled shoes and knew a good thing in footwear when he saw it; and liked it too, upon his wife.

For nineteen-year-old Dussie, tiny, radiant, absurdly finished and mature, was a bride of five weeks' standing. She had run away from the aunts who had taken her, and married Luke.

'And of course he had no right to marry me,' she said.

'Not so soon. He's only a student – students aren't supposed to get married. But he'll be a doctor next year.'

With that Martha looked at the lanky youth. Hitherto she had paid no attention to him. How could she, with Dussie running on like that? But she gave him now her grave consideration, and he returned her a scrutiny as grave.

'It's a holy pilgrimage,' he said. 'All the haunts of her childhood. A devotee's processional.'

Was it some sort of joke, Martha pondered, walking by them out of the wood. Dussie certainly had laughed extravagantly, though on her life she could not tell whether Mr. Cromar had meant it for a joke or not; and he was very earnest when he asked if they might see the cottage.

Martha asked them in. Dussie, quick to catch her hesitation, cried 'No!' But Luke was quicker and said, 'Of course we're coming in.' So in they came.

Martha's trepidation had cause. Emmeline was complacent that afternoon and therefore tolerant. The tolerance was manifest. Dirty dishes, a bit of pudding, old cast clouts and old rotten rags, broken bark, twigs and jags of firewood, a sotter . . . . Emmeline herself had just completed the current instalment of the serial story in the *People's Treasure*. An insatiable reader, like her daughter: but seeking apocalypse in fiction, not in fact. Peeragesque, her novels. Or if there were not titles enough (bold, bad and foreign in default of English) to go round, let them at least portray the Fortunate, their reversals be from misery to style: and never, dear fate! depict a ploughman, or a ploughman's wife and family.

She had just remarked to Madge, 'I bet you she'll mairry yon chap an' come oot a great swell yet,' when the door opened and the visitors arrived.

Married she was, though not the she of the novelette. Remember her? Well, to be sure! One didn't keep a black besom under one's roof three years and forget her in such a suddenty as that. And, looking her up and down,

'Ye're nae muckle bookit, onyway,' she said. Martha was a good four inches taller. A scoring point for Martha, and scoring points had been hard to find: would be hard still, she realized, studying Dussie more closely. Martha, clothe her how you would, would never look like that. Martha's figure went straight up and down, her blouses were always in bags or escaping at the waist, her skirts drooped, her hair was stribbly and in moments of preoccupation even yet she sucked its ends. Emmeline had a sudden movement of furious hatred against this shapely apparition that rose in her own house to mock her for her daughter's lack of presence. It was imperative to disparage Dussie for the sake of her own self-respect.

'A terrible-like chase ye were in to get merriet,' she said. 'But you aye did a'thing by stots an' bangs,' – and added, her eye on the husband,

'But what a tang'l! Ye micht a' chosen ane wi' mair beef on him fan ye were at it. Like a forty-fittit Janet up on end.'

Dussie's lip stiffened. Their call was brief.

'Yes, we must go on, mustn't we?' said the bridegroom. 'There's that wonderful Aunt Josephine. We have to see her.'

Aunt Josephine! Martha felt relief. Of course, they would go there, all three of them. Aunt Josephine's hospitality was equal to any strain. Martha had been wretched; the sloven kitchen, her mother's rudeness, Dussie's pretty hauteur, sank her in embarrassed shame. The young man's voice revived her. But there he was taking leave of Emmeline with a grave courtesy that was embarrassing too. Beef or no beef, the forty-fittit Janet up on end had manners. Martha was not accustomed to men who were polite to her mother. She felt incredibly shy.

Not much grave courtesy out of doors, however.

He had Dussie by the hand.

'Gorgeous heap of stones. Come on!'

'O Luko!' she breathed, ecstatic; and away they went, stumbling and shrieking, helter-skelter between the barley and the dyke.

They stood all three on top of the cairn, breathless.

Martha said: 'It's very old. It's supposed to commemorate something.'

Luke said: 'I like this place. There's such a lot of sky round about here.'

Dussie said: 'But aren't we going to see your father?'

From her point of vantage she swept the surrounding fields. How Geordie had kittled her, let her climb upon him, sheltered her from storm – Emmeline and the elements, both.

Martha was secretly glad that he was out of sight and call. It would have meant a shame the more. Her father, with his great crunkled boots, straws caught between the soles and uppers, sharn in spatters over them, his trousers tied with string, his empty speech, his roaring gales of laughter. . . .

They set out for Aunt Josephine's.

Mary Annie was visiting Miss Leggatt.

The years had made little difference to Aunt Josephine. She had no capacity for growing old. Mary Annie, too, was hardly altered: she had grown so old already, so many ages were graven in her anxious face, that nine years or so could only trifle with the indentations that furrowed her.

Apologetic, she tried to creep away.

'Noo, noo, Mary Annie,' said Aunt Josephine. 'Ye were bidden to tea an' ye'll bide to tea. We'll hae wer tea a' thegither. It'll be a party, ma dear' – she enveloped Dussie, excitement and buckles and all, with her slow shining gaze – 'just a party. Ye canna ging awa', Mary Annie, an' Jeannie oot. Ye canna bide yer lane.'

Fetching a profound sigh at the mention of her loneliness, Mrs. Mortimer sat down again.

Mary Annie's man was dead. He had died three months after getting a complete set of false teeth. Unlucky all the ways of it, those teeth. He hadn't had them three weeks when he had a drop too much. Some late in coming home, he was, and not so able to hold his liquor as he used to be . . . 'an' him spewin' a' the road hame, in ahin dykes an' sic-like.' . . . It was next morning till he noticed that he had shed the teeth . . . 'An' a terrible palaver there was or they got them.' The police poking about in all odd corners. And he hadn't had them three months when he died.

Mary Annie's plaint against the horrible uncertainty of life started always from the teeth and returned back upon them. They symbolised for her the tragedy of life's waste. She had wrapped them in a handkerchief and put them between the folds of the nightgown laid aside in her kist for her own last

dressing. She would have given them a more prominent
place among her gear had it not been for awe of her daughter
Jeannie. Jeannie, and no cataclysm of nature or the soul, had
tortured Mary Annie's features into their ghastly fixedness of
dark anxiety. She was preyed upon by the perennial sense
that she was unworthy of her daughter.

Jeannie indeed had certain powers beyond her mother's
comprehension. In her early teens she had developed ways of
her own and displeasures for which her mother could see no
kind of reason. Her withering young disapproval ran across
the household. Mary Annie set herself against innovation
and Jeannie had no more than looked at her father.

'I dinna see fat ye need conter the lassie for,' said he to his
wife. 'Dinna quarrel her. Jeannie's nae to be contered.'

Mary Annie, painfully conscious of the honour he had
done her in lifting her from her estate of servant lassie at the
Leggatts' to be mistress of a four-roomed house, had sorrowfully acquiesced. Her daughter bewildered her. She was
of her father's mould, superior to the breed of servants. Her
own shortcomings loomed heinous in view of Jeannie's
assured and incomprehensible managements. But one day
when the girl was sixteen she had appropriated a crimson
sateen bodice trimmed with black bugles, that had been her
mother's pride some eighteen years before. Never worn
now, it yet retained its valour in her memory. It was like a bit
of materialized experience. Mrs. Mortimer entered by
chance her daughter's bedroom (without knocking: a practice that Jeannie in vain had indicated to her as objection-
able) just as the second slash was making in the crimson
stuff. The girl (who did not even pay her mother the idle
compliment of deceit with regard to unapproved proceed-
ings) told her coolly that she was doing up the bodice to wear
when Tammie Gleg took her next week to the Timmer
Market.

'Ye needn't be in sic a takin' aboot it,' she said, the scissor
poised for another cut, 'it's gey cheap-john lookin' stuff.'

Mary Annie had long ceased expostulating with her
daughter by word of mouth. She simply grabbed the crimson
bodice and wrested it by main force from its captor. Jeannie
let go, to avoid rending it, secure of her own ultimate

victory. But Mr. Mortimer, to whom the sentimental value of the garment was fudge, nevertheless on this occasion sided with his wife. He had no mind to see a lass of his gallivanting in the Castlegate with a merry-andra like Tammie Gleg, 'skraighin' an' chawin' nuts, an' nae mair sense in their heids nor the timmer spurtles.' He forbade the occasion for the bodice, whispering behind his hand to Jeannie.

'Never heed the boady. Ye'll get a better ane to yersel whan ye're a bittie aulder.'

Jeannie never forgave her mother the interference. She took a terrible, if unintentional, revenge. She took to religion. In one of her turbulent adolescent moods she underwent conversion. The process was passionate and thorough, nor was there any reason to doubt its sincerity; but she early learned to master a force that might otherwise have mastered her, and use its currents for her own purposes. Henceforward the thwarting of her will became impossible. She had leadings from above and resorts to prayer in every complicated situation. She cultivated the habit of praying – aloud – for the soul of anyone who crossed her will. Mary Annie was gifted with a humble and ignorant adoration for all that had to do with religion. She had no genius for it herself. For many years it had been the secret craving of her heart to make up a prayer out of her own head, till the attempts had shrivelled of their own useless accord and been forgotten. When therefore her daughter graduated in piety, Mary Annie abased herself and worshipped. Thenceforward she was haunted by her own unworthiness of such a daughter. There was no conscious hypocrisy in Jeannie's conduct: her life indeed was one of extreme rectitude, just as many of the innovations she brought to the home were in themselves excellent: she merely allowed herself to be deluded in accordance with her desires.

She was now a woman in the middle forties, of powerful build and marked features, that gave her the impression of a strength of character she did not really possess. She was thrawn, not strong.

Aunt Josephine was making tea.

'Ye cutty 'at ye are!' she would interrupt herself to say to Dussie.

'And shouldn't Marty get married too?' said Dussie, preening herself.

'There's Andy Macpherson has a gey ill e'e aifter her, I'm thinkin',' said Aunt Josephine complacently.

'Rubbish!' cried Martha in a savage scarlet. Andy Macpherson, who sold bacon and sweeties in a grocer's shop at Peterkirk, had considerably less to do with her present scheme of the universe than had Hannibal or Robert Peel. Her annoyance, however, rapidly subsided. A day earlier she would not even have blushed. But something in Dussie's presence, her dancing and observant eye, troubled the waters in Martha's soul. Only momentarily: anything so alien from her common world of ideas had little power to hold her mind.

'You must come and see my house,' Dussie was saying.

'House!' scoffed Luke. 'Two rooms and a half, four stairs up.'

'In Union Street,' Dussie explained.

'Union Street!' echoed Martha. Funny place to live – all shops and offices. She had not thought that folk *lived* there.

'Oh, right on the top,' said Dussie. 'Above the shops and offices. Right up at the roof.'

'And you get out on the leads,' – Luke added his touch to the picture – 'grand view. All up and down Union Street. Some sky and a few gulls besides. You must be our guest next coronation procession. Splendid facilities.'

'You must be our guest a jolly lot sooner. Waiting for any old King, indeed!'

'Well, the Torchlight, then. That's better than a coronation. You shall view that from our top shrubbery – no, it hasn't any greens, just a way of speaking. Oh, but I forgot. You'll be a student yourself by the next Torchlight. You'll be waiting in the Quad, of course, not a spectator from the gods.'

And Martha listening had a sense of widening horizons, of vistas opening insecurely on a foreign country.

There was less foreign in the country when, a week or so later, she went to tea in Union Street, four stairs up, above the shops and offices, and Luke showed her his row of books. She was at home there, glowing visibly as she touched

them, turned their leaves, read in snatches. She even found a
tongue, and questioned. A listener, too. Her very listening
was speech, he thought. She was eloquent by what she did
not say.

'Young Pantagruel!' he laughed at her: and to her look of
enquiry read aloud:

'"These letters being received and read, Pantagruel
pluck't up his heart, took a fresh courage to him, and was
inflamed with a desire to profit in his studies more than ever,
so that if you had seen him, how he took paines, and how he
advanced in learning, you would have said that the vivacity
of his spirit amidst the books, was like a great fire amongst
dry wood, so active it was, vigorous and indefatigable."'

She went home with as many books as she could carry.

'Saw ye ever the like o' that in a' yer born days?' cried
Emmeline. 'Faur are ye ga'in to pit them a'? Fat were ye
needin' wi' sae mony a' at aince? There's a mids i' the sea.'

And Luke, four stairs up in Union Street, was saying to
Dussie,

'Your Marty's worth the knowing, you know. She's so
absolutely herself. There's such a white flame of sincerity in
her. So still and self-contained too. She's like – well, if one
could imagine it – a crystal of flame. Perfectly rigid in its own
shape, but with all the play and life of flame.'

He liked his simile and reverted more than once to it in
thought.

For Martha, she was happy in the possession of his books
and gave no thought to the owner.

In October she went to King's.

SIX

Expansion of the World

Martha snatched. There was no time to build a cosmos. Her
world was in confusion, a sublime disordered plenty. Some
other day, far off, she would order it, give it structure and
coherence. . . . Meanwhile there was the snatching.

She snatched because she lived in fever. Greedy, convulsive, in a jealous agony, she raced for knowledge, panting.
Supposing, in the three years of her course at King's, she
should not be able to gather all the knowledge that there
was. . . . When, in March, she sat her first degree examination, and passed, she had a movement of profound disil-
lusion. 'Is this all I know? I thought I should know
everything.'

She understood that a graduate may be ignorant.

By that time her panic was over. The grey Crown, that had
soared through so many generations above the surge and
excitement of youth, had told her that wisdom is patient and
waits for its people. The greed went out of her as she looked
up morning after morning at its serenity. It was like a great
rock amid the changing tides of men's opinions. *Knowledge
alters – wisdom is stable*. It told her time and again that there
was no need for haste. In the long Library, too, with the
coloured light filtering through its great end window, and its
dim recesses among the laden shelves – where thought, the
enquiring experiencing spirit, the essence of man's long
tussle with his destiny, was captured and preserved: a desic-
cated powder, dusted across innumerable leaves, and set
free, volatile, live spirit again at the touch of a living mind –
she learned to be quiet. One morning she thought, standing
idly among the books: 'But they might come alive, without
my mind.' And she had a moment of panic. The immensity
of life let loose there would be terrifying. They might clutch

50

at her, these dead men, storming and battering at the citadel of her identity, subtly pervading her till they had stolen her very self. She so poor, and they with their magnitude of thought, of numbers. . . . The panic passed, and elation possessed her in its stead. She stood a long time in a dark corner, watching the people come and go, touch books, open them, read them, replace them, carry them away: and at every contact she thrilled. 'Spirit is released.' The great room tingled with it. Even when no one was there, it might turn back to spirit, that dried powdering of words that held the vital element. But the thought no longer gave her fear. It liberated. She walked in a company.

From the company she kept in the flesh she took less consciously material for her building. She had not yet discovered that men and women are of importance in the scheme of things: though she allowed an exception of course in favour of Professor Gregory. She owed to him one of the earliest of those moments of apocalypse by which life is dated.

'Gweedsake!' said Emmeline. 'Sic a lay-aff. You and yer Professor Gregory! You wad think naebody had had a tongue in their heid afore to hear you speak.'

Martha spoke no more of Professor Gregory, but thought much. The moment of apocalypse had come in his opening lecture. She had climbed the stair, jostled a throng that pushed and laughed and shouted. Everyone was going to hear Professor Gregory's opening lecture. Martha felt herself carried violently on by the pressure from behind. At the top of the stair, separated from the girls she knew, she was flung suddenly forward. She lost her balance and her breath. . . . Then she found herself held securely. She had been pitched against a stalwart in navy uniform, who quelled the impetuous rioting throng with a gesture, a glance. They surged round him, chattering and shouting, 'I say, Daxy –' 'Hello, it's old Dak –' 'Daxy, you're a sight for sair e'en, man –'

Daxter, Sacrist of King's, an old campaigner, like Odysseus full of wiles from warfare in the East, greeted them all with one eye and marshalled them with the other; and all the while held Martha firm in a little island amid the stream.

'Now, miss, you go in.' And the way was clear for her. The old Logic class-room was filled. Greetings were shouted. Voices ran like the assorted noises of a burn. And then two hundred pairs of feet were pounding the floor, and Martha, looking round, saw a long lean man come in, spectacled, with a smile running up his face that drove the flesh into furrows.

'Funny smile,' Martha was thinking. 'Not a smooth space left anywhere.' But she forgot the corrugations when he began to speak. He spoke like a torrent. He digressed, recovered himself, shot straight ahead, digressed again. He forgot his audience, turning farther and farther round till he stood side on to them, gazing through a window and washing his hands with a continually reiterated motion while he spun his monologue. Then suddenly he would turn back upon the class with a wrinkling smile and swift amused aside; and a roar of laughter would rise to the roof, while the feet thundered on the floor. His theme was English literature, but to Martha it seemed that he was speaking the language of some immortal and happy isle, some fabulous tongue that she was enabled by miracle for once to comprehend; and that he spoke of mysteries . . . .

The confines of her world raced out beyond her grasp. When he had ended she felt bruised and dizzy, as though from travelling too rapidly through air. The strong airs had smote her. But she had seen new countries, seen – and it was this that elated her, gave her the sense of newness in life itself that makes our past by moments apocryphal – the magnitude of undiscovered country that awaited her conquest. She was carried downstairs in the crowd and at the bottom met the Sacrist, who gave her a look of recognition. At the moment Martha was thinking: 'And I shall go on travelling like that. There will be more new countries.' And she was radiant. For sheer joy she broke into a smile; but perceiving that she was smiling straight into the face of Daxter, went hot with confusion and hurried away.

Daxter, however, accosted her as she was crossing the quadrangle some days later. Shortly she counted his greeting a normal part of her day. He claimed friendship with her as from the beginning.

'You see, miss, you smiled to me the very first day you came.'

'Oh,' cried Martha, 'but I didn't mean to –' and stopped abruptly, confused again. A tactless thing to say. But Daxter did not seem to be offended. He took her into his den, a narrow room at one corner of the quadrangle, the walls and table of which were covered with photographs. From the photographs 'Daxy' could reconstruct the inner history of the University since he had become Sacrist. Here were the giants who had been on the earth in those days. He told Martha tales, such as appear in no official record, of the immediate past of the University, and tales of his campaigns in India, making her world alive for her in new directions. One day he showed her some strips of silk. They had been part of the colours of a regiment – a tattered standard that had hung in the Chapel of King's till its very shreds were rotting away. He had been ordered to remove it: but round its pole the silk was still fresh, and he had kept the remnant. He cut two snippets of the silk, a snippet of cream and a snippet of cerise, and gave them to Martha.

'That's history, that is, miss.' And he put them in an envelope for her.

Martha carried the envelope in her pocket for nearly a week, deliberating where she might keep her treasure safe from predatory fingers. She had so few possessions and no stronghold for storing them. Madge, on the verge of the teens, had developed an inordinate interest in her appearance. She brewed herself strange scents from perfumed flowers and water, and decanted the product into an ink-bottle, sprinkling her garments lavishly with the concoction; and rubbed her lips and cheeks with purloined geranium petals. Martha caught her once sneaking out of a garden where geraniums were bedded out, and preached her a very pretty sermon on the heinousness of her deed. Madge's only reply was to march without the slightest attempt at secrecy into the next geraniumed garden and abstract a goodly handful of scarlet petals. She was quite capable, if she caught sight of them in the bedroom, of using Martha's scraps of silk for personal adornment. In the end Martha flattened the envelope, that was crushed and smeared from its sojourn in her pocket, and laid it between the pages of a heavy algebra text-book that stood on the high triangular shelf in the corner of the room: with hooks on its under surface to serve the girls for wardrobe. Sometimes she slipped the envelope from its hiding-place and touched the bits of silk that a regiment had followed. At such times it seemed to her that she was touching the past.

While her universe was thus widening both in time and in space, Scotland grew wider too. Hitherto her own blue valley, the city with its spires and dirty trawlers, had been her measure of Scotland. Now it grew. The North came alive. Out of it, from cottar-houses and farms, from parlours behind country shops, from fishing-villages on the Moray Firth, from station-houses and shepherds' houses and school-houses, manses and mansions, crofts on the edge of heather, snow-blocked glens, clachans on green howes beneath the corries, where tumbling waterfalls lit the rocks; islands in the Atlantic, gale-swept, treeless; thatched cottages where the peat reek clung in stuff and fabric and carried east in clothes and books – there flocked in their hundreds her fellow-students, grave, gay, eager, anxious, earnest, flippant, stupid and humble and wise in their own conceits, dreamers and doers and idlers, bunglers and jesters, seekers of pleasure and seekers of wisdom, troubled, serene, impetuous, and all inquisitive; subjecting life to inquisition.

Out of the Islands Martha found her friends. Chief was Harrie Nevin. Harrie came from Shetland. She had the Vikings in her bearing and Martha worshipped her from a distance: until she discovered that Harrie was doing the same by her. Then they wrote each other wonderful letters. . . .

Martha suffered bitterly because she could not ask Harrie to her home. Harrie, with her regal port, in Emmeline's haphazard kitchen! In compensation she was able to introduce her to Luke Cromar.

It had not occurred to Martha that knowing Luke was a matter for public congratulation; but the girls who saw him leave a group of talkers in the quadrangle at Marischal and dash across to Martha when he saw her pass, put her right as to that. She perceived that knowing Luke gave her a social status in University affairs; but rated that at less worth than simply knowing him.

University affairs, indeed, made much of Luke. He was in everything. He was President of the Student's Representative Council and on half a dozen other committees as well. And in the flat, four stairs up, Dussie waited for him and entertained his guests. They lived on little. Luke had been an apprentice shoemaker, an orphan boy who had dreamed while he cobbled shoes of mending all the philosophies of the world. A legacy had enabled him to go through college. But Dussie played eagerly at economy. Gracious, petulant, fresh as rain, she was the delight of all his friends. She made a hundred mistakes, but proclaimed them aloud with such a bubbling candour that they were only so many assets the more to her popularity. The men loved to hear her own rapturous recital of her indiscretions, her social *faux pas*.

In the summer they held tea-parties on the leads – 'Luke's sky-highs,' Kennedy called them; and the name caught.

Martha came to few of their parties, though Dussie, whose childhood's adoration had lost none of its vehemence, would have had her come to all. She was too shy, too awkward, and her Sunday blouse and skirt were out of place. Besides, time was short. Piles of stockings to darn, of dishes to wash, ate too far into it. Emmeline, it was clear, regarded the time she spent on books as leisure, her recreation. To have pen and paper about, and open note-books, protected her: but when her pulses raced to the choruses in *Atlanta*, or, rapt away by thought, poring over *The Marriage of Heaven and Hell*, she stared out motionless upon the strangeness of its landscapes, Emmeline's voice would break in:

'Is that yer lessons ye're at?'

It took many skirmishes with her conscience to convince her that she was justified in saying yes: and by that time Emmeline was convinced to the contrary. A 'poetry book' was for fun, and its reader might legitimately be interrupted. *The English Parnassus* she recognized as a lesson book. It had been bought, not borrowed from the Library at King's; and on winter nights that were too chill for her bedroom, Martha carried *The English Parnassus* to the kitchen; she read it from cover to cover, fairly secure from onslaught.

Her leisure therefore she would not devote to parties: where, to say the truth, she was not over-happy. She went however to the Friday evening Societies – to the 'Lit.'; and to the 'Sociolog,' because Luke was its President and had made her a gift of a membership card.

'Raw ripe red wisdom every Friday at seven,' he proclaimed.

She sat astounded at the discussions she heard. Wages, industrial unrest, sweated labour, unemployment, mental deficiency, syndicalism, federation – words to her! She had given so little of her thought as yet to the present; and it amazed her increasingly to hear her fellow-students, some glib, some stuttering, some passionate, some sardonic, talk of these matters. *We are the people*, they might have cried.

In particular she stared cold-hearted at the 'Vice'. The Vice-President was a girl: Lucy Warrender by name. No matter what the theme, Miss Warrender talked with authority. She had already an Honours degree in Philosophy and was studying now for History and Economics. She seemed to know existence to its ends. Martha gulped in sheer terror sometimes when she heard her talk: so competent, flawless, master of her purposes.

'Oh, a mine of information,' Luke called her, when Martha stammered her dismay. Was it praise or disparagement? She could not tell: and when, puzzling it out, she looked at him, his long face told her nothing.

But astonishing as were some of the things she heard, Martha took them all in. One must not throw away a fact. Knowledge grew sweeter the more one ate of it. Sharp-flavoured too, though, acrid at times upon the palate.

This widening world of ideas grew more and more the true abode of her consciousness. The cottage did not reabsorb her afternoon by afternoon: it received her back. She was in its life but not of it. Its concerns did not concern her nearly. Still less did she feel herself concerned with her neighbours, the Andy Macphersons and the Stoddart Semples. She had no point of contact with these: or thought so. In this she was mistaken. The contact was there, though she did not feel it.

Its existence, however, might have been detected, less than a month after her session began, on a day when Aunt Josephine Leggatt walked down from Crannochie to Wester Cairns.

SEVEN

Sundry Weathers

Aunt Josephine, hodging steadily along the soft road in the direction of Wester Cairns, met Stoddart Semple lounging by the dyke.

Stoddart had never forgiven his February dismissal into the sleet. Having backed, in that dispute, the side that lost, he went away convinced of Martha's uppishness; and as Martha did not like the man, tasted moreover no salt in the jokes he relished with her father, and never stopped to give him a crack by the roadside, he supposed himself in her contempt when it was merely she who sat in his.

Meeting Miss Leggatt, he began to grumble sourly.

'Ye've gotten a lady in the family noo.'

He put a bitter emphasis on the *lady* and stopped to look at Miss Leggatt.

'I see the muckle feet o' her takin' awa' doon the road,' he added.

'If it's Matty ye're meanin',' said Miss Josephine – and she said it without the shadow of an alteration in mien or accent – 'she's been a lady sin' ever she was the littlin.'

'A bonny penny she'll be for books,' he grumbled.

'I wadna say. Ye get naething for naething in this warld.' Miss Leggat was quite unmoved at his grievance. She told him with an amiable serenity, 'An' naebody's biddin' *you* pay. Ye needna talk as though they hadna a penny to rub on t'ither.'

Once launched, he could not leave the theme. There was east in his weather. The old sore itched. He scratched. Moreover he was curious. He wanted to know many things – matters of price, for instance, and such gossip as he could glean regarding the *terrible lang chiel* that came about the doors sometimes, and his wife, that was here when she was a

58

bairn. He had questioned Geordie, to be sure, but Geordie's knowledge did not go very far.

'He's a terrible ane to speir,' Aunt Josephine said to Emmeline. She had given him little satisfaction by her answers.

'Speir!' cried Mrs. Ironside. 'He wad speir the claes aff'n yer back an' than speir faur ye tint them.'

She resented his prying into Martha's affairs, and – remembering February – stiffened her resolution to see the girl through her Odyssey.

'I'll show him,' she muttered to herself. 'Speirin' indeed.'

She 'showed him' a few days later. Martha fell sick. She recovered, but dragged her limbs.

'The cyclin's ower muckle for ye,' said Emmeline. 'Ye'll get a season ticket in the train.'

Thenceforward Martha went by train, tramping down the rough brae morning by morning.

The cross-country road, through the bright winds of October, had been pleasant: but she was glad enough to put away the cycle in these faint November days. December came with rain, black pitiless unceasing rain, that hurled itself upon the fields for days together, paused sullenly, and spewed again upon a filthy earth. It was on such a day of rain that Martha went with Luke and Dussie to her first opera. Luke insisted on coming home with her, although she warned him that he could hardly hope to catch the last train back to town.

'No matter,' he said. 'I like a soaking now and then. Good elemental feel it gives you.' And he steadied her by the elbow at the turn of the road.

The road was swimming. A flat of slimy mud lay across the bottom of the brae. Cataracts poured ceaselessly into it, carrying soil from the brae. The wind drove from the east.

'Just an April shower,' he said, crossing to the weather side of her as they turned.

She looked at him, swiftly. She could not see him. It was too dark. But she had an uncanny impression of having seen his smile. Oh, it was in his voice! – that smile that she had not been able to locate. He had a laughing voice.

They were both laughing as they stumbled among the

mud and the loose stones. Weather was a joke, it seemed! And the stormy chords from *Tannhäuser* beat upon her sleep, mingled in a colossal harmony with the beat of the elemental storm, through which his laughing voice recurred like a song.

January changed the wind. The stir of spring was in the world almost as soon as the year came in. Soft airs, faint skies plumed with shining wisps of cloud, blossom on the whins, bursting willow catkins, blackbirds fluting, a gauze of gnats against the sun, and everywhere the strong clean smell of new-turned earth – a wholesome kindly world: too mellow perhaps; without the young astringency of spring.

But at the end of February, out of a cold black north a dozen meandering snowflakes fell. They drifted about the air like thrums – blown from the raw edges of the coming storm. Next morning colour had gone from the world. Shapes, sounds, the energies and acutenesses of life, were muffled in the dull white that covered both earth and sky. No sun came through. The weeks dragged on with no lifting of the pallor. The snow melted a little and froze again with smears of dirt marbling its surfaces. To the northward of the dykes it was lumped in obstinate seams, at the cottage doors trodden and caked, matted with refuse, straws and stones and clots of dung carried in about on clorted boots. The ploughs lay idle, gaunt, like half-sunk reefs among the furrows.

'We'll hae wer sax weeks' snaw in March the year richt eneuch,' said Geordie, beating his arms across his chest to quicken the circulation.

Baby Flossie wailed miserably and sucked her frozen fingers. They were hottest in her mouth. When Emmeline caught them there she pulled them out and smacked them till they tingled. That heated them too.

Martha, buffeted in the bitter winds, struggling to keep her footing on the rutted ice of the brae, arrived listless at the lecture-room. Often her fingers were dead. She could not write notes. She sat, in the chill room that gathered a clammy warmth from a hundred breaths, heavy-headed, her interest subdued: but by noon, when Professor Gregory lectured, she was alert again, fleet-footed after knowledge. No ice, no battering winds, could hold her from that pursuit.

The spring term had ended before the frost gave.

One afternoon the wind veered. It rushed out of the south-west, hot and sweet, like the breathing of a cow against one's face.

'The snaw's gotten a fleg,' said Geordie jubilantly. He leaned against the door-post, a thumb in his arm-hole, watching the wind lick the surface of the world clean. Martha, plodding home with a bagful of groceries, looked at him listlessly and made no answer. She was heavy-eyed and round-shouldered. Knowledge is inexorable to its devotees and sets its own price high. The mild air softened her resistance to her own weariness. Her month's vacation dragged.

And meanwhile the sun was gathering strength. The earth was steaming like a wet clout held to the fire, with a steam so thick and close that it floated over the fields like heavy morning mists on an autumn valley. The fog-horn boomed; and the slopes beyond the river were out of recognition, flat and pale.

The sun gathered strength. The roads blew dry. In three days' time the dust was flying. The plough land changed its colour – sharp sandy brown at last, ready for the seed. Larks sprang and shrilled, operatic, mechanical, in a series, as though a multitude of catches were successively released in the grass and stubble. The sowers were out and the harrow was on the fields.

Geordie cried to Stoddart Semple down the gale that lifted the earliest clouds of dust – a roaring, rollicking, tattering, clothes-line-walloping gale – 'Ay, ay, man, the land's dryin' fine.'

It had been Geordie's daily remark since the thaw set in. He said it to everyone he met outside, and three or four times a day at home as well. A matter of such importance could not stale.

Stoddart, slouching by the dyke, made answer,

'It would dry some quicker if your missus stood oot o' the way a bit.'

And he looked at Emmeline where she stood full in the sun, stretching out after the tail of a shirt that reared and curveted on the clothes-line.

'I see she's gettin' a terrible-like size,' he said.

Emmeline in the last few months had been putting on flesh rapidly, achieving a shapelessness that was far from her old rounded grace. The shadow she cast, standing there in the sun, was considerable. It was a sore point, and luckily she was too far away to catch either Stoddart's sneer or the reply made by Geordie, quick-witted for once as he watched the surface of the earth scatter upon the wind.

'O ay,' he said, 'gran' for keepin' the grun' doon in a gale.'

Martha, however, had been near enough to catch both. She pondered, standing by a bush of whin, plucking at the golden scented blossoms and rubbing them on her palm until her skin was yellow; she pondered whether her father's answer was really as crass as it had sounded. She remembered Luke Cromar, who was polite even to Emmeline. And behind her Geordie went off in sudden uproarious laughter, as though his witticism, so natural in face of the blowing dust, had only now occurred to him as being witty.

Martha went back to the house and read *The Land of Heart's Desire* – a silver and azure world where she did not recognize that there walked the peasant folk of her own acquaintance. Like Emmeline, she hardly desired the stories that she read to deal with ploughmen: not at any rate with sharny boots and hacked hands seamed with dirt.

In the summer term she spent her afternoons studying Natural History. The Professor, in a quiet voice that he never raised nor quickened, peopled for her the airs, glancing waters and grassblades, and the cold dark grave profundities of the sea. He had the tongue of a poet and of a humorist: a tongue like that of the fabled story-teller of Arabia, whom no one could hear without believing every word he uttered. When he spoke, incredible shapes moved through an unimaginable past; and an unimaginable present surged in on one, humming with a life one had not seen before, nor even suspected. So full the world was, and so clamorous! And placidly, without haste or emphasis, he conjured up its press and clangour, its multitudinous anxieties.

'Like Aunt Josephine,' Martha found herself thinking: and her own temerity frightened her. But she was right. He had the same luminous unhurrying serenity as Aunt Josephine, the same sure capable grasp of life.

She lunched, between her two diets of worship, between King's in the morning and Marischal in the afternoon, on a hunk of bread and a bit of cold bacon.

'Not good for you,' said Luke. 'You must lunch with us.'

Dussie seconded eagerly. She served up every dish in her repertory, and invented a few new combinations of material. Martha had never eaten so many unfamiliar things in her life.

Dussie objected: 'You are not a rapturous eater, Marty. Now Luke is. He really pays attention to what I make for him.'

And to Luke she pouted: 'She might just as well be chewing at her hunk of bread. She doesn't care what it is she's eating.'

To which Luke made answer: 'Well, of course, you know, flame is fairly indiscriminate as to what it takes for fuel.'

'Oh,' she cried, exasperated, 'you are crazed with your flame. Marty has a stomach like the rest of us, I suppose, and she should be made to know about it.'

'Lord forbid!' he said. 'The people who know about their stomachs are the devil.'

Her exasperation effervesced into laughter.

'But you know what I mean, Luke. It's only because I love her so much that I want her to be like other people.'

'I should have thought that was a reason for wanting to keep her as she is.'

Dussie's brows went up in pity. Really, to be so clever, Luke had sometimes astonishingly little common-sense.

If Martha was indifferent to the provender, she was not indifferent to the joy of sharing it. As May ran on, indeed, she was glad of the heat and the shelter. The weather changed to a black cold, hard skies, hard edges to the earth, bitter winds. Then the skies loosened at the edge, puckered into cloud.

'Ower mony upcastin's,' said Geordie, eyeing the solid lumps of cloud *birsed* up into the sky.

Next day a plaster of snow deformed the opening leaves and hung in wet semi-transparent blobs on the clusters of lilac.

'The cauld Kalends o' May,' Geordie called it.

'Fourth winter for the season,' said Luke, helping Martha out of her dripping coat and chafing her white dead hands. And such a lunch as Dussie had for them – 'hot as sin,' Luke proclaimed.

Luke graduated early in July, coming through his finals with a star. One of his professors – who had warned him against his own enthusiasms – told him drily that he had no right even to have passed. Luke seemed to spend his days doing things he had no right to do, and doing them triumphantly: marrying Dussie, for example. They were radiant both. Their weather was golden, crisp, vibrant with energy. The dark gods had little portion in their love. It was of the sunlight and flashing winds, clear and merry.

Standing in the quadrangle after his graduation, Luke held a petty court. Half the University surged up to congratulate him; and when it became known that old Dunster had asked him to stay on the following session as assistant, they surged back and congratulated him again.

'It's not official yet,' he kept saying. 'Has to be ratified by the Senatus. Doubtless they'll rise in a body and refuse.'

Professor Forbes, who had told him he had no right to pass, shook hands and said cordially,

'So you're to be one of us next session, I hear.'

Next day they left for the Continent, where Luke was to study for six weeks in a hospital. Martha saw them off. Harrie had gone too. The islands and the glens and the fishing villages and farms had taken their bairns back. Martha's life was bounded again, in its externals, by the slovenly kitchen with its heat and clatter, the low-roofed bedroom where all the family clothes were stocked and where Madge smeared her lips with her geranium petals and studied the effect in a spotty mirror that had a crack across its upper corner; by meals for which her father cast his coat and kicked his boots aside, where the bairns wrangled and slobbered, Emmeline raged, Flossie whimpered. Her privacy was in the open; and in her thoughts. There like a wrestler she tried all comers – the companies of new ideas that had crowded in upon her mind. She had received them all impartially, stored them away. Now she called them out again. Martha was beginning to think.

Emmeline had said, eyeing the newspaper on the day when the University lists were published and Martha's name appeared,

'They'll see't at Muckle Arlo' – a consolation that it required some strength of mind to accept for consolation; since she could not know that her surmise was correct. It was therefore by way of a flutter in the dovecot when Aunt Jean herself wrote to Martha inviting her to Muckle Arlo.

EIGHT

Leggatt Respectability

Emmeline was fluttered and took some pains to make Martha presentable. The girl herself had not much interest in her outfit. She was so much accustomed to her own dowdy appearance that she accepted it as in the nature of things and made no effort to alter it: but the visit itself was an excitement. Here was she a traveller, at last; though the travel carried her only twenty miles. And it thrilled her immoderately to climb a stair to her bedroom. She had never slept upstairs before and never had a bedroom to herself. She sat on the edge of a chair, when she had said goodnight and shut the door, and clenched her hands together to keep within measure the waves of excitement that washed over her. So new the world was! When the door opened gently and she looked up with a start, she was prepared for any unaccountable vision to meet her eyes.

The vision that met her eyes gave account of itself at once. 'It's just the Syrup of Figs,' Aunt Leebie was saying, creeping across the carpet with her shapeless figure hunched together. 'Yer Aunt Jean aye gars the bairns tak' a dosie the first nicht they come.'

She was standing above Martha, struggling with the cork, the spoon thrust by the handle in her mouth while she fichered. Her dim and anxious eyes searched the girl, noting the bones that protruded at her throat, the shadows round her eyes. Leebie was a kindly body. Taking her cue from Jean, she was ready to translate her relenting even more liberally than she had formerly translated her disapproval.

'A sup cream wad dae ye mair gweed,' she was moved to say. 'But yer Aunt Jean . . . . Whan the bairnies comes – ye wunna ken aboot the bairnies?' She shot off at a tangent, glad of the excuse. Mrs. Corbett's elder son was married; the two children came frequently to stay with their grandparents. Castor-oil, Aunt Jean believed in. That was the thing when she was young and her bairns after her.

'But their mither, she has notions o' her ain. Nae castor-oil for *her* littlins. She's a prood piece,' said Leebie confidentially to Martha, edging up until the Syrup of Figs was almost at her nose.

'Terrible ful, an' aye wears a tailor-made.'

In spite of her kindliness, Aunt Leebie was inexorable over the Syrup of Figs. The tilt of Aunt Jean's chin had commanded.

Leebie, it was plain, was spokesman. The weather being wet and the ground soft, Martha could never return from a walk, or from picking, between showers, the black currants in the garden, but Aunt Leebie, mounted dragon over the immaculate fleece of the carpets, would be meeting her at the door:

'Noo clean yer feet, aifter a' that muck. We'll hae a hoose nae common.'

Martha grew to have a fondness for Aunt Leebie; though her reprimands pursued her. She liked the funny soft giggle in which her sentences ended. Round-shouldered, wrapped always in a grey Shetland shawl that was matted by frequent washings, she watched the girl's every action, and found fault with many. On washing day it was Martha who carried out the rugs and beat them on the green. She paused for breath, too soon.

'That's nae the way,' cried Leebie from the window. 'Startin' aff like that at a bicker an' then haein' to stop.'

The aunts had undertaken Martha's domestic education with more thoroughness than consorted with holiday. She made beds under supervision and learned how silver should be laid away and the due and proper method of buying and storing yellow soap. They talked as though she knew nothing.

'But I've stayed with Aunt Josephine,' she said, 'I've seen . . .'

Leebie sniffed. 'Josephine does a'thing by instalments.'

And Aunt Jean added, in one of her rare bursts of eloquence,

'Josephine will dee by instalments.'

On the last evening of her stay they called her into Leebie's room. The half-drawn blinds, the starched Nottingham curtains, the dressing-table with its swivel mirror set straight across the window, made the room dark: Aunt Jean, sitting very upright on a cane-bottomed chair, made it portentous. Leebie sorted her parson-grey Shetland shawl. 'It's aye slippin',' she complained, ending on her soft giggle. And pulling it closer to her throat, she moved up to the bed. 'Come richt in,' she ordered Martha over her shoulder.

On the bed was laid a lustre frock – ivory, that had deepened with age. Its voluminous skirts billowed over the quilt.

'Ye'll try it on,' Leebie said.

Fingering the folds while Martha took off her blouse and skirt, 'It was richt gweed stuff,' she muttered; and pouncing, at sight of Martha's underclothes,

'The Lord preserve's, look at yer slip-body – that's yer safety-pins. Pinnin' yer skirt up!' ('It won't keep without,' Martha pleaded.) 'Canna ye wear stays, like a Christian body?'

She dropped the gown and with her hands explored the leaness of Martha's haunches.

'There's naething there to support a skirt. Ye *maun* get a pair o' stays.' She continued to fumble with her hands at the girl's hips, muttering, as though she had a personal grievance in the make of her lanky figure. Then she lifted the lustre gown and fitted it upon her grand-niece. The full skirts sprang from the waist, covering her thinness, and at the back trailed slightly on the floor. Aunt Leebie struggled with the fastenings of the bodice, dragging Martha round, pulling her from point to point in the room to catch a clearer light. The bodice was fitted to a shaped lining, that fastened down the front with close-set alternating rows of hooks and eyes.

'It's some grippit in at the middle,' she complained in the aggrieved tone she had used with which to talk of stays. 'But ye cud sort that.' And again she giggled softly.

Martha perceived that the frock was given to her.

She wondered vaguely what she could do with it. No room at Wester Cairns for frocks like that – hardly room to store it!

And as for wearing it – ! Of course it could be remade – there were yards of stuff: but plainly that was not Aunt Leebie's purpose. *Sort* the waist, shorten the skirt a little, and there you were! Martha gave a gulp of sheer panic at the thought of wearing the gown; and she was no facile needlewoman, to transform it for herself. Shirts, underclothing, yes: but when it came to the tricksey wiles of fashion . . . she remembered Dussie's frocks and felt that she would rather die than snip and alter at this ancient dress till it was wearable.

But what was it that Aunt Leebie was saying? – She must make some sign of gratitude; and plunging she said,

'I could wear it when I'm capped.'

Her graduation was so infinitely remote – two whole years away. One could make rash promises for two years hence.

'I'll keep it for then,' she said. And fearful that her gratitude had not been warm enough, she put her arms round Aunt Leebie's neck, rubbing upon the parson-grey Shetland shawl, and kissed her. 'But where am I to keep it?' she was thinking.

Aunt Leebie was pleased. She helped Martha to take off the gown and lay it carefully across the back of a chair.

'Ye maunna fold it yet,' she warned. 'Let it air a whilie.' And anxiously, with her head pushed forward and her bent shoulders pressing in the direction of the girl, she added,

'See ye guide it noo ye've got it.'

It was plain that the maxim emanated from Aunt Jean (seated there so upright and so silent on her cane-bottomed seat), and issued by way of her square-set chin through Leebie's mouth, although the frock was Leebie's and the impulse to give it Leebie's too.

Martha suddenly wanted to kiss Aunt Leebie again. 'But must I kiss Aunt Jean as well?' she queried. And a wave of shyness flooded her.

Next morning she had to unpack the Japanese basket hamper (frayed to a hole at one of its corners) in which she had brought her clothes. She had to unpack it because Aunt Leebie came into her room too late to see her fold the gown.

'I canna hae it whammlin' aboot in there,' she said. And she giggled her soft giggle.

That Martha was affected by this solidity and order, the Leggatt respectability towards which her mother yearned in vain, the girl herself did not perceive: though she gave certain signals of it after her return. Indifference to the household laxity, the unconcern with which, sunk in a dream or hot on the tracks of knowledge, she had viewed domestic turmoil as no affair of hers, altered – spasmodically only, it is true – to irritation and that to hesitant rebuke. Emmeline took the hints with unexpected meekness. She had the makings of respect for her daughter now that she was reconquering the citadel whence Emmeline had been exiled. Martha had visited at Muckle Arlo: henceforward she was allowed to be an individual. Emmeline accepted an occasional innovation, not because it was cleanly and made for order, not even because Aunt Jean arranged her matters so, but because Martha had been at Muckle Arlo. That Martha had been at Muckle Arlo was a step on towards the shining goal round which her fancies fluttered, the respectability she had foregone: though how indeed was she to reach it? Respectability was a habit of mind beyond her powers.

It was a habit of mind beyond Martha's intentions. When the winter session opened in October, and her mind was steeped again in book-learning, she forgot household management. Respectability according to the Leggatt canons had little reality in a world of passionate pursuing, where the quarry, phantoms from a dead past flitting in shadow, grew more and more alive the hotter one's pursuit. Her contact with it had nonetheless strengthened, unknown to herself, an inborn timidity that shrank from unlikeness to its fellows. It made her more sensitive to the deficiencies of her personal appearance. It was it that operated in her, on a day in the winter session, when Luke had said,

'Oh, but you mustn't go away, Marty. You must stay to tea. Old Dunster's coming.'

His professor! Tongue-tied though she knew that she would be, Martha longed to meet him. But she said.

'Oh, I can't, Luke! Not with these old boots on.'

The *old* was a concession to public opinion. They were not really old; nor had she any better; but they were rough, clumsily cut, of thick unpliable leather that had crunkled into lurks about her ankles; country boots, and all the more unsuitable for the reception of Professor Dunster that Dussie was wearing the daintiest of black court shoes, with buckles whose silver gleam was lit with blue that answered the blue shimmer of her frock.

And Luke said,

'Oh, your boots! – My dear Marty, do you suppose any one would ever look at your boots who could see your eyes?'

'My eyes!' she echoed, in such genuine astonishment that Luke and Dussie laughed aloud.

'They're nice eyes, you know,' said Dussie. And she plumped herself on a cushion at Martha's feet and craned up into her face.

'If you had said Dussie's eyes – ' Martha began.

'Dussie? – Oh, she uses eye-shine. Pots of it. You have stars in yours.'

He loved to disparage Dussie's beauty. She loved him to disparage it, paying him back with hot-head glee.

Seriously, he said,

'You are a very lovely woman, Marty.'

'Oh well,' objected Dussie, 'not very lovely, you know . . .' and Martha, flinging up her head, was crying, 'I don't know what you mean, Luke! I'm ugly.'

'True,' he answered promptly. 'Out of the running, you and I. We have both big noses.'

It was the same sensitiveness to any external oddity that operated on an afternoon in early spring when Luke, she felt resentfully, put her to public shame.

NINE

Beatrice among the Pots

She was wearing shoes that afternoon, trim, black, new –
big, of course, because her feet were big; but respectable by
any Leggatt standard, though, to be sure, they showed up
the clumsiness of her ankles in their four-ply fingering
home-knitted stockings. She was wearing also her Sunday
costume. Emmeline had grumbled at both shoes and
costume: wearing them to her school – a pretty-like palaver.
Emmeline continued to talk of Martha's University classes as
'school' and of the hours she spent in study as her 'lessons'.
So did Geordie, for the matter of that. 'But they will never
understand,' Martha sighed to herself.

Emmeline's displeasure notwithstanding, Martha wore
the Sunday shoes and costume. Dussie had a tea-party and
there was no time to come home and change. The tea-party
in the parlance of the hour was a 'hen-shine': until Luke
came in at five o'clock, bringing Macallister, there were no
men present. Martha felt herself a dullard in more than
clothing. The chatter was edged, and Miss Warrender, now
President of the Sociological, with her raking wit and air of
authority, turned the world inside out to the discomfort of
one at least of its inhabitants. It was after Luke came in that
someone, discussing another theme, took for granted
Martha's Honours course.

Martha said, 'But I am not taking Honours.'

'Not taking Honours? Everyone thinks you are.'

They overhauled the position. Miss Warrender in her
adequate way ('rather foolish, isn't it?' she asked) persuaded
the assembly that in these modern days the passman was a
nonentity.

'An ordinary degree is cheap,' she said. 'Everyone spe-
cialises.'

She disposed of Martha's pretensions to a share in the sunlight of the teaching profession without specialisation and an Honours degree, with the same thoroughness and decision wherewith Stoddart Semple and Mrs. Ironside had disposed of her pretensions to a degree at all.

'Even financially, the extra year is worth it.'

The thought of Emmeline obtruded itself on Martha's mind and she realized, hating the knowledge, that she did not wholly belong to the world in which she sat.

She became aware that Luke was speaking. He was speaking magisterially, with an air of authority that equalled Miss Warrender's own.

'That's nonsense,' she heard him say. 'It's quite wrong, most of this specialising. For teachers, anyhow. Teachers shouldn't specialise – except in life. That's their subject, really. A man doesn't set out to teach mathematics, but life illuminated by mathematics; or by literature, or dancing, or Double Dutch, or whatever it is he chooses with which to elucidate the mysteries. Miss Ironside is specialising in life. She does it rather well too.'

'Illuminated by what, if one may ask?'

The speaker was Macallister, the only other man in the room. A huge full-blooded bovine fellow, with inflated hands and lurks of fat ruffling above his collar, he was reading for Honours in Philosophy.

'I wish to goodness you'd stop asking that Macallister here,' said Dussie. 'He never looks precisely at any particular spot of you, but you feel all the same as if he'd been staring the whole time just under *here*. Such a sight too – all those collops of fat.'

Here indicated the waist-line. She referred to Macallister's way of looking as 'the Greek statue glare'.

'That's what comes of philosophy, you see,' said Luke. 'Aren't you thankful I gave it up? – Jolly acute mind, though, for all the encumbrance.'

He continued to bring Macallister to the house. He liked to know the latest developments in philosophic thought, having never quite forgotten that as an apprentice shoemaker he had constructed a system of philosophy which he dreamed would revolutionise the world. Macallister was a useful asset.

'Illuminated by what, if one may ask?' Macallister was saying, waving his cigarette towards Martha and giving her the Greek statue glare with his continually roving eyes.

'Illuminated,' said Luke, 'by the sun, the moon and the eleven stars. Also by a little history and poetry and the cool clear truths of the wash-tub.'

And again before Martha's quickening eye came the figure of Emmeline, towsled and sluttish, and of herself on the sloppy kitchen floor thrusting her arms in the water. Emmeline's voice rasped. 'Ye've scleitered a'ower the place,' she was saying. Martha felt sure that every other girl in the room was seeing the same vision as she saw, and her heart burned hot against Luke.

'Luke, you gumpus!' cried Dussie's ringing voice. 'Cool and clear indeed! Much you know about the wash-tub.'

And a girl in an immaculate white silk shirt said pettishly,

'My blouses are being ruined, just ruined! In digs, you know – but what can one do? Last week – '

The conversation drifted to more important matters than specialisation.

'Spanking night,' said Luke when the guests had gone. 'Say, Duss, let's walk Marty home.'

'You can walk her home if you like, but I've an ironing to do. – No indeed, Marty, you shan't stay and help.'

She despatched them into the dusk.

'Quarries car,' cried Luke, 'and out by Hazelwood.'

The twilight was luminous, from a golden west and a rising moon. The whole sky glowed like some enormous jewel that held fire diffused within itself. Slowly the fire gathered to points, focussed in leaping stars. They struck through Hazelwood. Stark boughs vaulted the sky, and they walked below in silence, along paths that the moon made unfamiliar. There was no purpose in breaking a silence that was part of the magic of the place and hour. Luke walked on in a gay content. Troubled, in a low voice, Martha at last remonstrated with him on the disclosure to which he had subjected her. 'They will despise me.'

He heard the low words with some astonishment, not having supposed her susceptible to a worldy valuation. For a moment he realized that her nature might be other than he had perceived, but speedily forgot it and saw her only in his own conception of her.

'Let them then. It's not worth minding, Marty. Merely the price you have to pay for my determination that they shall know there are people like you in the world. They don't think, these women – they don't think anywhere farther up than coffee in Kennington's and partners for the next dance.'

'Oh Luke, that isn't true. They know such a lot – things I don't know. All those books they've read and plays they've been to, and concerts. I've never heard of half the names they used.'

'Ornamentation, Marty. They wear them because they're in the fashion. When they really *think*, it's of how to remove an incipient moustache. Oh, they're not all like that, thank God, but that little lot mostly are. I want them to know you – what you're like. To understand that there are qualities of mind that make common labour grace and not disgrace the purest intellectual ardour.'

'But I'm not intellectual.'

She did not know what she was, never having analysed herself; and the disclaimer was not coquetry but disbelief.

'No,' he answered, 'you're an Intelligence – a Phantom Intelligence.'

She let the accusation pass, not knowing how to refute it; and followed her own thought.

'But Miss Warrender, she's not – she's – '

'Oh, she's different, of course. Talks well, doesn't she? Tremendously well-read. Get Miss Warrender talking and you're sure to learn something you didn't know. A perfect pit of knowledge.'

'Then you shouldn't have classed her with these others – should you, Luke? The ones that just wear what they know.'

Martha spoke slowly, pondering the question, which evidently exercised her.

'I am rebuked, gentle guardian.' Martha shrank. Luke in obeisance before her was troubling. If she were sure that he was only bantering – ! She guessed too that he was aware of her trouble. 'Of course I shouldn't. Not so very different either, though. Her knowledge is merely hers, not her. It makes no sort of alteration in the essential man. She knows a

few hundred times more now than when I met her first, and
she hasn't grown an atom with it all. It gets no farther in than
her brain. When her brain suffers dissolution, so will the
knowledge. Food for worms. She'll waken up to her next
incarnation with horribly little to put on. Now you, on the
other hand, Marty – you know things with the whole of you.
Your knowledge pervades your whole personality. It's pure
spirit. A rare and subtle essence.'

He took an arrogant delight in troubling her, having
decided that she was insufficiently aware of her own worth
and ought to be made to see herself through other eyes. He
had a fine intellectual apprehension of her quality and tried
to show her herself as he perceived her.

'You are big enough to stand the knowledge. Nothing will
spoil you, Marty – there's flame enough in you to burn the
danger up.'

She began to comprehend that she was for him an earnest
of the spiritual world; its ministrant; his Beatrice.

'I don't worship you. You worship a goddess through
flame, don't you? – But I have learned through you to
worship flame. The flame of life. Like Beatrice. Making me
aware of hierarchies of being beyond our own. – I'm not
making love to you, you know, Marty.'

She said, 'Luke!' with a tongue so astounded that he
laughed audibly; and in a moment so did she. The absurdity
of the idea was palpable.

'I suppose to some fools it would sound pernicious,' he
reflected. 'To tell a woman that you love her and at the same
time that you haven't the least intention of wooing her –
well! – It can be done, though.' He was a little magisterial
again, liking his theories. 'There are two sorts of woman to
whom one can say these things with impunity. There's the
quite worthless woman, frivolous, nothing in her. The ichor
of her life's too thin and weak to receive anything in solution
– all her experience is precipitated immediately – it doesn't
even cloud the liquor – simply doesn't touch her. You can
say any mortal thing you like to her and be safe. And then
there's the woman in whom the life is so strong and powerful
that it receives all experience into solution – makes a strange
rich-flavoured compound of the liquor; and crystal clear.

You can trust a woman like that with any knowledge. You
can tell her the truth. We lie to most of the women we know.
I'm telling you the truth.'

She remained silent so long that he turned to look at her.
They had left the woodland and the moon was strong. He
saw her face, held straight ahead and as though she walked
without seeing where she went. Rossetti's picture of the
Annunciation came irresistibly to his mind. She had Mary's
rapt tranquillity.

It did not occur to him that that was her very mood; that
she carried it home with her; that, lying still on her bed,
among threadbare sheets that were patched with stuff of
different tone and texture from themselves, under matted
and dun-coloured blankets, she was undergoing the awe and
rapture of annunciation. Humbly she cried, 'I am not
worthy,' and the wonder deepened within her till it
brimmed and flooded her consciousness. She lay without
moving, nor were there articulate words even in her
thought; but her whole being was caught up in passionate
prayer that she might be able for her destiny. The place was
holy; neither Madge's noisy and rancid breathing, nor
Flossie's muttering and the constant twitch of her limbs,
could disturb its solemn air. Let the whole world despise her
now, in Luke's dower was her peace. He made her great by
believing her so. Because unwittingly she loved him she
became the more fully what he had imagined her. She fell
asleep in ecstasy, and woke in ecstasy, carrying to the tasks
of early morning a sense of indwelling grandeur that
redeemed them all. So strong and bright was this interior life
that the things she touched and saw no longer wore their
own significance. Their nature was subjugated to her
nature; and she handled without disgust, in the confined
and reeking closet where the boys had slept, the warm and
smelly bed-clothes and the flock mattress that had sagged in
holes and hardened into lumps, because her mind had no
room for the realization that they were disgusting. As she
cleaned the bairns' boots, there fell on her so strong a
persuasion of the very immediacy of unseen presences that
she stood still, a clumsy boot thrust upon her fist, staring at
the stubbly brush.

'You're a dreamy Daniel as ever I saw,' cried Emmeline as she poked fresh sticks beneath the kettle. 'A real hinder o' time, you and yer glowerin'. Fa's the time to wait on you? – Haud, Willie! – ye thievin' randy.' And she clutched Willie's *nieve, birsing* the cakes he had been stealing into mealy crumbles that spilt over the floor.

Martha returned to the brushing of the boots without comment, tied the strings of her petticoats for Flossie, who was wandering about half-clad among everyone's feet, and went back to the bedroom to make ready for town.

'Am I the daughter of this house, or are you?' she found herself asking Madge, having rubbed her sleeve against some of her untidy pastes that Madge had larded on a chair-back.

Madge, fourteen years old and done with her education, required, like Martha herself, a wider life than the cottage allowed, and was finding it in the glare of publicity afforded by the baker's shop, whither she took her jewelled side-combs and fiery bows attached to the very point of her lustreless pigtail, to enliven the selling of bath-buns and half panned loaves and extra strongs, and the delivery of morning baps and 'butteries' at the villas round Cairns. She ate in these pleasant precincts more chocolates and pastries than were at all good for her complexion, which had considerably more need now of her geranium petals than it had had two years before; instead of scarlet, however, on the assumption that the more of pallor the less of plebeian was accused by one's appearance, she spent her meagre cash on the cheapest variety of face powder, which she smeared with an unskilful hand across her features. Martha shrank from her tawdry ostentation, but was worsted in every attempt at rem-onstrance by Madge's complete indifference to what she had to say. It was useless to lose one's temper with Madge; and quite ridiculous to waste one's irony. She stared and answered, 'You are, of course,' and completed the tying of her pigtail bow. Madge would go her own way though the heavens fell upon her: or though Emmeline fell upon her, a much more probable, and to the girl's imagination more terrifying, catastrophe. She asked no one's advice and sought no one's approval. Martha was grateful for at least her silences, dearly as she resented the visible signs of her presence. She had long since ceased to share a bed with her, allowing Madge and Flossie the one respectable bed the room contained, and sleeping herself on a rackety trestle-bed underneath the window. There she could watch Orion, or hear, in the drowsy dawn, a blackbird fluting and the first small stir of wings.

On this particular morning she stood by the window watching clouds like green glass curving upward from the east horizon, and dressing her hair – a little perfunctorily, it must be admitted – while she gazed. She had wiped the chair-back clean herself, being in no mood to break her own interior peace by altercation with Madge. She studied now to dwell in peace. That she had suffered what was obnoxious in her surroundings – whether Madge's conceits, or Emmeline's sloven hastes and languors, or Geordie's grossness – had until now been by instinct; not from the tolerance that comes of understanding, but because, not having begun to understand them, she lived her real life apart from them, within herself. But she was now more consciously resolved to shrink from nothing in her laborious and distasteful life, subjecting herself in a glow of exaltation to the rough sand-papering of her daily courses. She would in no wise dishonour her fate. If the spirit had chosen her for shining through, she would be crystal clear. Crystal clear! Luke had used the very words. And again there rushed on her a sense of abasement that was in itself the sharpest joy. Incredible and sure – it was she who had been chosen for this rare privilege. Luke, whom she honoured, had desired her too. But what did they all see in her eyes, she queried, staring in the dull and spotty mirror. She could not even tell their colour exactly: they had something in them of Nature's greens that have gone brown, of grass-fields before the freshening of spring. What did they all see in them? She looked in the mirror longer than she had ever looked before, searching for her own beauty. It was not to be found there.

'Fat are ye scutterin' aboot at?' cried Emmeline from the kitchen. 'Ye'll be late for yer school.'

She jammed a hairpin into place and pulled her blouse awry as she poked it under the band of her skirt. The end of a shiny safety-pin looked out from below her waist-belt. The mirror had more cause than ever not to reflect her beauty.

Spring wore to summer and Martha lived in an abiding peace. She was disciplined to exaltation. Doubtless her critical faculty suffered. A course of Muckle Arlo would have done her no harm; and Emmeline fell ill, to the advantage of Martha's domestic, if dubiously (in her own eyes) of her spiritual economy.

On a day in early June she sat and read upon the cairn.

The country was indigo, its austere line running out against a burnished sky to the clear enamelled blue of the mountains. Rain at sea, a soft trail of it like grey gauze blowing in the wind. And an enormous sky, where clouds of shadowed ivory and lustrous hyacinth filed by in vast processional; yet were no more than swayed in the wash of shallows when the eye plunged past them to the unfathomable gulfs of blue beyond. Martha lifted her head from the pages and looked out on those infinitudes of light. She was reading history that year. The slow accumulation of facts and dates was marshalled in her brain, waiting for the fire from heaven to fall; and as she turned from reading and gazed on that wide country gathering blue airs about itself; saw the farms and cottar-houses, roads, dykes, fields, river, she was teased from her own inner stillness by an excitement to which all she had been reading anent the press and stir of centuries contributed. Looking up, she thought suddenly, 'I am a portion of history,' and between her glancing from the pages and the formulation of the words, that she had spoken half aloud, there passed the fraction of a second, which nevertheless was crammed with furious thought. She had seen the riotous pageant of history peopled with folk who were like herself. Wheresoever they had gone, whatsoever had been their acts and achievement, they had all begun in a single spot, knowing nothing, with all to find and dare.

'This place as well as another,' she thought; and then she said, 'But I am part of it too.'

She perceived that the folk who had made history were not necessarily aware of the making, might indeed be quite ignorant of it: folk to whom a little valley and a broken

hilltop spelt infinity and who from that width and reason-
ableness of life had somehow been involved in the monstrous and sublime unreason of purposes beyond their own
intention. The walls that shut people from people and
generation from generation collapsed about her ears; and all
that had ever been done on the earth – all she had read and
heard and seen – swung together to a knot of life so blinding
that involuntarily she closed her eyes and covered them with
her hands. She could not keep still for the excitement and
almost ran in her haste to the wood, forgot the supper-hour,
and walked hither and thither at random; but noting that
north of west the skies were flecked with saffron, and that a
June sunset is late, she turned home to resume her part in
the making of history.

Geordie was leaning against the door and seemed glad to
see his daughter.

'Yer mither's feelin' drumlie kind,' he told her. 'She's
had a dwam.'

Martha recalled her thoughts from the All and considered
this ingredient in it. Emmeline was not wont to be ill.

They went indoors together.

Emmeline, flushed and querulous, manifested a valiant
disinclination for bed. They got her there at last, and at
intervals throughout the night she proclaimed stoutly that
she was a better Leggatt than the best and 'that sair made
wi' thirst that she could drink the sea and sook the banks'.

'She's raivelled kind,' said Geordie.

In the morning it was plain that Martha must turn
sick-nurse. It was hardly the contribution to history that she
desired to make. Her examinations were coming on and
Emmeline ill was a handful. She broke every regulation the
doctor laid down. Fevered, she hoisted her bulk from the
bed and ran with her naked feet upon the floor to alter the
angle of the window screens.

'Sic a sicht ye hae them,' she grumbled to Martha when
the girl expostulated with tears. 'If ye wunna pit things as I
tell ye, fat can I dae bit rise masel'?'

'Temperature up again,' said the doctor to Martha. 'I
hoped you would have managed to keep it down.'

'Fat'n a way could *she* keep it doon?' cried Emmeline.

'Wad ye expect her to haud ma big tae to keep doon ma temperature?'

She was indignant now on Martha's behalf as she had been against her earlier. Indignation was a fine ploy when one lay idle and condemned. Emmeline was in high good-humour with herself. It was long since she had felt so important as she did lying mountainous beneath the bed-clothes, deriding her medical adviser's opinions and diagnosing her every symptom for herself with the aid of nothing more artificial than mother-wit; while round her in the heated kitchen the fervours of life went on – the steam of pots, the smell of food, the clatter of dishes, the hubbub of tongues, the intimacies of a sick-room toilet. Martha made a clearance of such articles as she could do without and Emmeline enjoyed a fresh attack of indignation. Demanding news of the whereabouts of something she had missed,

'There's a'thing ahin that door but dulse,' she cried, being told. 'Easy to tidy up when ye jist bang a'thing in ahin a door. But wow to the day o' revelations.'

'But where am I to put things?' Martha asked. 'There's just nowhere. There's nowhere in this house to put things. You shouldn't have so many of us – it's not as if they were ourselves.' And forgetting under the pressure of life the way of life she had purposed – her jubilant acceptance of every roughness – she allowed a secret desire to break cover.

'You should put these boys away now, mother. Why should we keep them when we haven't room for ourselves?'

Emmeline lay astounded. To be sure they had not room. And to be sure the boys were not her own, and stripped her stores like locusts, and brought no counter benefit in cash. The meagre sum she received for Jim and Madge was still forthcoming, but for Willie there had been more promises than pence. But put them away!

Alter an arrangement that had hardened to the solidity of a law! It was, and therefore it was right. – A belief that Emmeline was not singular in holding.

Martha did not push her argument. She dropped it, indeed, hastily, as though she had touched live coal. But the presence of the boys, their claims upon space and time, burned acidly in her consciousness. Jim she could endure, big hulking loon though he was, with Madge's own stolidity and a genius for unnecessary noise; but Willie, the younger boy, she was coming to dislike very fervently. He was dirty in habit and in attitude of mind. He sniggered. He used accomplishments hard-won at school for nefarious purposes, writing up obscene words on gates and outhouse doors: a procedure quite unredeemed in Martha's eyes by a certain merry insolence of bearing, not unattractive in itself. Her father's crassness, Martha could recognise from contact with Willie, was wholesome.

It looked like a month before Emmeline had recovered sufficiently to allow her to resume her classes. Actually the time had been so short that Luke and Dussie had not discovered her absence. But they had so many preoccupations! Luke was writing detective stories. He wrote for dear life, as though he had never had a hobby before and could not conceivably have another.

Dussie collaborated, criticising with a contemptuous common-sense the more outrageous effronteries of his plots.

They had had one accepted.

'Stout old yarn,' – Luke was telling Martha all about it, about its cruise among the editors, its ultimate haven – 'We'll go down to posterity yet: Sherlock and Missus.'

They were dreadfully – and quite sincerely – sorry to hear that Emmeline had been ill, and eagerly gave Martha the magazine to read that contained their detective story.

TEN

Dussie Enters on an Affair of Moment

Dussie had all this while been engaged on an affair of moment: to find someone for Martha to fall in love with. Happy herself, she longed to make her friend as happy, and knew only one way for doing it. But the men to whom she was introduced made little of Martha. She did not repulse them; but she seemed not to know that they were there.

'I can't get her to see,' Dussie said.

'Why should she see?' Luke asked. – 'No, she's not too innocent. She's not innocent at all. She's integral. Herself. And a singularly rare self. It would be criminal to alter it.'

Philosopher though he fancied himself, he had fallen into the plain man's error over Martha. He had made up his mind about her and was satisfied with that. She was the spirit made visible in flesh; tangible thought. He forgot that she was alive.

'No man in his senses would want Marty changed,' he said.

'A woman in her senses would,' retorted Dussie.

But Dussie did not get far that summer in the management of Martha's affairs. In August she bore a son, who lived an hour. Dussie was very ill too, for all her splendid vitality.

Luke took it hard. He had wanted his son. But in her weakness Dussie became dearer. She made no lamentation over the dead child; but sometimes in the darkness, slipping from her bright defiant capriciousness, with low words that were maternal in their solicitude, she consoled him for his loss. He divined that in comforting him she comforted herself and loved her as he had never loved her before, this new tender Dussie, comforting him in the night.

When the winter session was in swing again she was ready for company. There were merry meetings in Union Street;

but she refused passionately to have Macallister in the house again. The Greek statue glare. . . .

Luke laughed, and talked philosophy with Miss Warrender instead.

'A most informative lady,' he called her.

Martha had never lost her early fear of Miss Warrender. Less diffident now, she talked in company; but if Miss Warrender were present she sat mute, anxious and self-distrustful.

'But why?' persisted Dussie. She rather liked Miss Warrender herself. She talked so well – kept a conversation going. Martha, Dussie reflected, must be cured of this over-sensitiveness: now that she herself was growing well again it was time to resume that important undertaking to which she had vowed herself – the finding of someone with whom Martha could fall in love: but meanwhile it was pleasant to dissect Miss Warrender.

'O shut up, will you!' cried Luke from the other side of the fireplace. 'Can't you see that I'm engaged on a deathless work?' He waved his sheet of paper, and read aloud:

'Strange that the spirit's infelicity

Should rob the world of beauty –

'That's deathless, but I can't get any further.'

'Didn't know you were a poet,' said Dussie.

'Neither did I, until today.'

He mouthed the lines again.

'That's a magnificent opening for a man's first sonnet, you know.'

He continued to write poetry. Magnificent openings that reached no conclusions. He had none of your young poet's diffidence in showing them off. No hole-and-corner self-consciousness. He displayed his accomplishment gratuitously. Why not? Had he possessed a Cloisonne vase, a fine quartz crystal, a son, he would have showed them off with the same eager gesture. Like his faculty for verse, they were among the myriad enticements that life offers to the curious.

In spring he announced the advent of his first long narrative poem.

'It's about the Archangel Gabriel. He gets tired of

hopping about heaven, so down he comes, moons about on earth for a bit and does a star turn.'

'I don't wonder – much more fun out of heaven,' said Dussie.

'Nonsense! More fun out of heaven? Fat lot you know about it. Much more fun in heaven than anywhere else. Isn't it, Marty? Don't you expect fun in heaven?'

Martha looked at him, a slow considering look. She was not an eager talker. *I can wait*, her willing silences implied; but her pauses were not hesitant, giving rather a sense of hoarded powers. Now she said, slowly:

'Of course. There will be so much to discover.'

'Of course! Hell's the sort of place where everyone sits around with a teacup and wonders what on earth to say next. O, they're a dull lot down in hell. Sensible. Everyone as like everyone else as ginger-beer bottles. Nobody with a mind of his own. Whereas in heaven you'll have all the really interesting people, the cranks and eccentrics, the fanatics and fools, all the folk who aren't afraid to be really themselves. No, my dears, there will be neither originality nor style nor humour in hell.'

'I hope we'll get some humour in heaven, then,' said Dussie. 'It would be awful to be serious all the time.'

'Never you fear. Heaven isn't serious. How do you imagine we could stand being as wise as we shall be if we weren't able to laugh at ourselves? You take my word for it, a sense of humour's a paradisal possession. It's the liberating agency. You go crawling about under a heavy tombstone, suitably inscribed, Wife of the Above and all the rest of it, until suddenly one day you see how confoundedly funny it all is, and then you come out with a great shout of laughter at yourself, and hey presto! up you walk to the next ring of the circus.'

With his arm round Dussie, he began to declaim his lines.

'What's that?' she asked. 'The new pome?'

'My latest and greatest. Wait till I tell you about it.'

Eager, impetuous, he spoke: as though the doings of the Archangel Gabriel were all that mattered in the world.

'You see, he grew tired of heaven, because he wanted to know what God was really like to the people on earth. So he visited a man, and took him up to heaven. Tremendous experience for the man, of course, but that's not what really matters. What really matters is what Gabriel discovered by taking the man up. But I've got them hung up between earth and heaven just now, and I can't get any forrader.'

He swung into the lines again, chanting them, hypnotised with his own creation:

> 'But the full certainty of understanding
> Was his not ever. He had oft to go
> Among the worlds, and knew their fierce demanding,
> Sharing their troubled littleness, their woe
>
> 'Not little. For only thus could he endure
> Divinity upon him, and unfold
> Its thousand-fold intensity. The lure
> Of the worlds had called him and their tale untold.
>
> 'So grew he, oft surrendering complete
> And rounded silences and brimmed desire,
> And chose bewildering war: but deemed it meet.
> For though he had learnt the All, and might not tire
>
> 'Of knowing it, he knew not yet the whole
> Of those inconstancies and alterations
> That dwell resolved in God. God of his soul
> He knew the fulfilment, but –'

'Luke dear, now listen,' said Dussie firmly, climbing on his knee and covering his mouth with her hand. 'Do you remember that we have a supper party tonight?'

'Yes, of course,' he answered, coming promptly out of his absorption. 'Fraser and young Kennedy and the beautiful Mrs. K., mostly frocks and fal-la-la-la – what Marty's mother would call with equal truth and eloquence a flee-up.'

'Well. – Don't be soulful in front of Mrs. Kennedy, Luke.'

'I shall be myself, my love. If the self chances to be soulful, all the worse for the beautiful Mrs. K.'

Soulful the self chanced to be, the beautiful Mrs. K. notwithstanding. He discussed at length the scheme and purpose of his narrative poem and declaimed the complete contents of the manuscript.

'If you'd cut out two-thirds of it and sharpen the rest, Luke,' said young Kennedy, 'you could make something of that.'

'Cut out two-thirds! My dear fellow, there's two-thirds yet to write.'

Kennedy grinned. With his Buchan accent he developed his criticism.

'It's like a half-hewn statue just now. Imperfectly disengaged from the block. You want to hew much deeper – '

'My good youth, am I a hewer of wood and a drawer of water?'

He wrote his poetry easily. Like going to heaven, it was fun; and without the travail of his soul he was satisfied.

Martha spoke little during the supper party. She sat very quiet, smiling to herself with a still, shining smile. She was intensely happy. How Luke could take her secret thoughts and transfigure them! – as though she had not always known that when the angel visits the man the deeper spiritual experience is the angel's. Since he had begun to write poetry (would he be as great as – oh, not Milton! one could not expect that – as Tennyson perhaps? or Mr. Yeats?) he had written nothing but had responded, like the vibration of a stringed instrument, to some tune within her own being. She did not look at him, but once or twice amid the nonsense he was talking he caught her eye. There passed between them a spark, swift, momentary, the flitting of a gleam, a recognition from their external and perfect selves.

Fraser called across the quadrangle next morning, 'Hello, Luke, how's the Archangel Gabriel?' It became a three-weeks' fashion to greet him with, 'Hello, Luke, what's the Archangel doing?'

The Archangel Gabriel remained in a parlous state between earth and heaven, and Luke was unable to extricate him from his plight.

'After all,' he explained, 'light takes a few hundred years to make the passage. You can't expect an Archangel to do it in a month.'

Doubtless the Archangel accepted the situation with grace

and humour, that paradisal attribute. The only person to suffer seriously from the delay was Martha, who was passionately exercised over the climax of Gabriel's experience. What did he discover about God? She wished Luke would reveal it; and brooding, devised conclusions for herself, even setting one of them, impatiently, to rhyme; though to tell the truth her verses were by no means as beautiful as her eyes had been when she tramped the Quarry Wood beating out the metre. Preoccupied thus, less than ever did she yield her inclinations to Dussie's Cupid-mongering.

ELEVEN

The Lustre Frock

'She's to hae a goon like the lave o' them,' said Geordie.
'She's nae to be an ootlin.'

Emmeline fingered the stuff of Aunt Leebie's lustre frock,
holding it taut and running her thumb along its weave.

'It's richt gweed stuff,' she said. 'Yer Aunt Leebie'll be
terrible offended if ye dinna wear it.'

Martha had said, when she brought the frock from
Muckle Arlo:

'I promised to wear it when I'm capped.'

Graduation had looked immeasurably distant then, but
how rapidly the years had sped! She had still her year of
professional training to go through before she would be a
'finished teacher'; but her University course was almost
over. Another month, and she would be dismissed into the
world with a little tap on the head to signify that there was
learning there . . . *Initium sapientiae* . . . .

Meanwhile there was the question of the frock. Martha
considered it with a bad grace. The sacrificial mood was in
abeyance. She had conceived a horror of the out-moded
garment and would have repudiated her own hasty promise
with great good-will. It was Dussie whose quick eye saw the
possibilities of the lustre, her hands that transformed it.
Martha was astonished by the result.

The Graduation morning arrived.

Geordie, Emmeline and Aunt Josephine came through the
archway slowly. Of the three, Aunt Josephine was most at
ease. She was superbly at her ease. She had travelled. She
knew the ways of the world. She moved at her steady sober
pace down the quadrangle, doubting nothing of the
homeliness of those towers and pinnacles of granite towards
which she floated with sails full-set. She would have made

port as cheerfully in a barn.

Neither was Geordie perturbed, though stiff and awkward to appearance in his Sunday suit; and though he stood within the very haunt, the breeding-ground of that jeopardy that menaces a comfortable world, the virus of brains. For, holding still to his opinion that brains were a vexing agitation, he had yet of late kept silence on the matter and ruminated over what he saw; since he saw Martha reaching the very crown and proper end, the acme – as he supposed, being uninformed to the contrary and knowing nothing of the cunning whereby the university makes mention to her sons of only the beginning of wisdom* – the acme of instruction, without any alteration so far as he could see in her power or willingness to wash his sweaty socks and clear away the remnants of a meal. Moreover he had the reassuring persuasion that he had the right to be where he was. He set foot in the precincts with the confidence of a man for whom a place is prepared. Had not his daughter won it for him? And no gliding motors, no proud and peacocked women, could take away his security. It was Emmeline with her pretensions to gentility who was embarassed. Waddling under her load of fat, smelling of perspiration, with a button missing from one of her grey cotton gloves, she stared around uneasily, convinced that the majority of that animated throng had eyes for her; and with a good conceit of herself in spite of her uneasiness, keeked about in the presumptuous hope of being seen by someone who might admire and report her state. Being recognised by no one but Luke (who existed merely as husband to that Dussie) she yielded herself with but a hoity grace to his guidance, and followed behind his lean length up the stairway of the Mitchell Hall, indignant at his easy thinness and turning a critical eye upon the company with which she moved. 'Some gey ordinary jiffs,' she thought. She had been very uncertain what she was to see in a concourse gathered under the roof of the great hall of the University, and was secretly reassured by seeing numbers of men and women not too unlike herself.

* Motto of Aberdeen University: 'Initium sapientiae timor Domini.'

From the glens and farms, the fishing villages and country towns, the fathers and the mothers had come.

Here, and not in the granite walls, not in lecture-room nor laboratory nor library, nor even in the mind and character of those who taught, was the true breeding-ground of Geordie's jeopardy. Here, for this one day, was the creative power behind the University's glory and achievement. Twice a year she gathered for an hour the sources of her life, that he who would might look and understand. Geordie was part of this great spectacle, no spectator merely. By his ploughman's gait, his misshapen shoulders, his broken nails and fingers ingrained with earth, his slow rough speech, his unabashed acceptance of himself, he brought into that magnificent hall the sense of a laborious past, of animal endurances, of the obstinate wholesome conservative earth. With him came the mind's humbleness. He symbolised its ultimate dependences, its elemental strength.

Part also of this spectacle for the imagination was Aunt Josephine, who had been piloted by Dussie to the gallery and sat pleased with all she saw and pleasing all who saw her. In her was manifest that substantial Leggatt imperturbability, sure of its own worth and ways, positive, that gives direction and stability to the questioning mind.

Part too was the woman who sat on Geordie's farther side, and shared with him her printed list of graduands, Emmeline having fixed very securely on to the sheet served to them. With her exquisitely gloved finger she pointed out to him the name of her son ('my youngest') and he sought for Martha's and showed it her, pressing his thick discoloured thumb on the paper ('ma auldest an' ma youngest tae. I've bit the ane – ma ain, like,' he said).

'Yon was a gey grand duchess I had to sit aside me,' he told them later, at lunch in Dussie's flat. 'A terrible fine woman.' A woman of race, mother of sons who were to make an illustrious name yet more illustrious in government and law and literature.

Part also was the washerwoman with ragnails and sucked hands where the flesh had swollen in ridges round her wedding-ring, whose daughter went in crêpe-de-chine; and the minister, hollow of cheek and with the eyes of a fanatic, and his shabby sunny wife, clapping her hands at the antics of the laddies, at heart a *halarackit* boy herself.

Martha, as part of the obvious spectacle, discovered that graduation was after all not very exciting. It was ordinary and inevitable, like stepping out of a train when you reach your destination. She was excited none the less; and her secret excitement had a double cause. Half was in Luke's parting words to her that evening – 'We're off tomorrow. Mind, you are coming to stay with us.' The other half, surprisingly in a Martha who seemed to care so little for the outer integuments of living, was the lustre frock. It was so different from every other frock she had possessed. Dussie called it her inspiration. Everything had gone right in its making. Wearing it, Martha had an uncanny sense of being someone other than herself; as though she had stepped carelessly to a mirror to dress her hair and had seen features not her own looking out from the glass. The mere wearing of the frock could not have changed her: but like the mirror it served to make her aware of alteration; and she seemed to herself farther from her folk and her home. Wearing the lustre frock, she had no Ironside instincts. She did not belong to the Leggatts. Across the mirror of lustre there flitted an unfamiliar Martha with alien desires; and when some days after her capping she received one of Aunt Jean's brusque notes of invitation, that specified the dates on which she was expected to arrive at and depart from Muckle Arlo, Martha set it aside and did not answer. The following day brought another note, as brief and as peremptory as Aunt Jean's:

DEAR MARTY,

The Beyond at whose Back we are meanwhile situated is a Gloomy Mountain Pass much infested by midges. Come at once.

LUKE

'But ye canna nae ging to yer aunt's,' said Emmeline aghast.

'I could go later.'

'Deed ye'll dae nae sic thing. Ye maun ging whan she's bidden you.'

'Not if I'm going elsewhere,' said Martha. 'I shall write and ask if I may come to her afterwards.'

Emmeline bickered for the next two days. This was a strange riding to the ramparts of the citadel that she was counting on Martha to reconquer. When the portcullis had been lifted, that the girl should turn in the saddle and canter away to other ploys! 'She wunna lat you come,' she said to Martha.

'I suppose I shan't miss a very great deal,' Martha answered. Queer contagion from a frock!

Aunt Jean having signified that the later date was approved, Martha went to Luke and Dussie.

Her fortnight in the hills had no reality. The hours floated past. Night glided after night. Muckle Arlo was on another earth. After two years Martha was amazed to find how similar everything was and how differently she regarded it. The black currants were over but there were red currants and rasps to pick. Martha again gathered currants and Aunt Leebie cried to her to wipe her feet; and Aunt and Uncle Webster came to Sunday dinner.

Yet nothing was the same. She was not excited but bored by her bedroom, and Leebie with the physic bottle was ludicrous; and when she changed on Sunday morning, after breakfast and the making of the beds, to her best apparel (which was of course the lustre frock), she chafed a little at kinship. Relations . . . but what relation had they to her soul? She set out for church living again in ecstasy her days among the hills.

'Ye've connached it,' Aunt Leebie was saying. 'Clean connached.'

She was pulling her lustre frock about, scraping with her nail at its embroidery. But what right had she to be displeased? She had given the frock. And Martha remembered how Luke had approved it and Dussie had waltzed her round the room when she saw it on.

'That's gey guideship it's gotten,' the old woman was muttering.

Martha had no leisure to be touched.

'I'm nae nane cornered wi' Matty this time,' Leebie said to Jean.

A relation . . . but what relation had she to their soul?

TWELVE

Torchlight

Martha's year of professional training began badly. After a dozen tentatives, rehearsals as it were for the grand affair, Emmeline took that autumn to her bed in sober earnest.

'There's naething ails her but creish,' grumbled Stoddart Semple.

He still came in about and smoked a pipe by the fireside while Emmeline lay, lumped and shapeless, in the kitchen bed. He would slouch about the doors: sometimes Martha, glancing up, saw him glowering through the window.

'Foo are ye the day, missus?' he would cry through the window to Emmeline; and abroad, report, 'There's naething ails her but creish' – a diagnosis that speedily came round to the lady's ears.

'So he says,' quoth she a little grimly. 'He says a'thing, that man, but his prayers.'

If *creish* were the ailment, certainly it did not serve to swacken the patient's temper. Martha was *trauchled*.

'Ye can keep Madge at hame to notice ye,' said Geordie. But Madge was earning money (if but a pittance), Martha merely expending it by her daily labour. It was obvious to plain common-sense which of the two might best be interrupted.

Martha, however, was resolved not to have her work interrupted. She knew that Emmeline would fare well enough alone by day. There was a modicum of truth in Stoddart's dictum. Emmeline was ill, though not so ill but that she might have been better had she wished. She had perhaps a pardonable temptation to indulgence in the importance that hedges an invalid about. Emmeline had been unimportant for so long! – Now her neighbours talked of her, and talked with her, comparing her ailment with their own, their sisters', their mothers', their aunts'. . . . How could Emmeline resist such dalliance? Fortified by the doctor's authority, Martha determined to do her college work by day and her cottage work at morning and evening; but stated early in family conclave the condition upon which alone it would be possible: that the bairns should be put away. Her reasoning was too cogent to be dismissed. Even Emmeline yielded; and other homes were found for the boys and Flossie. Madge remained, parting from her brother with no emotion on either side. Flossie screamed and kicked. She had had scoldings and buffetings enough in all conscience; and yet immoderate huggings too, and jammy *pieces* at illegitimate hours; and always Geordie's slow affectionate devotion.

Martha was not much concerned as to where they might be ultimately tossed. She had other absorptions. Even apart from her enraptured inner drama, her life was full enough to keep her thoughts engaged. She came home from long crowded days in schools and lecture-rooms to make the supper, set the house to rights, prepare as far as she could the next day's dinner; and rose in raw black mornings to get breakfast ready and attend to Emmeline's wants. Never, through all the weeks of Emmeline's illness, had she to clean the stove, light the fire, or carry water. Slowly and clumsily, but without fail, Geordie did these things; and he and Madge between them dished up some sort of dinner, while Aunt Josephine came frequently about, and the neighbours ran in and lent a hand. By and by Emmeline rose again, and sat heavily by the fire, putting her hand to an occasional job; and the winter wore through.

Meanwhile Martha's private drama had spun more fiercely. She had discovered, on the opening of the Training Centre session, with something like dismay, that Miss Warrender, now with Double Firsts, had been appointed to the lecturing staff; and that she would spend an hour a week under her tuition. Her reason repudiated the dismay. To feel a fool in the presence of a brilliant woman when one meets her socially, is no excuse for dread of her as a teacher: but reason was not particularly successful in her arguments. Martha continued to feel constraint in Miss Warrender's presence.

Others of the girls, who though her juniors had been the year before the young lecturer's fellow-students, were less abashed. The student's inalienable right to criticize his teachers became doubly a right when the teacher had been a fellow student the previous year. Martha therefore heard, in the Common Room and corridors, much discussion of Miss Warrender's affairs. It was thus that one afternoon, waiting in the lecture room for the lady herself to appear – for with all her brilliance Miss Warrender had no very accurate ideas on punctuality – Martha heard her name coupled with that of Luke Cromar, and coupled lightly. Luke, it appeared, talked philosophy with Miss Warrender elsewhere than in Union Street. She was reported to have said that he counted her his greatest friend. The tone implied that species of friendship that has laws outwith the common moral law. It was the tone, even more than the disclosure, that played havoc in Martha's brain. She tried to shout, 'It's a lie, a lie,' but her lips were parched, her tongue was too clumsy for her mouth. Miss Warrender came in. Martha could distinguish words but no ideas in the lecture. Her pulses were pelting and in a little she rose and went out. 'Are you sick?' her neighbour whispered. She paid no attention, walking straight past the lecturer's desk to the door.

Outside she stood still in a fury of anger. This breaking of the third commandment! But was it true? The blood thundered in her ears and wave after wave rushed hotly to her brow. She hurried at random among the mean streets that surrounded the Training Centre, but recollecting that her fellow-students might come out from lecture and meet her, directed her steps towards Union Street. A filthy lie. – But if he had given it circumstance? His walking with Miss Warrender was so hateful to herself that she saw it as a dishonour to his nature. That Luke should stain his honour! – could even act so that foul breath might play upon his honour.

In Union Street she met Dussie. Dussie cried, 'Do come and see this frock!' and dragged her to a window. 'That golden-brown one. Marty, you'd look lovely in it.'

'Duss,' blurted Martha, staring through the plate-glass window, 'I heard something abominable just now. Some

girls talking. They suggested that Luke goes too much with
Lucy Warrender.'

'Pigs,' said Dussie.

Martha had spoken from an urgent impulse to thrust the
knowledge outside herself, but regretted at once that she
had thrust in on Dussie.

'I oughtn't to have told you. I –'

'Why ever not? You'll better tell me next who the
damsels were, so that I can claw their eyes out when I meet
them.'

She had broken across Martha's slower speech, so that
simultaneously Martha was saying:

' – didn't mean to make you unhappy.'

'Oh, *that* doesn't make me unhappy! It's rather fun than
not to be properly angry. I could slaughter the lot of them
and then dance upon their reeking corpses.'

She made a mouth at the shop-window and laughed at it
herself so heartily that Martha was compelled also to laugh.

'I suppose,' she said thoughtfully, 'a thing like that
couldn't make you unhappy unless you weren't sure of
Luke.'

'Marty! – You're the pig now.'

'Oh, I don't mean *you*. I mean anyone. I was only – ' after
a perceptible pause she concluded – 'theorising.'

'Don't, then. Theorising's stupid. Sure – ! I'm as sure as
death. No, as life. That's a lot surer.'

'I know you are. No one could be not sure of Luke.'

Her anguish nevertheless was because she was not sure.
Not that she doubted his faithfulness to Dussie! But she
feared lest by a careless gesture he had marred his own
shining image, made himself a little less than ideally perfect.

It was at that moment it dawned on Dussie that Martha
was in love with Luke, and the irony of her own procedure
struck her. But immediately after she was moved with a
grave pity for her friend. 'How unhappy she must be.'

But Martha was not unhappy. So long as she was unaware
of it, to be in love with Luke was bliss; and she was not yet
quite aware. She was however at the moment in an agony of
fear for him. Her love was ruthless on his behalf and would
have nothing less for him than her imagined perfection. For

two days she supped and slept with her agony, rose with it in the morning and carried it to every task she undertook. She began to understand the Incarnation. It was the uttermost shame for her to offer rebuke to the man who had dazzled her eyes until she could not see his human littleness; but if one cared enough for a person one would be thankful to suffer any shame, humiliation, misunderstanding, if so be the beloved could be saved from becoming a lesser man than was in him to become. God, put gladly to shame and reviled, because that was a lesser anguish than to see men and women fail of their own potentialities. . . . By the third day she had tortured herself into the persuasion that she must do violence to her nature and tell Luke that he had laid himself somehow open to public reproach.

She told him what she had heard.

'Do you happen to know one George Keith, fifth Earl Marischal?' he said, in the curious voice that she used to think had a smile in it.

She turned enquiring eyes, as though to ask what the Earl did there.

'As you may have heard,' Luke proceeded, 'he founded Marischal College, of which I am an unworthy member, in the year of grace 1593. Rather a magnificent Earl he must have been, since he did of his own prowess what it required kings and such-like bodies to do elsewhere – founded a University. The only one in Britain, you know, founded by an Earl. It was a separate University then, a sort of rival grocer's shop across the street from King's – whence it results that Marischal had a motto which I daresay you have heard.'

She wished he would be serious.

'What's good enough for an Earl is good enough for me.' And he quoted the old motto: 'They haf said: Quhat say they: Lat them say.'

So! – He had not understood.

She made her point clear – the high perfection he must not violate; and lifted her eyes to him, suffering mutely, imploring his acquiescence with all her simplicity of soul.

'You precious saint!' he said. 'Beatrice from the Heavenly Towers. There's an impromptu beginning for a poem. Shall

I continue? Or has any other blighter used it before me?'

But though he jested she touched him with a kind of awe. Impossible ideas she had, of course; not of this world: but her speech was like a lit and potent draught. What fools men were, to think the spirit could not be manifest in human flesh!

She kept herself in hand until the last of the evening's tasks was over, undressed herself in darkness and went to bed. Then she let her strung nerve snap and sobbed with abandon. He had smiled at her and she all earnestness. . . . Thinking after a time that she heard a movement in the room, she quieted herself and lay, tense and listening. So lying, she became aware of moonlight, and turned her head; Madge in the other bed had raised herself upon her elbow and was watching her with curiosity.

'What' up with you?' she asked.

'Nothing's up with me.'

'What're you crying for then?'

'I'm not crying.'

'Oh, all right, then.'

Madge dropped to her pillow again.

Shortly she said, 'If you'd fash yourself to do your hair a bit decenter, you'd easy get a lad.'

'What do you mean?'

'Oh, well,' said Madge, 'you're near twenty-two and hinna a lad yet.' And after a moment's pause she added, 'I'll lend you my side-combs if you like.'

Her side-combs were set with a glitter of sham blue brilliants.

Martha said sharply:

'I don't want either your side-combs, or a lad, thank you.'

'Oh, all right, then,' said Madge again. She turned her shoulder, rubbing her greasy hair about on the pillow till she found a comfortable nook. Soon she was sleeping heavily.

Martha was indignant at the supposition that she occupied her thoughts with anything as vulgar as a *lad*: though if a *lad* be considered as a young male who cares for one and for whom one cares in return, that was exactly of

what she had been thinking with persistence for some little
time. But what relation was there between Luke and a *lad*,
any more than between Martha and an Ironside or a
Leggatt? He had set their intercourse on too high a plane for
the one, and kept her in her exalted mood too long for the
other. Thinking of him (and no longer of his honour) she
fell asleep.

The following week Miss Warrender spoke to Martha
after lecture.

'Are you quite better now?' she asked. 'I was sorry you
weren't feeling well.'

Martha stared, having forgotten the manner of her exit
the previous week. Talking at the classroom door with the
young lecturer, she was swept by a hurricane of hate. She
wanted to hit her. Her fingers clenched of themselves . . .
she could feel them closing on Miss Warrender's throat . . .
and all the time she was saying calmly, with a smile, that she
had not been very sick and was quite well now; that the sky
was threatening; there had been too much wet weather lately
and it would be most unfortunate if the coming Rectorial
Election were marred by rain.

'For the peasemeal fight and the torchlight procession – it
would be too bad,' Miss Warrender said.

Martha walked away. The corridor was endless. It seemed
to roll away, like a barrel on which one tried to walk. She
supposed she was tired; and, Good Lord! how she ached,
now that she let herself relax. Into that imagined strangul-
ation had gone the energy of a week's work.

She went home, climbing the long brae very slowly.
There was dirty weather in the offing. A grey south; and a
diffused yellow crept through the grey, giving it a still dirtier
look. As Martha plodded on, absorbed, her blue-paper-
covered child-observation note-book, in which she had to
write her observations on every lesson she saw taught in the
schools, slipped from among the books on her arm and fell
in the soft road. She was annoyed at its griminess and wiped
it hastily with her coat-sleeve. The smear looked uglier.

'Stupid!' she thought. 'I should have let it dry.'

And she stood staring at the stain, but it was not the stain
that she was seeing. She felt as though with every step in her

slow ascent she had been turning very carefully the revol-
ving lens of a fieldglass, and had come to rest with her
picture focussed to a perfect clarity.

She understood now that she was in love with Luke.

Reason told her that there should be black depths of
horror in the knowledge, but all she could feel was wild glad
exultancy, the sureness of a dweller in the hills who has
come home. One loves – the books had taught her, though
she had given the theme but little attention – as one must,
perhaps against one's will and inclination: but she, sucked
under without awareness, had loved the greatest man she
knew. Judgment approved. She counted herself among the
blest. Besides, this secret and impossible love had a wild
sweetness, flavoured and heady, luscious upon the palate, a
draught for gods. It was eternal, set beyond the shadow of
alteration in an ideal sphere, one of the concentric spheres
of Paradise. It would satisfy her eternally. There was
nothing possessive in her love; or rather she possessed
already all that she desired in him – those far shining,
terribly intimate moments of spiritual communion.

She thought that she would love Luke forever with
hidden and delectable love. It was a consummation, the
final fusion of their spirits in a crystal that would keep
forever its own exquisite shape, timelessly itself.

But some crystals founder in some fires.

The rain began, hesitant at first, then powerful as from an
opened sluice. Martha pulled off her gloves, and throwing
her face and palms upwards, let the water rush upon her
naked flesh. She felt light, as though her body were
sea-wrack floating in the deluge of waters; or as though an
energy too exorbitant for her frame, coursing through her,
had whipped her into foam.

'Ye maun be soaked,' Emmeline was saying. 'Yon was
hale water.'

Martha only laughed, standing in the doorway with the
water streaming from her clothes. She was remembering
what Luke had said, one stormy night when he had brought
her home from town: 'I like a soaking now and then. Good
elemental feel it gives you.' Elemental! – That was it.
Washed by the rain she felt strong and large, like a wind

that tosses the Atlantic or a tide at flood –

'Ye micht shut tae the door,' Emmeline complained.
'We'll be perished wi' cauld.'

Martha smiled to herself and shut the door. She had done
the biggest thing she had ever done: she had fallen in love
with Luke. It was the crown of her achievement. And
without changing her wet garments she began briskly to
prepare the supper.

'Ye're raised the nicht,' her mother said. 'Fatever's ta'en
ye?'

Martha laughed again, catching the tails of her dripping
skirt for joy of the feel of water through her fingers. Raised!
– of course she was – upraised to the highest heaven because
she had had the wit to fall in love with Luke and with no
other man on earth. And still laughing, and squeezing the
hems of her skirt, she began to waltz round and round very
rapidly on the kitchen floor.

Martha's procedure was by way of pantomime to her
mother. Emmeline found the days very long. 'We're better
wantin' yon canalye o' kids,' she acknowledged; but she
missed the stir. When Aunt Josephine did not walk down
from Crannochie, and none of the neighbours stepped in
about for a crack, and not even Stoddart Semple flattened
his nose against the window and called 'Foo are ye daein'?'
her days were very empty; nor did her evenings provide
much entertainment. Geordie might have a curran remarks
to make anent the doings at the farm, and Madge, when
directly asked, would detail the customers who had visited
the baker's shop and what their purchases had been; but
Martha, with her head in the clouds, or absorbed by the
mysteries of School Hygiene and Child Psychology, had no
news to give her mother. Emmeline therefore enjoyed the
departure of Martha's impromptu by the fireside, though
her mind, untrained to the true analysis of its own enjoyments, insisted that she was distressed.

'Are ye gane clean gyte?' she asked; and anxiously:
'Haud oot ower fae the dishes. – There ye are noo! – a' tae
crockaneeshion.'

Martha was still laughing. The clash of the broken
crockery was like cymbals to her. Stooping she swept the

pieces together with her wet hands, flung them with a clatter in the coal-scuttle and ran to her own room.

She was still laughing. She wished that she could stop. It was folly to laugh like this because one had got wet. Her clothes were clammy now and she was shivering from her exposure. Her teeth chattered and suddenly her weariness came back upon her. She sank to the floor, one arm upon the bed. The walls and roof seemed to recede to an interminable distance. The whole house was flying away; and through an unobstructed clearness, but very far off, she could see Luke. There was nothing between him and her and she knew that she could reach him. She knew that she had reached him. Her spirit flowed out upon him, encompassing and permeating his. She could give herself to him forever by the mere outpouring of herself. She put herself at his disposal, and rising from the floor very quietly, changed her clothes and returned to the kitchen.

The weather cleared. The night of the Torchlight Procession was dry and cold, and very dark; but cold only heightened the ardour of the students and the dark threw up the torches' glare. They poured out of the quadrangle on to the crowded October streets – devils and pirates, wivies with mutches and wivies with creels, knights and grinning deaths'-heads, Japs and Maoris, *tattie-boodies* and emperors – lit fantastically by the gleam of the torches they carried. Spectators lined the streets, and the bairns of the poorer quarters, yelling and capering, pressed in upon the revellers; some marvelled, some in a fine scorn criticized, some tumbled to the tail of the procession and followed on with shouts and mimicry. In the remoter streets, away from the glare of the shop-lights, the procession trailed its length like a splendid smouldering caterpillar, with fire and smoke erect like living hairs along its back.

Dussie had pranked Luke out in a sailor suit, from which his inordinate length of neck and limb protruded grotesquely. Though no longer a student, he was too much a boy to hold back from the fun of a Torcher.

'Wish I could go too,' Dussie had pouted as she stitched at the sailor collar. 'Luke – couldn't I? Dressed up – no one would know.'

'Rubbish!' said Luke. 'The size of you – it would give you away at once.'

Miss Warrender was in the flat that evening. She laughed and said, 'The men's monopoly, you see, Mrs. Cromar.' Miss Warrender was noted for an ardent feminist. Luke laughed also, and said, 'Oh, you want to share Torchers as well as Westminster, do you, Miss Warrender?'

'Why not?' she said.

'I'd do it,' cried Dussie. 'I'd do it in a twink, if I were tall enough.'

'Oh, no need to wait for your growth, Mrs. Cromar. One should do such things openly, or not at all.'

'Would you?' challenged Dussie.

Miss Warrender shrugged her fine supple shoulders and flung her arms above her head in a careless gesture.

'Why not?' she said again.

'You'd make rather a jolly gipsy,' said Luke watching the play of her arms.

Miss Warrender laughed again.

'For a freak,' she said, 'I believe I'll do it. You'd better come too, Mrs. Cromar – show yourself off. We'll let them see we are not afraid of them.'

She spoke mockingly. Luke took her in jest but Dussie in earnest; seeing which 'Rubbish!' cried Luke again, sharply decisive. 'You can hang around in the Quad, Duss, and welcome the warriors home.'

By the evening of the procession he had forgotten the jest; nor did it recur to him at all, when, marching through the streets, he found himself puzzled by a Spanish gypsy lad who walked in front of him. Something in the figure was familiar. It teased him for a little, then was forgotten.

When the roysterers had made their round of the city and gathered in the quadrangle again to fling their torches on the blazing bonfire, Dussie slipped from the crowd of waiting girls. Flushed and excited she sidled among the torch-bearers seeking Luke. Some of the men, recognizing her, shouted a welcome. 'Come on, Mrs. Cromar – into the ring!' Luke, excited himself, grabbed at her arm. At the same moment he felt his other arm seized. Turning, he saw the Spanish gypsy whose identity had puzzled him in the street; and with something of astonishment recognized him for Lucy Warrender. In the hilarious confusion that arose as the torch-bearers thronged to dance around the bonfire, she had manoeuvred herself close to Luke and thrust her arm firmly into his. He glanced aside at her. She was wearing heavy gold ear-rings that glittered with a barbaric inconstancy as she swayed; and he was startled by something lascivious in her eyes and posture, as though the Spanish costume, like Martha's lustre frock, was a mirror that reflected sharply an unfamiliar aspect of the woman. He did not like the sharp reflection. Revolted, he flung her off brusquely and drew forward Dussie, who had been pushed back in the scrimmage, putting his arm around her possessively. For the first time Miss Warrender perceived that Dussie too was in the ring of dancers, and with a savage energy she threw her torch on the bonfire and slipped back into the shadows. A tongue of light pursued her for a moment but shifted rapidly, and her gorgeous finery was flattened out against the blackness and melted in it. Her torch, flying high and falling short of the central fury of the bonfire, spat back a shower of sparks and smuts that lit on Dussie.

The incident made Luke thoughtful. He was still thinking of it next morning, as he walked briskly down Union Street through a frosty haze. In his preoccupation he whistled as he went. Luke had a passion for making the world comfortable. He liked setting people at their ease, humouring them into a satisfaction with themselves that made them the best of company; and if he had humoured his living-mine-of-information-and-perfect-pit-of-knowledge into a belief that she meant more to him than she did, well, he must disabuse her, that was all! But he hated the necessity. He had taken all she offered him so long as it was to his mind, and now that she was offering that for which he had no manner of desire . . . Luke turned into Broad Street, making for the University, and continued to whistle.

As it happened, Miss Warrender was already sufficiently disabused. Her pride was fiercely hurt by the manner of her throwing off, and she made public the opinion she had always held of Dussie – a poor thing to be mated with a man

like Luke, illiterate. She could give him so much that
Dussie could not give.

'A poor thing but mine own,' Luke said to his wife with
the voice that had the smile in it. He had told Dussie plainly
of Miss Warrender's outburst. There were always birds of
the air to carry the matter.

'I prefer to be the dicky-bird myself,' he told her.

Dussie meditated, saying nothing. Then, flinging her
head back and laughing merrily:

'Do you know, Luko,' she said, 'I once tried to make
myself literate. I read and read at your books – oh, for hours
– when you weren't in. I thought you'd hate me for being
ignorant, but I gave it up 'cos you didn't seem to like me
any better when I knew things out of books, and just as well
when I didn't. But I was dreadfully unhappy about it for
awhile.'

'I didn't think you were ever unhappy.'

'Oh! – lots of times.'

'Over what, for example?'

She looked at him with her mouth askew.

'Not over that Warrrender creature, anyhow!' she said at
last.

They agreed that the Warrender creature was not worth
unhappiness.

'You know, Luke,' said Dussie by and by, 'Marty never
liked that Lucy Warrender. I used to try to argue her out of
it, and you see she was right.'

'Marty has a way of being right on points of judgment.
Spiritual instinct. She's clear-eyed. Like day.'

It were hard to say whether it was by reason of spiritual
instinct that Martha disliked Miss Warrender, but very easy
to say that she liked her lecturing no better as the term went
on. No doubt but that Miss Warrender knew her subject
and lectured, as she talked, brilliantly and with authority;
but she had no power to fuse the errant enthusiasms of the
young minds before her, to startle them from their preoccupations and smite them to a common ardour to which all
contributed and by which all were set alight. She had not
discovered that lecturing is a communal activity. For once
Martha found that the getting of understanding had no

charm, and confounding theme with lecturer, she hated
both; though as far as Luke was concerned she gathered
from both Dussie and Common Room conversation that she
need fear nothing more to Luke's honour from Miss
Warrender. She was therefore shining again with gladness,
rejoicing that he no longer laid himself open to the mis-
representations of the scandal-mongers and quite unaware
that Luke was raging inwardly at that disgusting feminine
folly that will not allow a man plain Monday's fare, a little
rational conversation on topics of current interest, without
the woman's obtruding her womanhood on him and forcing
upon him the meanness of repulsing her. He had no more
desire to offer love to a woman other than Dussie than to
offer her a used teacup; but with his avidity for exploring
other people's minds, he wanted as much intellectual
comradeship as he could obtain, from men and women
alike. He wanted to go on talking philosophy to Miss
Warrender as he had always done, and being unaccustomed
to repressing any of his energetic and multitudinous
impulses, resented the make of human nature.

Seeing no alteration in Martha's shining calm, and
clearly persuaded that she was in love with Luke, Dussie
thought: 'She is heroic.' But Martha was not heroic. She
had her paradise within herself and it sufficed her. What she
possessed was more to her than what she lacked.

Luke continued to believe her a spirit: but her spirit
haunted him. He was arrogant but not conceited; and that
she might love him had not crossed his mind. Indeed he felt
a subtle fear of her; and fear is not the way to truth. But
during that spring Luke began to grow up. Though he
hardly admitted it, Miss Warrender had sobered him; and
Martha's rebuke had gone deeper than he knew. He was
thoughtful, brooding sometimes until Dussie marvelled. He
would turn from her finest dishes, light a cigarette and fling
it untasted on the fire.

'A burnt offering,' he said, answering her remonstrance.

'A burnt . . . what on earth?'

'Well, a sacrifice to the gods. You set fire to valuable
things, you know.'

'And what god do you sacrifice cigarettes to?'

He said: 'An unknown god.'

'But what *is* it, Luke?' she cried one evening. 'You don't eat or anything. You seem hardly to know that I'm here.'

'I don't quite know, Duss,' he said, rumpling his hair. He was rueful and puzzled; a boy who had remained a boy too long and found maturity difficult.

'It's . . . some sort of spiritual adventure, I suppose,' he said.

And he began to talk of Martha.

'Remember the time she told me I shouldn't be so friendly with Lucy Warrender? All nonsense, of course. Oh, in this particular case she happened to have some justification, but in principle she was quite wrong. But somehow afterwards I couldn't get her out of my mind. Herself. Not what she said. But her nature. Her nature is like an exquisitely chastened work of art. She does without. Rejects. Takes from life only its finest. And she doesn't *want* the other things. She's amazing, you know – to want so little and to lack so much. She doesn't really want the things we want – chocs and shocks and frocks and things – all our social excitements. But it's not because she's satisfied with a thin and empty life. I expect it's because she has something much more wildly exciting of her own. I thought and thought about it till I wanted to have it too – to get at the positive side of asceticism. What it gives you, not what it denies. It was really an intellectual curiosity – wanted to know what it was like. Inquisitiveness, you know.'

He could not humble himself far enough as yet to acknowledge that it was more than an intellectual curiosity.

'You're awfully funny, Luke,' said Dussie. 'Imagine punishing yourself out of inquisitiveness.'

'It's what scientists and explorers and people do. But it isn't punishing myself. That's the great discovery. It's the most thrilling excitement – refusing yourself things. Things you normally enjoy. The thrill of doing without them is far more exciting than having them. Comes to be a sort of self-indulgence. A Lenten orgy. A feast of fasting. A lap of luxury. I shall take to lashing myself next as an inordinate appetite. Like smoking, you know. Strokes instead of whiffs. Shan't you love ironing my hair shirt?'

Dussie's heart had gone cold. Was he in love with Martha? She turned to the piano and played a ranting reel.

'You'll have to look after your costume yourself,' she cried over her shoulder. 'I don't know how to dress for spiritual adventures. I never have any, you see. Shouldn't recognize one if I met it in my porridge.'

They were both growing up and afraid at first to share their knowledge.

THIRTEEN

Crux of a Spiritual Adventure

Throughout that spring Martha had walked enchanted. A spell was on her that altered the very contours of her body. Unlike the maleficent spells of the witches, that shrivel the flesh and destroy the human semblance, the spell that was on Martha rounded her figure, filled out the hollows of her cheeks, straightened her shoulders. In spite in her harassed and laborious winter, she had never been so strong and well. Her limbs were tireless. She carried her head high. The philtre she had drunk was of very ancient efficacy. Under the influence of her conscious love for Luke, she was rapidly becoming what Luke loved her for not being – a woman.

'That's grand hurdies ye're gettin' on you, lassie,' said Geordie, slapping her as she passed him. 'The wark suits you better'n the books.'

Martha was indignant. She felt obscurely that a change was coming on her, and though hardly aware of its cause knew well enough that it was not housework. Scornful, she tossed herself from her father's reach and strode up the brae towards Crannochie.

'Spangin' awa' up the hill in some style,' her father reported.

'Weel, lat her,' said Emmeline. Now that she had recovered sufficiently to resume most of her household duties, she was willing enough that Martha should take her liberty again. Besides, it was Sunday evening – an April Sunday – the very time of the week for young people to go walking. Madge was out too.

'Awa' oot aboot wi' her lad,' said Geordie.

'Lad!' quoth Emmeline contemptuously. 'Fat'n a way wad she hae a lad?'

'Weel she tells me whiles aboot him.'

'O ay, a' a speak. It's easy to see fa her lad wad be – a palin' post.'

On this occasion Emmeline was wrong. Madge had a lad. He came from Glasgow, clerked throughout the week in a wholesale paper store – a very genteel business – wore his tie through a ring with a flashy diamond and had alberts to his watch chain. Altogether a satisfactory person, and given to the week-end pursuit of rural delights: among which was numbered Madge's sturdy little figure. At sixteen her breasts were already swollen and her hips pronounced. Madge, when she caught gawkishly at the alberts as they walked along the road, was already in possession of her share of the spiritual mysteries. Her perceptions had attained their apotheosis. She had other uses now for her side-combs than offering them to Martha.

Martha, swinging uphill on the April Sunday evening, had no more use for the side-combs than she had had on the October night when they were offered. She was feeling splendidly alive. Life coursed through her veins, and she was glad, in a way she had hardly known before, of the possession of her body. It was a virginal possession. On the solitary uplands, throwing her arms to the winds, breasting the hurricane, laughing with glee at the onslaught of the rains, she felt as Diana might have felt, possessing herself upon the mountains. She rejoiced, as a strong man rejoices to run a race, in her own virginity, the more, as she came to fuller understanding of life's purposes, in that she felt herself surrendered eternally to a love without consummation. Her virginity was Luke's, proudly and passionately kept for him.

So strong was the life in her as she walked onwards in the tossing April weather, that she could afford to be prodigal of herself even to the extent of throwing a greeting to Andy Macpherson, who was walking, also alone, on the uplands. So might Artemis, of her condescension, have graced a mortal with a word. But Andy knew only one way of talking to a girl, and be sure, given the opportunity so long denied, made use of it: whereupon Artemis, who had amassed a very considerable vocabulary during her researches in history and literature, and in her new-found arrogance of spirit discovered she could use it, chid him with such hot scorn and vehement indignation (after making the first advances too!) that Andy's blandness frothed to bluster and his bluster collapsed like a paper bag at a Sunday school picnic; while Martha marched ahead with her chin a little higher and her shoulders more squarely set. O, cruel! – But these goddesses are notoriously unfeeling, up yonder on their Olympian crags. When Artemis takes to the heather, ware to the soap-selling, bacon-slicing helot who would follow.

Artemis was very happy on the heather. She swung up through Crannochie, hailing Aunt Josephine as she went; and on to the Rotten Moss, where she clambered upon the boulders and plunged among the heather-tufts; and like a votary of the fleet-foot goddess (for to goddess her were hardly fair and she so near the discovery of her humanity), ran races with her own swift thought; and wind-blown, mazed with distance, drunken with height and space, danced fiercely under a bare sky. Diana would have trembled, could she have seen her votary. Such wild abandon was hardly virginal.

May was a frail blue radiance. Was there ever such a summer? Day after day the sun rose softly and night after night sank in a shimmering haze. The hills trembled, so liquid a blue that they seemed at point of dissolution; and clouds like silver thistle-down floated and hovered above them. Stifling one night in the low-roofed bedroom, where Madge's cheap scents befouled the air, Martha rose exasperated and carried her shoddy bed outside. There she watched till morning the changes of the sky and saw the familiar line of hills grow strange in the dusky pallor of a summer midnight. Thereafter she made the field her cubicle and in its privacy she spent her nights. She did not sleep profoundly, but her vitality was too radiant to suffer from the privation. Sometimes the rain surprised her and she was compelled to shelter; sometimes she let it fall on her, soft unhurrying rain that refreshed like sleep itself; sometimes she awoke, dry and warm, to a cool wet world where every grass, each hair on the uncovered portions of her blanket, each hair about her own forehead, hung with its own wet drops. But oftener the nights were clear, marvellously lit. Darkness was a pale lustrous gloom. Sometimes the north

was silver-clear, so luminous that through the filigree of leaf
and sapling its glow pierced burning, as though the light
were a patterned loveliness standing out against the
background of the trees. Later the glow dulled and the trees
became the pattern against the background of the light. The
hushed world took her in. Tranquil, surrendered, she
became one with the vast quiet night. A puddock sprawled
noiselessly towards her, a bat swooped, tracing gigantic
patterns upon the sky, a corncrake *skraighed*, on and on
through the night, monotonous and forgotten as one forgets
the monotony of the sea's roar; and when the soft wind was
in the south-west, the sound of the river, running among its
stony rapids below the ferry, floated up and over her like a
tide. She fell asleep to its running and wakened to listen for
it; and heard it as one hears the breathing of another.

In the third week of June Luke said: 'We deserve a change
– we're positively grey with dust.'

The hot air quivered above the bogs. There was no wind to
blow the cotton-grass. An insubstantial world, hazed upon
its edges, unstable where the hot air shook. Midsummer: at
their feet the sweet pink orchises, the waxen pale cat-
heather, butterwort: the drone and shimmer of dragon-flies
around them: and everywhere the call of water.

They were drowsed with happiness. Sometimes they
walked, sometimes they stood and gazed, sometimes they lay
in the long brown heather, smelling the bog-myrtle, listening to the many voices of the burns. A butterfly – a tiny
blue – glided over and over them. It floated on the current of
their happiness.

At twilight long shadows came out upon the hills. Their
darknesses were tender purple, and stars, too soft to shine,
hung few and single above. The skies were dust-of-gold.

There were no stars too soft, no purple too tender, no
dust-of-gold too paradisal, for their mood.

Tomorrow – the trance will break.

Martha tossed the bedclothes off and sat up in bed. She
was in the house, in the low hot room with Madge and her
reek of face powder. She had been too weary, coming home
from the afternoon among the hills, to carry her bed outside.

They had gone, the three of them, in an excursion train, up-country among the Saturday trippers, and back at night in a crowded compartment where sleepy children squabbled and smeared the windows with their sticky hands.

It was long past midnight when she abandoned the effort to sleep and sat up. She was not weary now, but through her body there ran a tantalizing irritation. She thought: 'It isn't pain – but what is it? It's in me. It hurts my body.' And she writhed, twisting herself upon the bed. 'I want the eleven stars,' she thought. 'But are they enough?' Her wants felt inordinate and she too small and weak. She battled against a sense of impotence.

She moved again, tossing an arm, and her hands met and clenched. She was so sunk in her absorption that for a moment she did not realize it was her own hand she had closed upon. She felt the firm impact of the grip . . . oh, it was her own! Queer, her own hand there. And then, with the suddenness of light when a match is struck, she knew what it was she wanted. Luke's hand, just to touch his hand: that would allay the agony that tore her, the pain that gnawed and could not be located, that was in all her body and yet nowhere.

She knew now. She wanted Luke. All of him, and to be her own. And the torrent of her passion, sweeping headlong, bore her on in imagination past every obstacle between her and her desire. The thought of Dussie was like a straw tumbled in a cataract. Let the whole world be swamped and broken in this cataract, so it carry her to her goal. The Ironside in her blood was up. Like her father who had swept the proud Leggatt beauty on to marriage, masterful until he had his will; like her Aunt Sally who had defied opinion and eloped with the man who roused her passion; Martha was ready to spurn the whole world and herself as well, in the savage imperious urge of her desire. Leggatt respectability! – She wanted Luke with an animal Ironside ardour. And was he not already half in love with her? – or more than half. 'I could make him love me,' she thought; and the sense of her own power rushed over her with a wild black sweetness she could not resist.

A curious part to be cast for a Beatrice. Martha was going

out of her rôle. But in truth she was neither Beatrice, nor
Artemis, but Martha Ironside, a woman: of like dimensions,
senses, affections, passions, with other women. If you prick
her, will she not bleed? And if you wrong her –

But it was a little later till Martha began to consider
whether she had not been wronged.

Morning came at last, and she could rise without exciting
comment.

The day was Sunday. Impossible to see Luke that day. She
passed the time in restless walking, and had one thought
only: 'I can make him love me.' She had never had a strong
sense of the complex social inter-relationships of life: now it
was gone completely.

At night she slept in the field. Slept! – Sleep was past
imagining. There was no darkness; and the diffusion of light
was strange and troubling. In the very early hours of morning she slipped from bed, put on her clothes, and went to the
wood.

There the light was stranger still. The wood was bathed in
it; a wood from another world; as though someone had
enclosed it long ago in a volatile spirit, through which as
through a subtly altering medium one saw its boughs and
boles. She was almost afraid to enter in; and when, ahead
through the glimmering gloom, she had a swift glimpse of
fire, as though a match had been struck and extinguished,
she shook with an undefined terror and plunged hastily in
another direction.

Roaming thus through the wood, she came in sight of
Luke himself, standing among the trees. She knew of his
night-wandering habits, but nonetheless at finding him there
just then, an intoxication seized her. Her blood raced; her
heart thumped; she could hardly stand: but recovering
herself she went straight towards him. 'I will have what I
want. I can make him give –' But as she glided on among the
boles of the pine-trees, and he saw her coming and stood
watching where he was, there was no alteration in her that he
could have seen. The boiling fermentation of her passion was
all within; and her habit of self-control and silence was too
strong to be broken soon or lightly. The Martha who
advanced through the strange shimmering night came tran-

quilly, stole in an exquisite quietude to shatter and plunder and riot. In her heart was havoc, in face and movement a profundity of peace. Luke, watching her coming, did not stir. She stood beside him, and neither he nor she spoke a syllable. They did not look at each other but at the night. Moon and afterglow and the promise of dawning were dissolved together in one soft lustre. They stood side by side and looked at it. After a long time Martha swayed a little, made a blundering half-step backwards, as though numbed with standing and seeking the support of a tree. He put out an arm and she swayed against it; and stood so for some minutes longer; and imperceptibly her head drew closer until she laid it at last upon his shoulder and looked up full, for the first time that night, in his face. Her whole being cried, 'Take me, take me.' But she stood so still, so poised, that it did not occur to him that she was offering herself. After a while he stooped and kissed her on the lips. There was no passion in the kiss. It was grave, a reluctance, diffident and abashed, as of a worshipper who trembles lest his offering pollute the shrine. But the flame that burned within herself was fierce enough to transfigure the kiss. It seemed to blaze upon her lips and run like fire through all her body. She closed her eyes under its ecstasy; and opening them again, slipped from his arm and went swiftly away through the wood. He did not follow her, nor did she look back, nor had either of them spoken.

Martha did not perceive that she had not had her desire. She was drunk with the sense of her own power over Luke and gulped more and more of the perilous draught until she was incapable of distinguishing any other taste. She lived only for seeing him again, but would not place herself in his path. It was three days later that, walking along the street, she heard his voice behind her and turned. The look she gave him was a direct continuance of the look with which she had left him, as though all that had passed between had not existed and they were still at their moment of exquisite communion in beauty. But he was not aware of the look. He had been much occupied in the interval and plunged at once into the theme that engrossed him.

'Tremendous news, Marty. If you have tears, prepare, etcetera.'

And suddenly very grave:

'Marty, how long have you known me? – four years, is it? And have you seen me in all that time accomplish anything? Lord, I've strewn the street with corpses! – things I've begun and cast away unfinished. And you've seen it and never said a word. Why didn't you tell me about it earlier?'

'Tell you,' stammered Martha. How could she have told what she had not perceived?

'You should have stabbed me awake to it sooner. There I've been, junketting at a thousand occupations, while you walk steadily on at one. So that's why I'm going away.'

'Away.'

'Imphm. A spell of hard labour. Hard labour and prison fare. It's you that's sending me away, you know. Aren't you upset by the responsibility?'

'Sending you away,' she said again. She had not fully grasped his meaning. He always went away in summer; but, was there more in this? And her responsibility? Wildly self-conscious, remembering the night in the wood, she queried: Was he fleeing her? Afraid of her power? And black exultation shook her. But he was speaking – she forced herself to listen.

'We're bound for Liverpool, Marty. I've just completed the purchase of a practice – a fine slummy practice, plenty of work and little pay. I'm leaving the University – old Dunster has his hanky out.'

She stared at him without speaking. Her mind seemed to have stopped working.

'Got a shock?' he said, looking down on her. 'We're giving shocks all round, it seems.'

'It's so – sudden.'

'Yes. Well, no. Not exactly. It's been under consideration for awhile, but we didn't want to say anything till it was all settled.'

She asked,

'Does Dussie know?'

'Dussie? – Rather!'

'I mean, did she know? – before.'

'Before? – When? – But of course she knew. A man doesn't do that sort of thing without consulting his wife.'

He was still unaware that Martha loved him. Rapidly though his education had progressed in the last few months, he was still able to believe that a woman could be all spirit. He had told Dussie, with a certain defiant diffidence, of his meeting Martha in the wood.

'You know when I walked the other night – sounds like a ghost, doesn't it? And it was ghosty – you wanted to say a bit out of the Litany, that bit we used to say when we went the long way round home at nights, after theatres and things, in the out-of-way streets, you know – "Fae ghaisties, ghoulies an' lang-leggity beasties, fae things that go dunt in the dark, Good Lord, deliver us." Only it wasn't things that go dunt in the dark that you wanted protection from, but things that go lithe in the light. Ghosts of light, not of darkness. You never saw such a night! Moon up and the whole sky like silk – gleamed. So did the earth. You felt like – or at least I felt like – a stitch or two of Chinese embroidery. You know – as though you were on a panel of silk. Unreal. I went as far as Marty's wood – the Quarry Wood. You've no idea, Duss – you couldn't imagine what it was like. At least I couldn't have. You know that thing – Rossetti's – about going down to the deep wells of light and bathing. It was like that. Only it was like an ocean, not a well. Submarine. Seas of light washing over you, far up above your head, and all the boughs and things were like the sea-blooms and the oozy woods that wear – you know. It was like being dissolved in a Shelley ode. Your body hadn't substance – it was all dissolved away except its shape. You walked about among shapes that hadn't substance, unreal shapes like things under the sea. Even some of the horrid rapscallion fishes out of the sea-bottom were there – one was, anyhow. That great sumph of a man that lives near Marty – what's his name? – Stoddart something. I met him just inside the wood – like a monstrous unnatural fish, one of those repulsive deep-sea creatures. Meeting him's like finding a slug in your salad. It was that night, anyhow. He had his eternal pipe in his mouth, and when he cracked a spunk the lowe of the flame was like an evil eye winking. Horrid feel it gave you. But further into the wood you forgot ugly fishes. You forgot ugly everything, and when Marty came walking through the wood you knew she wasn't real – just a ghost of light. I've no idea why she came – perhaps it really wasn't herself but just her phantom. I don't know. I didn't ask. She didn't speak a single word all the time. Just glided in and stood beside me – stood at gaze, so to speak. We looked and looked for a long time. Then she got tired, standing so long in one position, and made a stumbling sort of movement. And I put out my arm to give her support – and kept it there. And then somehow or other – God knows why I did it – I kissed her.'

He had paused there, diffident. Dussie had made no answer.

'And she just melted away – if I were a mediaeval chiel I'd honestly be tempted to believe she was an apparition. A false Florimel. An accident of light. She never spoke, you see. A voice is rather a comforting thing, don't you think?'

He paused again: and suddenly his wife was in his arms, her bright capriciousness gone out, sobbing as though she could not stop.

When he understood her fear, Luke went through one of those moments that are like eternity, so full it was of revelation. In that moment his boyhood was over. When he had held Martha in his arms in the wood, he had felt no lust for her possession but only a solemn wonder at his nearness to a thing so pure and rare: but now as he held his wife in his arms, and understood her fear that he might love Martha more than herself, he was ravaged by desire for Martha. At that moment he felt like universal Man assailed by the whole temptation of the universe; and because hitherto he had taken exactly what he wanted from life, the shock was extreme.

But there was rock in the welter: he did not know that Martha loved him. Had he been aware of her passion, there could have been no straight issue. Blindingly it flashed on him that she might be assailed. He put the thought from him. The contest was unimaginable but so brief that when he came to himself Dussie was still sobbing:

'I know she's better than me, but I love you so, oh Luke, I love you so.'

Afterwards he could hardly remember that he had thought of Martha thus. The lightning had been too keen. He was not quite sure that he saw it. But he took his wife in his arms very soberly. They had done playing at love. Henceforward they were man and woman, knowing that life is edged.

Dussie kept her own counsel concerning Martha.

'She has just to get over it,' she thought.

So when, in the street, Martha asked, 'Did Dussie know?' he looked at her with some surprise.

Martha perceived that she had not been in his innermost counsels. Hardly aware of the action she began to chafe her hands, which were clammy cold. In common daylight the insanity of her supposition – that she might be more to him than Dussie – was glaringly apparent. Hot black shame consumed her. She was too conscious of it to grasp very thoroughly the significance of his departure, but with a resolute mastery of her thoughts she forced herself to attend to what he was saying. She heard much detail about the new practice, the house they were moving into, the date of their going.

'I wish you were coming too, Marty,' he said. 'We shall miss you horribly.'

She heard her own voice saying:

'I'd have been away from you this year anyhow. I don't know where I may get a school. Not at home, likely.'

He continued: 'You've meant an awful lot to us. You've no idea how much. And do you know, it's really you that's sending me off on this new enterprise. They've been glorious, these last three years, but too easy. My work – oh well, I've done it all right, of course. Old Dunster wouldn't be so sorry to let me go if I hadn't. But somehow – well, it hasn't used enough of me. There was too much over to caper with. Another year or two of this divine fritteration and I'd be spoiled for good solid unrelieved hard labour. I owe it to you to have realized that one must have singleness of purpose. Oh, I'm not condemning the fritteration. Capering's an excellent habit. But not for me. Not just now. I feel in need of a cold plunge – you know, something strenuous that you have to brace yourself for. A disciplined march. A general practitioner hasn't much leisure for capering. G.P.'s to be my disciplined march. Instead of a hundred things I'm going to do one.'

And something cracked within her. Suddenly, it seemed,

the new self inside, that in the wood had not yet worked out
to the surface, had issue. It surged out over her. It took
form in a jest. Gaily she cried, throwing her head back and
meeting his look:

'And what about the other ninety-nine?'

'Dussie will attend to them,' he said, gay like herself.

Her mind began to work again. G.P.! – But his
greatness? He was to have been – what was he not to have
been? She saw the destinies she had dreamed for him float
past, majestic, proud, inflated. . . . She found herself
saying – and how queer it was, incongruous, unforeseen,
that she was laughing over this also, twisting it to jest –

'So it's a P. after all. Remember all the P.'s we planned
you were to be? Philosopher, Poet, Professor –'

'Piper, Pieman, Priest. Sounds like prune-stones, doesn't
it? Or there's Policeman – I'm tall enough. Or Postman.
That would be a fate worth considering. A country postie –
I'd love that. There I am again, you see! Can't stick to one
thing. A real Philanderer.'

They had reached the door in Union Street.

'Dussie's begun to pack already,' he said. 'Oh, that's
what I must be – a Packman! Come on up.'

The next five days were like a dream to Martha. Dazedly
she helped with the preparations for departure, and stood
on the draughty station platform among the crowd that was
seeing the travellers off. There was chattering and jesting,
and a ringing cheer as the train steamed slowly out. Martha
chattered and jested with the others; but the jests she
bandied, and the thoughts she had been thinking, had no
reality. 'You have been a fool,' she told herself: but the
accusation had no meaning. Even shame was burned out;
nothing had reality but his going. He saw her from the
carriage window among the waving group; so gay, so
shabby. Almost, he thought – but it was not a thought, so
quickly it flitted, so unformulated it remained in the scurry
of his mind – almost, he thought, he had rather she had not
been gay; but still, a shining symbol, herself the counterpart of the image he had made of her.

She was gay because she was no longer a counterpart. She
did not know what she was.

Climbing the long brae home she was overtaken by the lassitude of reaction. She did not seem to have strength enough left in her for passion, but she did not understand that it was only a temporary ebb. 'I don't seem to care any more,' she thought; and later, walking wearily on, with her eyes to the ground, she said to herself, 'So that's over,' and she thought she had only to exercise her will to be again what she was before, passionless, possessed only of herself.

But Martha after all was very ignorant. She could not know that a cataclysm four years in preparing does not spend its forces so easily. The waters were loosened and not to be gathered back.

FOURTEEN

Trouble for Aunt Josephine

Martha went to the Graduation. She had intended to go, and though the sap and savour were gone from every avocation and she was indifferent as to how she spent the days, it was easier to drift on the stream of former intentions than to force herself to new. Besides, Harrie Nevin was graduating, with Honours in English Language and Literature. She realized with a shock how little she had seen of Harrie recently and how seldom she had visited her thoughts. Of course she must see Harrie capped! But it was a stimulated interest.

For a time she continued to sleep out of doors, though there was no joy in the changing lights or the many voices of the country. She could no longer surrender herself and be lost in the world's loveliness. She would as willingly have slept in the bedroom beside Madge; she was quite indifferent to where she slept, and it was easier to stay in the bedroom; but that would have provoked comment and question. Anything rather than that! But she was not sorry when the weather broke and she was compelled to stay within.

At the turn of July there was already a hint of autumn. The skies were heavy grey; everything closed in unexpectedly; the wind blustered and squalls of rain broke upon the country, laying the corn in patches. The hips and rowan berries were dull brown that sharpened every day. Soon, the barley was russet. An *antrin* elm-leaf yellowed. Birds gathered; suddenly on a still day a tree would heave and *reeshle* with their movement, a flock dart out and swoop, to settle black and serried on the telegraph wires; and after a little rise again in a flock and disappear within the tree. In the wood and among the grasses gossamers floated, tantalizing the face, invisible, but flaring as they caught the sun like burnished ropes of light. Moors and hillsides, railway cuttings

and banks beside the roads, glowed with the purple of
heather. In a blaze of sun its scent rose on the air and bees
droned and hummed above the blossom. Strong showers
dashed the sun and the scent. *Hairst* began. They were
cutting the barley. Scythes were out and the laid patches cut
patiently by hand. Sometimes a whole field had been devas-
tated, and through the yellow of the heads there gleamed the
pink of exposed stalks. Winds rose and dried the grain.
Stooks covered the fields. Nights grew longer and sharper.
One morning the nasturtiums and potato tops were black.
Leaves floated down. At every gust a light rain of *preens* blew
through the firwood. The bracken and the birches turned
golden and golden trails swayed from the laburnum trees, a
foolish senile mimicry of their summer decoration. Gales
brandished the half-denuded boughs and whirled the leaves
in madcap companies about the roads. The whole world
sounded. A roaring and a rustle and a creak was everywhere;
and dust and dead leaves eddied in the gateways.

But long ere these things Martha's path had turned. Late
in August she was appointed to a school at Slack of Mar,
some ten miles across country towards the Hill o' Fare.
There being no direct conveyance, it was not so near that she
could stay at home, though not so far but that at weekends
she could cycle back and fore. From Monday morning till
Friday night, and later when the nights grew longer and
darker from Sunday night till Saturday morning, she lodged
in a cottage near the school.

'A gey quaet missy – terrible keep-yersel'-tae-yersel- kin','
the folk around said of the new teacher. The other teachers
in the school tried to draw her out, but she refused their
advances. She was thankful to be left alone. Her inner life
was too turbulent, too riotous, and absorbed her energies too
fully to leave much possibility of interest in the external
world.

Martha had discovered that she was by no means done
with passion. The numbness of exhaustion worn off, she
found herself delivered again to its power. She let herself go
to it. Only in its flame did she feel herself alive. She luxuriated even in the black depths of pain to which her craving
surrendered her. They were the earnest of an intensity of life

beside which all else in the world was mean and flat. She
lived for the incidence of those cyclones of desire that lifted
her and drove her far beyond herself, to dash her back
bruised, her very flesh aching as though she had been
trampled. There were times when she felt the presence of
Luke so close and vivid that the things she touched with her
hands and saw with her eyes were as shadows. These were
the times when she had been accustomed to pour herself out
for him. Since the day when, dripping wet from the pelt of
rain that had overtaken her, she had crouched on her bedroom floor and felt for the first time in absence of her spirit in
immediate communion with his, she had satisfied by this
means love's imperative demand to give. Her life had seemed
to pass out from her and be received in his.

But love's imperative demand was now to take. She
wanted Luke, his presence, his life, his laughing vitality;
and it seemed to her, crouching mute upon the floor with the
mood upon her, that reaching him she could draw his very
life away and take it for her own. 'I mustn't. I mustn't,' she
thought. It was like rape. And her exultant clutching was
followed by an agony of shame. But next time the mood
possessed her she clutched again. 'He is mine. I can hold
him. I can have his life in me.' And she felt like a dabbler in
black magic, the illicit arts. There had been nothing illicit in
her loving Luke, nor in the outpouring of her spirit upon
him; but this reckless grabbing was like a shameful and
beloved vice. She fought frantically against it, only to
succumb to a blacker and more gluttonous debauchery.
Reason, that had been the adversary in her effort to give,
mocking her with the ultimate inability of the mind to know
that what she felt as true was actually so, was now her
triumphant ally. 'You cannot know,' reason whispered, 'that
you really touch him. It is only idea.' And as long as she
could not be sure, she could not exert her will to check her
thieving. Afterwards she was hagridden, with strained
miserable eyes. The hollows had come again in her cheeks.
Her face was hungry.

At home she was merrier and more vivacious than she had
ever been. Mirth was her hiding-place. Anything rather than
have them guess she had been hurt, and how! But she hated

the effort it demanded and was thankful that the larger part of that winter was spent away from home.

The road from Slack of Mar to Wester Cairns ran through Crannochie, and every weekend as she passed on her bicycle, Martha paid Aunt Josephine a visit; but preoccupied with herself she failed to notice, what the neighbours round about Crannochie were noticing that spring, that Miss Leggatt was less alert than she had been. Her straight shoulder and steady foot were failing her. She sat too often and too long by the ingle, forgetting time; sometimes, she forgot to rise; her blind was not drawn up, her door was not opened, till far on in the day; but always she had a ready word for a visitor, and Martha, for whom Aunt Josephine had been just the same since ever she could remember her, went on perceiving the familiar image and missed its alteration.

'Yer Aunt Josephine hasna come in aboot this lang while,' said Emmeline one Sunday in February. 'Is she weel eneuch?' If it was long since Aunt Josephine had been to Wester Cairns, it was longer since Emmeline had been to Crannochie. Emmeline, in the parlance of the neighbourhood, was like a house-side. Walking was not for her. The mountain could not go to Mahomet, and Emmeline was dependent on her daughter for news of Miss Leggatt.

'She was all right on Friday,' said Martha, staring out at the weather. A storm had broken the day before and she did not relish her ten miles' cycle run to the Slack.

'It's nae near han' by,' said Emmeline, peering out over her shoulder. 'See to that roarie-bummlers.'

Glittering bergs of cloud knocked against the south-east horizon, and turned and floated on again, and gave place to others; or stayed and piled themselves in toppling transient magnificence.

'The sooner I'm off the better,' said Martha. The ground was coated with a powdery snow; not enough seriously to impede progress, had it not been for the wind. Through the lifted snowclouds a ferocious wind seethed and twisted. One could watch its form in the writhing powder as one watches the reflection of branches broken in a pool. A dragon-shaped wind. With the sifted snow stinging her cheek and clogging on her spokes, Martha was glad enough to see Crannochie;

and too grateful for Aunt Josephine's fire and cup of tea to pay overmuch attention to Aunt Josephine's appearance. On the Friday of that same week, however, she could not be blind to the alteration of the old lady.

The cold snap had gone, giving place to a muggy Monday, Tuesday, Wednesday, Thursday, days without spirit or *smeddum*. But here was a day for you, blue as a kingfisher, pungent as tang'l! – tonic. Martha sprang on her cycle and came to Crannochie flushed and towsled with the spring.

Aunt Josephine sat in her chair, dull-eyed, *dowie*, indifferent. She was without enthusiasm and without food. Even from the cup of tea that Martha prepared she turned away her head. Aunt Josephine refuse a cup of tea! But when one has been sick for days –

Martha persuaded her to go to bed.

'I'll tell you what, I'll come back and stay with you. I'll run home first and tell them.'

By light of Saturday she saw everywhere the evidences of Aunt Josephine's unfitness. The house was grey with dust, clothes smelly with dirt were flung in a corner, on the pantry shelf she found a dish with scraps of stinking meat, hairy-moulded. *Scunnered*, she turned the contents into the fire and carried the dish hastily to the door. Peter Mennie the postie was coming up the path.

'But the dish smells still,' she said, 'even though I've washed it. Throw it away for me, Peter.'

'Bury it, lassie, bury it in the earth,' answered Peter, 'the earth's grand at cleanin'.'

And thrusting on her the bundle of letters he was holding, he took the cause of offence in his hand and strode with it round the end of the house.

'It's in ahin the white breem buss,' he said when he returned. 'You dig it up in twa-three weeks an' it'll be as sweet's the earth itsel'. There's mair buried in the earth nor fowk kens o'.'

With a spasm of dismay, an hour or two later, Martha was wondering whether Aunt Josephine might not soon be laid there too. Plainly she was very ill. There was hurrying back and fore . . . by night Miss Leggatt had been carried to the infirmary. They operated thrice in all before they sent her

home, haggard, shrunken, a ghost of herself; and with the
knowledge that shortly she must die.

'They should 'a' lat me dee in peace,' she said, weary of
hospital routine, of chloroform and the knife and all the
elaborate paraphernalia by which science prolongs a life that
is doomed like hers. 'They canna cure an' I micht 'a' been
deid ere now an' laid in the bonny grun', an' nae trouble to
naebody. Weel, weel, but here I am.' And contemplating
herself in her own bed among her own belongings, she
cantled up and looked around her with a shining pleasure.
'It's rale fine nae to be deid,' she pronounced. She *cantled* up
a little farther when Aunt Jean, who had accompanied her
from the hospital, began to tell her the arrangements made
for looking after her. 'A nice body that had been a nurse, nae
ane o' the hospital kind, ye ken – ' 'Nurse!' quoth Miss
Josephine; and with that she perked up and there was no
more word of dying. Never a nurse would Aunt Josephine
have, no, nor any hired woman. A pretty pass things were
come to, if she had to take a hired woman under her roof, she
who had relished her jaunty independence through so many
years. Oh, she knew there were unpleasant necessities, her
wound to dress and so forth, but the district nurse was
coming in about every morning to do that; and for the rest –

'There's Matty there,' she said, ''ll bide wi' me. That
would be mair wiselike nor a stranger body, surely. She can
easy get ower to the Slack on her bicycle. An' it's little that a
craitur like me'll want an' brief time that I'll want it.'

Aunt Jean approved the suggestion. Quite right for Matty
to make herself useful.

Martha was undergoing at the moment one of her fierce
revulsions from a bout of passion. She wanted to dash up out
of the waters that had engulfed her, to stand high and dry on
common ground; and it seemed to her that the more hard
work she had to perform, plain and ordinary tasks that
would use her up, the freer she would become. 'Even more
than I've strength for,' she thought, 'so that I'll be tired out
always and never have time to think.' There would be an
astringent quality in days that included an eight miles' cycle
run night and morning through all weathers, the tending of
an old woman stricken with cancer and the keeping of her

house, in addition to the day's teaching in school: something
antiseptic to draw out from her what at the moment she felt
as poison. *An ounce of civet, good apothecary.*

'Of course I will stay with you,' she said; and to her father,
who demurred a little at the arrangement, though conced-
ing, 'Ye'll hae to pleesure her. It canna be for lang,' she
repeated, 'Of course I'll stay with her. I can easily manage.'

Later, when the sharpest of her revulsion had worn off and
she no longer thirsted to scourge herself, she had a sagging of
the heart over what she had undertaken. 'Shall I be able?'
she queried: and with the insidious creeping in again of
desire she thought, 'I shan't have time enough for Luke.' To
gather her forces and pour them out on him seemed just then
the only worthy use in life: though in her heart she knew that
the outpouring would turn, as it always did, to grasping. She
wanted time for that too. . . . But it had never been in her
nature to step aside from necessary labour and she held
steadily to her task, stifling the impulses that sometimes she
counted madness and sometimes the noblest sanity she
knew.

Aunt Josephine made an astonishing patient. As Peter the
postie said, 'I never saw her in twa minds. She's aye grand
pleased wi' hersel'.' Pain, sickness, comfort, the kindliest of
attentions, the most wearisome of waiting, a clean house or a
dirty, won from her the same divine acquiescence. On her
worst days of pain she said, 'Weel, weel, ye canna mak a
better o't. There's fowk waur nor me.' 'If you knew where to
find them,' Martha said once. She was humbled by Aunt
Josephine's shining gratitude for attentions that were often,
tired as she was by the time she arrived back at evening,
scanted and hasty. 'That's richt, ma dear,' Aunt Josephine
would say, when Martha had not time to shake the mats or
lift the ornaments and dust behind them. 'They'll wait fine
till the morn. A lick an' a promise, that'll dae grand.'

'A dicht an' a promise – it'll serve my day,' she often said.
Yet as the weeks slipped by and summer came in, she
seemed far indeed from dying. Every day she took a firmer
grip again of life. She left her bed, sat most of the day in her
chair; then moved about the room doing odd jobs for herself; by and by could take a turn in the garden.

'I'm a bittie better ilka day,' she proclaimed delightedly. 'I'll seen be tae the road again at this rate.' And jubilation shining from her countenance, 'I'll nae keep sorrow langer nor sorrow keeps me,' she said.

Did she really think she was recovering, Martha queried of herself. If she still talked of what would serve her day, in the tone of resignation that suggested a brief day and a bounded, it was only, Martha noted, in phrases where to speak so had become a habit. When she was not simply making use of a phrase, Miss Leggatt's talk was all of life. No worms, nor graves, nor epitaphs had entry there. She had turned her back on the incredible folly of dying and was setting again about the excellent business of living with all the astuteness she could muster. 'Does she understand?' Martha thought. A few months at the most, the doctors had said. And she pondered whether she ought not to recall the old lady's galloping ideas. Was it kind to let her deceive herself, build false hopes that could have no foundation?

Miss Leggat understood well enough. She knew that she was dying: but she was not going to smirch what was left of her life by any graveyard considerations. And she said to Martha, 'It's high time the kail was planted out.'

'Kail!' Martha thought, with a queer contraction of the heart. 'Where will *she* be by winter? – But if it makes her any happier, where's the harm?' And she planted out the kail.

The old woman's gallant endurance of pain astounded her. 'But it's less awful than spiritual pain,' she said to herself hastily, ashamed a little of her own cowardice in face of her black nights of craving; and ashamed a little farther at the self-excusing, she would turn to Aunt Josephine with some tender ministration. She was not always tender. Passion, that seeks self very abundantly, left her at times a poor leisure for the concerns of other folk. When the crave was on her, it was dull companionship she gave Miss Leggatt. Luckily, however, Miss Leggatt had other companions. Peter Mennie, whether he had a letter for her or not (and Miss Josephine had no great correspondence), put his head every day round the cheek of the door and cried her good morning. Clem, from Drochety Farm, the rough country lass who since the death of Mrs. Glennie had been mistress in all but name of Drochety's establishment, and held her empire with an audacious hand, ran in on any pretext, or none at all, and bandied high jests with Miss Josephine.

'Ye're a great case,' Miss Josephine would say, gleaming in spite of her nauseating pain at some of Clemmie's audacities. Clem was a thorough-paced clown. She had an adaptable body. She could squint at will and her limbs were double-jointed. She would descend rapturously upon Miss Josephine with 'eyes that werena neebors an' feet at a quarter to three,' and take off again 'bow-hoched,' her tongue lolling; while the old lady sat in her chair and beamed with pleasure.

'She's a tongue in her heid an' she can use it tae,' she would tell Martha. 'She's some terrible up-comes. She's a caution, is Clem. A cure.'

A cure she was. The bluffert of her presence did Miss Josephine good. The very sound of her voice, strident and exuberant, carrying across the fields, was companionship in the long lonely days; and when Clemmie made jam, she gave Miss Josephine a taste; when she baked she brought her a scone for her tea.

And Stoddart Semple shambled in once or twice with his dambrod and gave the old lady a game; but she was 'tired some seen' for the game to be much of a success. 'We maun jist tire an' fa' tae again,' she said, 'that's fat we maun dae. Tire an' fa' tae again.' They fell to again, Stoddart having ample leisure to await her convenience and in his glum fashion enjoying the stir.

Mary Annie, too, old widowed Mrs Mortimer, would look in, hastily and deferentially, upon her friend. Her visits were conditioned. With the years Jeannie Mortimer had become increasingly peremptory and inquisitorial. She had carried her habit of bigotry from her religion into the minutest affairs of daily life; and surer every hour of her own salvation, grew proportionately contemptuous of the remnant of mankind. For Miss Leggatt in particular, who said straight out exactly what she thought of such a misanthropic variety of religion ('I'm ane like this,' Miss Leggatt would proclaim, 'fatever I think I say.' And she thought, and said, that Jeannie Mortimer was a *besom*. 'She's blawn up nae handy in her ain conceits. Religion's nae for plaguin' ye. A bit prayer's richt bonny in its ain time an' place, but yon's fair furth the gate. She's nae near han' soun'.'), for Miss Leggatt in particular Jeannie entertained an unconcealed distaste.

'I canna bide,' Mrs. Mortimer would tell Miss Josephine. 'It's an offence if I bide awa' ower lang.'

But when Jeannie's back was turned, Mrs. Mortimer, with her head poked forward, in her curious mode of progression that was half a walk and half a run, would sneak in by to Miss Leggatt. Some mornings she would arrive a little after ten o'clock.

'Jeannie's tae the toon, Miss Josephine,' she would say. And, jubilantly, 'I've on the tatties. I dinna need muckle breakfast, but I maun hae ma dinner. I'm nae nane o' yer gentry kind o' fowk. I'm jist the common dab. I jist eat whan I'm hungry.'

'The gentry has jist three meals a day,' Miss Josephine would answer. 'It's the common dab that has five or sax an' jist eat whan they're hungry.'

'I dinna ken' – all her old anxiety was in Mary Annie's voice and countenance – 'I dinna ken. I'm jist plain Geordie Williamson.'

And she would trot away, between a walk and a run, to eat gleefully of smoking hot potatoes and salt; and then pick and fidget at the meal she shared with Jeannie.

'I dinna need muckle mate, an auld body like me,' she said.

June was a hot and heavy month. Martha found the eight miles to Slack of Mar a little longer every morning. There came a morning when, nauseated by the odour that clung about Aunt Josephine's room, she sickened and could eat no breakfast. She climbed on her bicycle nonetheless and set off up the road.

'She has her ain a-dae wi' they littlins,' Aunt Josephine was saying somewhat later to the doctor, who chanced to call that morning.

It did not occur to her that Martha might have her own ado in Crannochie as well. How could she be a trouble to anyone, sitting there so quietly in her chair, with never a word of complaint upon her lips?

Quarter of an hour later the doctor came on Martha herself, sitting by the side of the road where she had stumbled from her bicycle, her head sunk in her hands.

'If you could take me on to the Slack – ' she said.

'The Slack!' quoth he. 'It's slack into your bed that you're going.'

And to Miss Josephine he said, 'You'll have to get a woman in to notice you, or I'll be having two patients instead of one.'

'Weel, weel,' said Miss Josephine, 'what we canna help we needna hinder. We'll jist e'en hae to dae't.'

But that evening as she sat in her chair her mouth was a little grim. A woman in to notice her indeed! What noticing did she require? It was not as though she were *raivelled*, as her old mother had been, poor body, or Miss Foubister of Birleybeg, who had been a terrible handful for years before she died, getting up and dressing herself in the middle of the night and trotting away down the road to the yowie woodie in search of a sweetie shop to buy her peppermints; or clearing the dirty dishes off the table into her apron and flinging them like so much refuse on the grate, where they smashed to smithereens. No, indeed, she was not like that. And a stranger body, too, meddling among her things, preventing herself perhaps from going and doing as she pleased. Her mouth was still a little grim in the morning.

'I'm fine, auntie,' Martha insisted. 'I'm quite all right today. Really I am.'

'Wi' a face like that!' said Miss Leggatt. 'Like a deuk's fit.'

Martha laughed. 'I've been waur mony a day an' nae word o't,' she said, giving Miss Leggatt back one of her own sayings.

The old lady's mouth relaxed a little.

'I shan't go to school today,' said Martha, 'but by tomorrow, wait till you see, I'll be as right as ever. The house can do without cleaning today.'

The mouth relaxed a little farther.

'The doctor thinks ye've some muckle to dae,' said Aunt Josephine. '"Hoots, awa', doctor," I says, she's managin' grand." "O ay, grand," he says, "but ye'd better get a woman in to notice you."'

'If only she would,' thought Martha swiftly. 'O God, I'm tired.' But she read the note of entreaty in Aunt Josephine's voice.

'We don't want a woman, do we?' she said.

The grimness went quite away from Miss Josephine's mouth.

'It gings clean by my doors,' she said, 'fat'n a way fowk can like to hae strangers aboot them. They're like the craws amang the wifie's tatties. I mind fine, fan I was stayin' wi' that cousin o' yer grandpa's, her that was terrible ill, there was twa fee'd weemen in the hoose – a cook an' a hoosemaid. I crocheted a cap to the hoosemaid, but nae to the cook. I didna dae richt. I should 'a' gi'en her a cap tae. But she was sic a discontented besom. She micht 'a' been mair contented if she had gotten a cap.'

Its natural pleasant line was restored to Aunt Josephine's mouth. She talked gaily on of the fee'd woman of half a century before and forgot the project to fee a woman on her own behalf.

'Matty and me'll jist scutter awa',' she said to the doctor. 'Her play'll seen be here. We'll manage grand.'

He looked at the girl's sunken eyes. They were not sunken because of Aunt Josephine, nor yet on account of the bairns at Slack of Mar: but that was her own affair.

'Term's nearly over,' she said. 'Of course we'll manage.'

'It can't be for long,' he told her as she saw him out.

But they had said that so often. The holidays came and Miss Leggatt was still smiling and serene, and viewed her growing kail plants with satisfaction; and Martha drew in her lip and wondered what was to happen about her visit to Liverpool. That visit had been promised for a year, and for a year she had luxuriated in the thought of it. Now – ? Aunt Jean and Aunt Leebie came occasionally to Crannochie, though Aunt Leebie was fragile now and ailing nearly all the time. 'Leebie'll dee first o' us a',' Aunt Josephine had always said; and Leebie herself accepted the probability as a distinction. It was a melancholy business for her to come and look on Josephine usurping, as it were, her right. She came but seldom. Aunt Jean came, brusque and brief, and found rust on the pan lids. Aunt Margot came, once only, harassed with flesh. But none of them offered to relieve Martha, and she was too proud to ask.

'She could get a body in for a whilie, surely,' said Emmeline, who knew of the invitation to Liverpool.

'She wouldn't like it,' Martha said.

'Oh well, ye'll need to humour her. She's gey far on her way,' Emmeline responded, and thought no more about it.

'There's mair last in her nor a body wad 'a' thocht,' said Geordie, who did not know of the Liverpool project but had overheard the last few words between his wife and his daughter before the latter left again for Crannochie. He was wanting his daughter home. Matty might have her head stuffed with queer notions, but he liked her presence about the doors.

'Fat way wad she nae get a wumman?' he asked Emmeline. 'Has she nae the siller?'

'O ay, she has the siller, but she has mair, she has the sense to keep it. What ill-will hae ye at Matty's bidin' wi' her?'

'O, nane ava', but that the lassie wad need her holiday.'

'Holiday eneuch for her to be awa' fae the geets, surely to peace,' said Emmeline. Remembering a disclosure Martha had inadvertently made anent Aunt Josephine's marketing, however, she added, 'But she's funny wi' her cash.'

'We're a' funny wi' something,' Geordie answered, stretching his legs out in the sun. Matty, he reflected, was funny with her notions about book-learning, and sleeping in the field – 'like the nowt,' he thought – and now there was Madge trying on the same caper; and Emmeline was funny with her notions about other folk's bairns. There he paused, ruminating.

Emmeline had designs upon another baby boy.

Unfair, Geordie pondered, to bring another bairn there without even telling Matty. It was for Matty's sake the others had been sent away, and Matty, it was to be expected, would not be long an absentee from home.

On Martha's next visit home, meeting her in the field on her way to the house, he told her of her mother's intention.

Martha's anger blazed. She broke out upon her mother.

'Where are you getting him?' she asked, after having

intimated her displeasure. Some illegitimate outcast, she supposed.

'Hingin' on a nail i' the moss,' said Emmeline shortly.

Martha could be conclusive too.

'Well, mind,' she said, 'if you bring that child here and you fall ill again, I won't look after him. So you can please yourself. I mean it, mind.'

'Ye're terrible short i' the trot the day,' said Emmeline.

Martha's anger blazed again.

'Well,' she said, 'I want to know what my bed's doing out in the field.'

'Oh, is't oot? That's Madge, the randy. Fancy nae bringin' it in a' day. That's her sweirness – '

'Do you mean to tell me that Madge is sleeping in my bed?'

'Weel, fat's a' the temper for? Ye did it yersel! Why sudna she?'

'It's my bed,' cried Martha passionately. 'She can take her own bed outside.'

'Yon lumber o' a thing – '

'And she's had my sheets. Hasn't she? I know she has – '

'The sheets'll wash, surely to peace.'

'I'll never sleep in them again after her.'

'Weel, dinna, then. Ye wad think she was a soo.'

'She's worse,' cried Martha in a transport of rage; she had no idea that she hated Madge so much; and the girl herself coming in at the moment, she emptied out the cataracts of her wrath.

Madge gave her a contemptuous stare and began to spread a bit of oatcake with jam. She did not trouble herself to answer back. There was something horrible in her self-possession.

'Mind you about that infant, mother,' said Martha, swinging round on Emmeline. 'I won't touch it, I won't look at it. If you're ill it can starve, for all I care.' And she made off up the field. A fortnight of her six weeks' holiday was already gone and there seemed no nearer hope of reaching Liverpool; and she had realized, in a ferocity of anger against herself, that through the whole year that had elapsed since Luke's departure, she had been living for the moment of reunion. 'I need him,' she cried desperately to the night. 'I must have him. I'm only really alive when I'm with him. If I can't see him now I'll die. I'll never go through another year without him. Without seeing him. Being revitalized by him. It's by his life I live.' And in daylight, taking the ashes from the grate, 'Good God,' she thought, 'am I such a slave as that?' She wanted to kick out at the whole world to prove how free she was.

'Fatever ails her?' said Emmeline, as she swung herself away from the family conclave. 'I hinna seen sic a tantrum sin' she was a bairn.'

'She's richt eneuch aboot the loonie,' Geordie said. 'If you werena weel again it wad be a gey trauchle for her.'

'O weel,' said Emmeline, 'I wunna bring him.'

In spite of aching muscles after a long day's work among the hay, Geordie walked to Crannochie that night to tell his daughter that the child was not to come.

'O, I'm not caring,' said Martha peevishly.

What did anything matter if she was not to see Luke?

But the next time she came home Emmeline was seated by the fire with a bundle cradled in her arms.

Martha's rage had fallen. She was toneless, apathetic. Three weeks of her vacation had gone.

'So you brought him after all, mother,' was all she said.

Emmeline had been in secret a little afraid of what Martha might say. She blurted, apologetically,

'Ye sud 'a' seen the girl's face whan I said I cudna tak him, Matty. . . . Besides, I'm rale fond o' the craiturs. I've been used to them a' ma days an' it's rale lanesome-like wi' you and Madge an' yer father awa' a' day lang an' me used to a hooseful. I like a bairn aboot to get the clawin's o' the pots.'

Martha said nothing. Encouraged by the silence, Emmeline drew aside the shawl that wrapped the child.

'Did ye ever see sic an imitation?' she said, displaying the baby. 'Ye cud haud him i' the lee o' yer hand. But he hadna a chance – the lassie was that sair grippit in.'

Martha glanced incuriously at the child.

'Sax months an' mair,' said Emmeline. 'An' ye wadna think he was three.'

Six months and more, Martha was thinking. Six months and more till she would see Luke. Half her holiday was gone. Aunt Jean had visited Aunt Josephine the day before and Martha, desperate, had gulped that she was invited to Liverpool. Aunt Jean had not seemed to realize that Martha could not go to Liverpool unless someone else stayed at Crannochie. She had not made the slightest motion towards help. She had said, 'Oh. Fa's there?' 'I've friends,' Martha had said. In Aunt Jean's presence it had seemed an utterly senseless proceeding to have friends of her own outside the family cognisance. But perhaps later Aunt Jean would realize the position, and write.

At the end of another week Aunt Jean had not written. Martha wrote. She wrote to Liverpool and told them that she would never be able now to get away.

Three days later Peter Mennie, calling out cheerfully from the garden so that they might know he was coming, strode into the kitchen and struggled with something in the letter bag.

'Is't a parcel?' asked Miss Josephine, all agog with interest.

'There ye go!' he said triumphantly, dragging out from the bag first one and then another huge potato. 'A makin' o' ma new potatoes to you. Arena they thumpers?' And while Miss Josephine exclaimed upon their beauty, he held a letter out to Martha.

'O ay, they're a terrible crop the year,' he said, striding to the door again; and stepping out cried over his shoulder to Martha:

'Ye'll be awa' to Liverpool ane o' these days.'

The postmark of her letter was Liverpool: doubtless Peter had taken a shrewd glance at it before he gave it up. Clemmie had trained him well in such habits of observation: especially in regard to the letters that were delivered before he came to Drochety.

Obeying a sudden impulse, Martha blurted out her bitterness of spirit to Peter.

Twenty minutes later Drochety's Clem burst open the door. 'Foo's a' wi' ye the day?' she shouted to Miss Josephine, and, lugging Martha outside the door:

'Dinna you fret, lassie,' she said, 'awa' wi' ye an' hae yer holiday. I'll come in-by an' sleep aside Miss Josephine an' dae her bits o' things. There's nae need to hae onybody in.'

Martha looked at her coldly.

She resented Clemmie's interference in her affairs. She had almost instantly regretted her impulse of confession to Peter and was furious that he had gone straight and told Clem. She might have known! – He told Clem everything. Every day as eleven o'clock approached, she watched for his coming and had his cup of cocoa ready when he arrived; and while he sat in the big armchair in Drochety kitchen and drank it, Clemmie relieved him of the bundle of letters he was holding. . . . Hence her unique mastery of the affairs of the neighbourhood.

'But she doesn't need to know mine,' thought Martha angrily: and she was short with Clem; refusing her offer in brief politeness. It was only when Clemmie insisted – 'Ye're lucky fond, lattin' them a' ride ower ye that gait,' she said. 'Yer play'll be up or they tak ony notice o' ye. O, I ken yon Mrs. Corbett. It tak's her a' her time an' a lot mair to see that her cap's set straught. An' Mrs. – the little ane – the Leebie ane – she's aye that sair made wi' hersel, ye wadna think ony ither body had an ill ava.' She wad be a sicht waur gin onything ailed her. Jist you tak yer ways awa' an' never heed them. Miss Josephine'll dae grand wantin' ye' – it was only then that Martha had the grace to tell the truth.

'It's awfully good of you, Clem,' she said, with an effort upon herself, 'but it's too late now. My friends are going off to Spain this week.'

Dussie had written, in the very letter that Peter had handed to her that morning, 'We're frightfully sorry you can't come, but since you can't we're to take our holiday at once. It suits Luke better. We're going to Spain.'

A couple of hours later Clem came running back with a plateful of scones. Clem was the most generous of mortals, with Drochety's goods. Since Drochety's ailing wife had died, a twelve-month after Clem had taken over the rule of the place, she had slowly and very securely gathered the power into her own hands. All the countryside knew that Peter had *speired* her more than once, but Clemmie had

always an off-putting answer. She had been putting him off
for fourteen years now. And meanwhile with a lavish hand
she distributed Drochety's belongings.

Martha ought to have been grateful for the scones. Clemmie's scones were a wonder and a treat. They melted in the
mouth. But at sight of them Martha's anger flared. 'How
dare she pity me?' she thought; and she pushed the plate
savagely away.

She persuaded herself that she did not care. Her mind
seemed to have gone dead, as her fingers went on winter
mornings. Too tired to cope with her thoughts, she turned
away from them and left them in confusion. School took up
again. She cycled to the Slack and cycled home, absorbed
herself as best she could in the bairns she taught and in Aunt
Josephine, and told herself that her emotions were exhausted
and nothing would stir them any more.

She had yet to reckon with Roy Rory Foubister.

FIFTEEN

Roy Rory Foubister

The coming of Roy Rory Foubister to Crannochie woke
queer old memories in Martha's heart. She lay far into the
night and heard, through the pelting rain, the creak of the
boarding above her head as he turned himself on the impro-
vised bed in the loft where he had insisted that he must be the
one to sleep; and saw, in vivid projection, an ill-dressed
awkward child of nine who stared at Aunt Josephine's hand
of cards and heard her doom pronounced. Her halcyon days
in Crannochie had ended because Aunt Josephine and her
guest had talked of Rory Foubister: or so it had seemed to
the child: and persistently as erroneous ideas will cling, she
had gone on associating the name of Foubister with evil
omen. The name had stuck: though to be sure that was not
wonderful; seeing that Aunt Josephine had told her a hundred times since then of Rory and his stars. 'The world fair
made for him, ye wad 'a' thocht . . . but he wasna a gweed
guide o' himsel . . . "I've been a sorrowfu' loon to ma
parents, Josephine" . . .' She had heard it all so often, and it
had had the conventionality of the long familiar. It was only
very recently, in the light of her own new comprehension,
that Martha had divined a broken romance in Aunt Josephine's past. The serene old lady, with her boundless assurance in the rightness of life, had know heartache too. 'But it
couldn't have been like this,' thought Martha, agonizing on
her bed alone. 'She never went through a hell like this.'

She lay then that night and thought, in a hazy and jumbled
fashion, of these old tribulations; and hearing the small
unaccustomed noises above her head of the stranger within
the gates, remembered feverishly the queer thump that her
heart had given when he had said, shouting at her through
the bluffert of wind and rain that made her hold back behind

the shelter of the door, 'Roy Foubister's my name . . . .
This is Miss Leggatt's, isn't it? She knew my father – '

'Oh yes,' she had said. 'You'd better come in, hadn't
you?'

'It would be wise,' he said. And he came in streaming.
'Gosh! but you keep some weather here. Oh, the rain's all
right. I could show you rain – ! But this cold gets into you.'

It was November, and bitter on these unprotected roads.
She knew it to her cost, cycling up to Slack of Mar in the
early mornings. That day was Saturday and she was at home:
and so Rory Foubister's son, seeking Miss Josephine, found
Martha.

Aunt Josephine was in a flicker of excitement. Rory
Foubister's laddie! Well, well! That she should have lived to
see this day! And hearing that Rory himself was dead, but
had bidden his son, on the visit home that had somehow
never happened in the old man's time, seek out Miss Leggatt
if she was still alive. 'Alive!' said Miss Leggatt quite indignantly. A funny-like thing to suppose she would not be alive.
'And Rory's deid,' she said. 'Peer laddie, he was young to
dee.'

'Young?' said the son Rory had left behind him. 'Oh no,
my father was never young. He was eighty when he died. He
was over fifty, you know, when I was born.'

And Miss Josephine, to whom Rory was an incarnation of
eternal youth, and who was seventy-eight herself, replied:

'It's been gey queer guideship he's gie'n himsel, I'm
thinkin', to be awa' sae seen. Weel, weel, we canna but feel
the way-ga'in' o' wer freens.'

She let Roy do the talking for a little then, and he talked
very pleasantly of his fruit-farm in the Transvaal. Breaking
across his evocation, for Martha's delight, of a thousand
golden oranges in their groves, Aunt Josephine came back
into the conversation with a hearty:

'Weel, weel, he's deid. Deid an' daein' fine an' ca'in' peats
to Paradise. He was gey sair keepit in aboot fan he was the
laddie, but I'se warren he's seen the ferlies sin' syne. I mind
now – ' Thereafter it was family history for what'll-you-
wager, thick and slab while Martha made the tea. And if Roy
told Miss Josephine twenty tales of what Rory had done

abroad, Miss Josephine told Roy twice twenty of what he had done before he ever went away from Mar. She even told him the famous tale of how Crookity Bella, the hotelkeeper's wife at Slack of Mar, cured Rory of the drink. 'A terrible drouthy chap he was, 'but he didna cairry it weel,' said Aunt Josephine sadly. 'Bella kent him weel an' ower weel. He cudna keep awa'.' But on a certain Saturday night she refused him his dram. 'She was as gweed at a joke as onybody, was Bella, but there was nae joke that nicht. She was in sober earnest.' Rory, it seemed, was neither sober nor earnest. 'He was in a bawlin' singin' kind o' humour, an' had mair in him already nor he kent hoo to cairry. Sae she jist said, "Na, na, Rory," though he craved her for't. An' there was him cravin' her wi' a bit sang an' a bit dird aboot the fleer, an' her gie'in Barny Tamson anither an' aye anither drappie. But nae his warst enemy cud 'a' said o' Barny that he cudna cairry his dram. He was aye drinkin' – a sodden lump – but niver drunk. Weel, fan Rory saw Bella handin' anither drap to Barny an' denyin't to himsel, he oot at the door in a flist, an' "Nae anither copper o' mine will she see," he says, "though she's in the peers-house." An' nae anither copper o' his did she see. He niver darkened her doors again, an' him was fou' ilka nicht afore. "He's ta'en the bung," Bella says. "Weel, weel, lat him tak it." He was grand company an' she thocht to tryst him back, but he cud set his mou' wi' the best o' them. She fair cured Rory o' the drink.'

'That's a great tale,' said Roy, very polite, though plainly a trifle perturbed at these evidences of a disreputable past in his immediate ancestry.

'It's nae only a tale, it's true,' answered Miss Josephine. And her eyes shone with delight. She was a girl again.

But when tea was over Roy altered the programme. He was very willing to entertain the old lady, but to entertain her by listening to her was out of his part. He liked to hear his own narration just as well as she to hear hers. There was indeed a superficial resemblance between the two. Both were pleased with themselves; both buoyant; but the old lady's imperturbable assurance in the rightness of everything was replaced in the youth by an imperturbable assurance in the rightness of himself: a distinction not immediately evident.

What was evident was that he was in spirits, hearty and pleasant. The world seemed made for Rory's son as well as for Rory; and already after a couple of hours in Crannochie he was stretching out his hand to claim a little portion of the world that he found there.

The little portion was Martha.

Martha was an uncommon listener. Tell her a tale, and you had her! And for so long she had had nothing fresh to listen to. Her life had been held in a schoolroom, a sickroom, and the room of her own dark passion. Absorbed in these, she had hardly realized how she was missing the intellectual excitements of college; and now here again came a talker who brought her light and air, space, widened horizons. Her face took fire: a subtle flattery that was not lost on the narrator. Very politely, but quite firmly, he claimed a monopoly in the conversation. Old wives' tales could rest. He seasoned his wares with a dash of cunning, watching their effect. The plain one was attractive when she listened! Such a wildfire light in her eyes. Those eyes again! But it was not for Roy to know that he was not the first to find that plain face quite redeemed by those shining eyes.

'But I've never been in London,' she had said when he expected her to understand his reference. 'I've been no-where. I've seen nothing.' And she had bent forward, digging her elbows in her knees, eager as a landward child for the first visit to the sea. Such a young-girl face! Its candour at the moment quite belied her twenty-three and a half years. Delicious, he thought, to find a girl so innocent, so frankly inexperienced. Martha was not acting the *ingénue*. She felt herself very aptly the landward child and was not ashamed of her eagerness for what lay beyond her borders; and sinking her chin in her hands as she listened, she made a curious inarticulate noise of contentment.

'Whinnied,' he thought, and smiled at his metaphor. 'I'll have her nuzzling me next,' he promised himself. A riderless girl! All he need do was to mount. And he put his hand to his pocket for the knots of sugar, added the Anthropophagi to his traveller's tales.

The November night had closed in long before he was wearied of talking or she of hearing; and when at last he sprang to his feet, stretched himself splendidly and cried out on the lateness of the hour, the rain was still battering on the window.

'But in that storm,' said Martha. 'And it's pitch – you'll never find the way.'

'Na, na,' said Aunt Josephine, 'ye maun jist bide. Ye'd be like a drookit rat or ye got the length o' Beltie an' it dingin' on like that.'

'If you think you could put up with sleeping in the kitchen –' Martha ventured.

'Oh,' he laughed, 'I've slept in many a worse place than your kitchen.' He had already been there, carrying the tray for her and drying the dishes when she washed them up. But when he realized it was her own bed she was surrendering to him, nothing would serve him but that he and not she should sleep in the loft.

'But it isn't even a room,' she said. 'Just boards. We just store things there. It hasn't a stair. You have to shove a ladder up through the trap-door and climb.'

'Top berth,' he said genially. Apparently everything was to please him. They placed the ladder and helped each other up and down as they made the eyrie habitable; and Aunt Josephine sat alone in her room and beamed at the sound of their laughter.

So it came about that Martha lay and heard the boards creak above her; and saw, between sleep and waking, the world spin giddily round. 'Top berth,' she murmured; the house was a ship tossed on billows, and the rain was the lapping sea; and herself, a child, leaned over the deck-rail and saw, far below, a tiny Aunt Josephine playing a hand of cards with a boisterous black-a-visaged man whom she knew to be Rory Foubister. Roy was leaning beside her over the rail, watching too; and she knew that she had grown up again. 'It was the cake,' she thought mistily. 'No, the bottle. Alice in Wonderland. I shut up and stretched out again.' She fell asleep dreaming of flying-fishes that skim the surface of the sea like swallows; and the Karroo at evening, transfiguring the light.

She woke to a soft blue world. The rain was over. The hills were faint and clear. Roy called down to ask whether he might descend. 'Or shall I be in your way?'

'Come and look at Lochnagar,' she answered. And when he scrambled down from his eyrie and came to the garden gate, from which they could see the long panorama of the hills, she said, softly, as though her voice might smudge the frail shimmering beauty of the morning, 'Distance upon distance. Wouldn't you think it would never end?'

'Wait till you've seen the Veld,' he said. His loud cheerful voice seemed to roll echoing about in the empty morning. 'You won't talk about distances then. Or going down to Delagoa – the Low Veld. You look down and down and down and there's always more of it. You begin to think it must be the sea, and it isn't. It's always more earth.'

Martha's heart was battering in her throat. 'Wait till you've seen the Veld. Wait till you've seen – ' The words hammered themselves against her consciousness. She hardly heard the rest of his sentences. 'Wait till you've seen the Veld.'

She escaped to the house and made breakfast.

In the afternoon she walked with him to Beltie.

'You'll come back and see Aunt Josephine?' she said. 'It's been a treat for her to see you.'

'Yes,' he answered. 'I'll come back and see Aunt Josephine.'

He chose to come back and see Aunt Josephine the next Saturday. He came suitably munitioned for seeing Aunt Josephine, with a motor-cycle and a side-car; and before Martha very well understood it, she was bundled into the side-car and whirled along the road. They were through Slack of Mar before she had quite collected herself.

'That's where I teach,' she shouted up at him across the rush of air.

'Lord, is it, though!' he answered. 'It won't be long.'

'No,' she rejoined seriously. 'Was Aunt Josephine telling you? I'm being transferred at Christmas. To Peterkirk. It's much nearer.'

'You precious innocent!' he thought.

She was by no means so innocent as he imagined. Martha knew quite well that she was being wooed, and an uneasy excitement possessed her. She had never been wooed before.

Oh, there was Andy Macpherson, of course, who once in a way leered in her direction. But she knew how much that counted for! Andy's conquests were numerical. He wanted to add her to his row of scalps. But this was the authentic thing.

'Why shouldn't I know what it is like?' she thought: but she gave no sign of her awareness. Under his insinuating speeches she was as quiet, as unconcerned, as though he were asking for another cup of tea. Roy was completely in the dark. Finding her inexperienced on the levels where he could test her, he failed to realize that there were other modes of experience. It did not occur to him that she had any sort of past. He had no inkling of the still black depths through which she had gone down nor of the depths of light through which her thoughts had soared and hid.

They sped on past the Hill o' Fare, across the river at Potarch, over the Sheetin' Greens and down by the Brig o' Bogindreep. Martha let her spirit fly out on the air; the swift motion whipped her blood and paralysed her mind. Better, far better, never to think! If one could rush like this forever, too fast for contemplation, too merrily for desire, without a goal! She belonged neither to her past nor to her future. Before they rattled up the long brae to Crannochie again the hills were a uniform sombre grey, the trees and bushes a wash of shadow; inside the cottage it was already dark.

'O, I'm sorry,' she cried to Aunt Josephine, who was seated in her chair with one hand over the other. 'I didn't mean to be so long.'

As though what she had meant, or hadn't meant, had had any authority once she was caught in the machine. She had surrendered her will and knew it.

'Ay, ay, you're gey far ben, my lady,' answered Aunt Josephine, smiling at her.

Aunt Josephine smiled with the air of a woman who knows a thing or two. She smiled very frequently as the weeks and the motor-cycle ran on, and by sundry sly pokes and digs at Martha expressed her delight in what she felt to be happening. Martha suffered the digs. She offered neither repartee nor denial. Why should she? She was gliding on over a surface. She knew it was only a crust and at any moment might crack and precipitate her through its fissures; but its very insecurity exhilirated her, and plainly foreseeing a period to the excitements she was enjoying, she snatched them while she could. They galvanized her to a very fair imitation of life. She let her excitement appear, as he plied her with new experiences – rushing rides to all quarters of the country, theatres, dances – and the candour with which she showed it made her very young. Knowing women, Roy reflected, were the devil. She drew him on by her utter lack of calculation, and he made no doubt but that he rode her fancy as he intended very soon to ride herself.

Martha was under no real delusion as to his quality. She saw plainly that he was generous for his own ends.

'An' we aye get a fairin',' Aunt Josephine told Clemmie with proud assurance. 'He's that goodwillie. There's aye a pyockie or a boxie.'

Roy was astute enough to offer on most occasions the *fairin'* to Miss Leggatt. It was Martha who realized that his politeness was policy. She was coming to a surer understanding of men and women and in the abstract judged the situation fairly enough. Roy's was a cupboard love of life. Taking life, like Aunt Josephine, with zest, he could not take it, as she did, for itself; but always for what he might take from it. It was plain that he would exact of life his pound of flesh and see to it that he was not duped with carrion. Martha read it in his impatience at any interruption to his purposed enjoyments, his indifference to her concern over leaving Aunt Josephine alone: but her judgment remained in the abstract. She had not yet quite learned that the importance of things lies not in themselves but in their relations. Roy as an isolated phenomenon she had appraised, but she was still blind to the fact that Roy was not an isolated phenomenon. If it did not occur to him that she had a past, neither did it occur to her that both he and she had a future. She knew that he was wooing her and she knew that she would not be won: between these two sharp certainties the whole world lay in a confusion that her deadened intellect made no attempt to clarify. That he might count her a cheat, and be justified therein, was at present outwith her comprehension.

Meanwhile the motor-cycle ran back and fore. It enlivened the road. Motor-cycles, particularly reinforced by side-cars, were not so numerous as they have since become; and on the Crannochie road were not numerous at all. Not much doing on the Crannochie road! Folk did not congregate there; or if they did, they were the known folk, whose affairs were common property. They made no *steer* when they gathered for a *collieshangie* at a dyke corner. But add a motor-cycle and a side-car, duly inhabited by two! – Two in that case made a rabble, and the neighbourhood was agitated by the rabble.

The agitation, however, did not reach to Wester Cairns. The wood lay between, and Wester Cairns looked naturally towards Cairns and the city, while Crannochie looked towards Beltie and Peterkirk. Emmeline and Geordie heard nothing of their daughter's on-goings. She had reported Roy's first visit to Miss Leggatt – 'the son of an old friend – somebody Foubister, Rory Foubister,' she had said.

'Oh,' said Emmeline, 'I mind aboot him fine. He sud 'a' merriet yer aunt, if a' tales is true. O ay, if a' tales is true, that's nae a lee. She was terrible come-at, I mind ma faither sayin', fan he up an' laft her. But he was gey gweed at ga'in' on the ran-dan. Some ill for a dram, I doot. But a terrible fine chiel. Ma faither had a great gweed word on Rory.'

And Geordie, stumping up on a Sabbath to pay his respects to Miss Josephine – and see his lassie in the by-going – met cycle and cyclist and was introduced.

He duly related the meeting to Emmeline.

'Is he as young's a' that?' said Emmeline, with the judicial air of solicitude that must be allowed in the circumstances to the mother of a marriageable daughter. 'Wad he be aifter Matty, div ye think?'

'Na, I dinna nane think that,' Geordie answered. 'He had anither lassie i' the cairrage.'

The other lassie was a neighbour's niece, who had spent her Sunday afternoon in Crannochie. She had chanced to come in on an errand to Miss Leggatt on her way back to Beltie, and Roy with his ready affability had offered to run her in to town. Hence Geordie's misapprehension. Emmeline accepted his diagnosis of the situation and thought no more of Rory's loon. Had she known that the motor-cycle, with her own lassie in the *cairrage*, had not returned to Crannochie till the small hours of that very Sunday morning, her thoughts might have been of another colour.

Roy had taken Martha to her first dance.

He had taught her her steps in Aunt Josephine's room. The dancing lessons had delighted the old lady. She was not blither at the barn dances of her youth, the reels and *Strip-the-Willows* that Rory had shared; and when the night of the dance arrived, she watched Martha don the lustre frock with a brightening of the eye that would have done the heart good had there been a heart near enough to feel its influence. There was Martha's heart, to be sure, but it was not susceptible just then to such influences.

'Haven't you a warmer wrap than that?' Roy was asking.

'Just you wait, just you wait.' Aunt Josephine was rising from her chair and making for her high old wardrobe. 'Just you wait. You'll get my cloak.' She fumbled among garments; and Martha going to her aid they pulled out between them a long black cloak with a peaked hood falling down behind. The old lady wrapped Martha up in it, drawing the hood close round her face.

'Noo, ma dear,' she said. 'Ye're in an' lookin' oot.'

'Is it a proper sort of thing to go there with?' Martha was wondering, her eyes on Roy.

'Enchanting,' he was saying.

She was sure it was the wrong word, but would not let herself suspect a duplicity. Since he appeared to be satisfied, she said, laughing up into Aunt Josephine's face,

'My evening cloak! Imagine me possessing one.'

'And you *will* possess one,' Roy declared to himself.

Miss Josephine heard the retreating clamour of the motor. She sat smiling at the blaze of her fire, following their progress in thought; and it seemed to her that fifty years had fallen away and she was again the lassie whose heart Rory had made to *dirl*. She lived again her girl's romance, all save its dismal conclusion; and made no doubt but that Martha was dancing through a romance as sweet. There was endless wonder for her in the way things had come to pass.

Early in the year, on a stormy Saturday when Martha was busy close by her, she chanced to say aloud what she had often already said in secret:

'Weel, weel, an' to think I should have lived to see this day. I've been keepit alive for this.'

Martha caught the *Nunc dimittis* of the tone. But giving thanks for what? She glanced sharply aside at her aunt. Thanksgiving shone from her face; she was radiant with it; and her eyes rested on Martha with a joyful satisfaction. *When you have seen the Veld.* The words hammered in the girl's head. But she had not supposed that other folk had noticed whither she was drifting. She had short time, however, for speculation. At the same moment her ear caught the approaching throb of the motor-cycle and her eye the spectacle of a face flattened against the window and peering. She started violently, staring at the face.

'It's jist Stoddart Semple,' said Miss Josephine, following her agitated stare. 'The muckle sumph. He aye glowers in like that.'

'How horrible,' Martha said.

'Ye needna fash yersel,' said the old lady unperturbed. 'Ye needna be sae vexed.' She was vexed enough herself at times at the bad manners of the man. 'He's nae worth mindin'. He hasna the manners o' a soo. He's some ill-fashioned – wants to ken a'thing. But lat him in. It's kindly-like to come an' gie me a gamie.'

Martha opened the door to him and saw Roy dismounting by the gate. Stoddart had had no more time than to say, 'Foo are ye daein'?' thrusting his face forward into Miss Leggatt's as he spoke, when the young man strode in; and almost immediately afterwards the rain, which had been threatening all afternoon, fell battering.

'No ride for you in that, my lady,' grumbled Roy. And he went out to cover his machine.

On his return, 'Here's another visitor for you,' he cried, ushering in Clem. Clemmie had brought along some chicken and sauce, decorated with a wish-bone.

'I sees aul' Auntie takin' doon the road,' she said (referring to a neighbour for whom she had no great respect), 'an' turnin' in-by wi' a hen in her oxter. "Ay, ay,"

I says to masel, "if Auntie's gotten the length o'killin' a hen, it'll be a gey auld ancestor o' a hen that she's kill't." Ye had had some dividin' or ye got yon ane divided up, I'se warren ye.'

Aunt Josephine dimpled over into the most disarming of laughter.

'Weel, weel, ye're sayin' it,' she said. 'As auld's the Hills o' Birse – she wad neither rug nor rive.'

'Sae, "I'll jist tak them a bit," says I, "to lat them taste the taste o' a hen."'

She laid her offering on the table, and began explaining to Roy, behind Miss Leggatt's back, while the old lady praised both the gift and giver to Stoddart, 'She's penurious wi' her meat, but cud ye wonder?' *Penurious* Aunt Josephine was not. 'It's wersh, wersh,' was the utmost of her complaining, when food had neither sap nor savour in her mouth. But Clem continued to explain to Roy, in her hearty fashion: 'Her digester's a' tae nonsense. She gets scunnered at a'thing. Ye wadna wonder, noo, wad ye? Matty's nae great hand at the cookin' – her awa' a'day an' a' – ' and breaking off hastily, she eyed Roy and burst into laughter. 'Losh, laddie, I didna mean naething. The lassie's awa' a' day. Bit she'll come at it – she'll be a grand hand yet.' And she gave Roy a dig with her elbow and winked at him lavishly.

Roy winked back.

'She won't need to bother,' he said. 'She'll have a black boy to cook for her.'

'Losh be here!' said Clem. 'That's nae mowse.'

These savoury asides between Roy and Clemmie were meant for their own private entertainment; but they paid so little heed to the modulating of their voices that their words could be heard quite clearly by the other three persons in the room.

Martha's heart stood still. What! she thought. Were her affairs thus publicly arranged? In the innocence of her heart she had been supposing this adventure, this voyaging after the fruit of the Tree, as secret and self-contained as her adventure with Luke; inward. Seeing it thus bounced and bandied in plain daylight, focussed for her through the consciousness of others, she saw it as common and tawdry.

She had cheapened herself for her apple. Good God! she must disabuse them, and that mighty quick. But how? She was quite uncertain how to proceed.

And as it chanced she was already a little late. The four persons gathered round her were very comfortably persuaded that she and Roy were making a match of it. To Stoddart, who had not come that way for awhile, and had seen Roy only once before, the idea was new; but he seized on it with avidity. He knew a thing or two concerning Martha; and he relished a bit of gossip. Greedy once after the secrets of the universe, now he was greedy after the secrets of his neighbours; and he loved his own importance when he could divulge what others did not know. Not that he chose always to divulge such knowledge. He had a sappy mouthful, for example, concerning Martha, which he had kept to himself. In that there was malice. He had never forgiven the girl for her indifference to himself, which he termed her uppishness, and he had saved his bit of knowledge, to be used when it might harm her.

The time was now.

He growled at her across the room: 'Ye'll be ooten practice in kissin' sin' yon lang lad o' yours took to his heels.'

Martha stared.

Back over her memory rushed the night of her only kiss. Its width, its shining exaltation, caught her anew. O, to escape, leap upwards again to that sure serene communion in loveliness that had been theirs! – And crashing horribly through her moment of reconstructed paradise came the query: How did this man know? Confusion was in her brain. Conscious that there was silence round her, and that it must be broken, she blurted, 'I don't know what you mean,' and immediately cursed herself for her folly. She should have ignored his insinuation, changed the subject swiftly. She was too late now.

'I'se warren ye kent fine fat *he* meant,' Stoddart was saying. 'If it wasna a kiss ye was seekin', fat gar't ye tak a dander intil a wood in the middle o' the nicht?'

'To haud you speirin',' cried Clemmie in her loud rough voice. 'Fat sorra ither?' And she went off into a prolonged crackle of laughter. She had no idea to what Stoddart was referring, nor apart from her natural love of knowing everyone's affairs, was she greatly concerned to know: Clem was ready to defend her friends from any charge, and accuse her enemies of any enormity, that the human mind was likely to devise; truth being secondary. 'An' fat's in an antrin kiss?' she asked. 'A lassie needs to be kissed to get her mou' in.'

Clem had her mouth out. She had worked her way round to the back of Stoddart's chair and was carrying on her antics behind his back but in full view of Aunt Josephine, to the old lady's unconcealed delight. Aunt Josephine was as blithe as a bairn at a Punch and Judy show. Clem was the deftest of mummers. *Sonsy* though she was, big and ungainly of body, with huge hands and feet, she was incredibly nimble in her movements. Behind Stoddart's chair she was mocking Stoddart's clumsy gestures, shoving her mouth out till one could have tied twine round it, rolling her eyes so that the pupils seemed to meet.

'It's a fine thing a cuddle,' Stoddart was sneering, 'i' the deid o' nicht.'

'It's a fine thing an ingan,' mimicked Clemmie, 'to them 'at likes't.' And bringing her arm down with a thump on the back of the chair, 'Yauch!' she cried. 'I've yirded ma airm.'

She made a great to-do about the arm, showing off the bruise to each separate member of her audience, and talking volubly about the pain. Stoddart's drawling speech was lost in her clatter, as she had meant that it should be; and if he muttered something about lying in the arms of a man, Clemmie's arm was guarantee that no one knew distinctly what he said. And now Miss Josephine, deprived of her raree-show, was beginning to feel discomfort from the wintry air that penetrated by every chink.

'It's a wild-like nicht,' she said, drawing her shawl closer and huddling towards the fire.

The wind was rising, and the rain turning to sleet.

'O ay,' said Clemmie, 'I cud 'a' tell't ye last nicht there was a storm on the road. The moon was in the midden.'

'Yes,' Martha answered, 'she had a halo round her.'

She answered Clem's remark resolutely, holding her shoulders back and her head high. She had remembered a

forgotten detail – how light had winked suddenly in the
darkness of the wood and scared her: Stoddart with his
pipe? Knowing the man's night-roving habits, she knew
that her guess was probably correct. He had seen her hour
of apocalypse. She had not time just then to realize into
what foul-mouthed travesty he might turn it: all she cared
for was to get his slouching evil self out of her presence; and
thankful that she had noticed the *broch* around the moon the
night before, she held resolute conversation with Clem
anent the weather.

And luckily Aunt Josephine desired no game that afternoon. The chill was hard on her. She shivered. She was
feeling sick. Her guests must go. Stoddart slouched away.
He cast at Martha, 'Fan dirt begins to rise it gings an awfu'
heicht,' and drew no flicker on her impassive face. She
wished him good afternoon; with her chin lifted. Clem was
off too, *dirdin'* on through the sleet; and Roy must follow.

Martha raised her eyes and looked at Roy. They
inhabited different worlds. She had always known it,
though she had chosen not to see. Now she saw; and desired
nothing but to have him gone: forever if he liked. She felt
she would not care. But it flashed upon her suddenly that he
had not shared her experience of the afternoon; that for him
there had been no re-focussing and he considered her still at
his whistle. She revolted from the thought. How to disil-
lusion him? If it could be done without overt explanation,
by significant withdrawal of herself! Her mind played
wildly round the problem as she followed him to the door.

'Come to the door with me,' he had said peremptorily.
And she had obeyed, walking as in a dream.

'Look here,' said Roy in his loud bumptious voice, 'will
you kindly tell me what that person meant?'

'Which person?' Martha asked. She was looking at him
but hardly seeing him, absorbed as she was in her own
thoughts.

Roy jerked his head backwards towards the road where
the sloven figure of Stoddart Semple could still be seen
through the sleet.

Martha came half-way out of her absorption and realized
that Roy also had undergone that afternoon the necessity for

re-focussing. With that half of her that was still absorbed
she answered, using mechanically the same form of words as
she had used to Stoddart:

'I don't know what you mean?'

'Well, you had better discover what I mean. Double
quick time, too. Were you, or were you not, in a man's arms
at midnight in the middle of a wood?'

Martha came three-quarters out of her absorption and
realized that Roy was offended.

O, admirable! All unconsciously, Stoddart had played
into her hand. She was very willing just then to offend
Roy.

'It wasn't midnight,' she said. She said it without calculation. Her mind was running on that June hour that was
neither dawn nor dark, and instinctively, as she might have
corrected in school a child's inaccurate statement, she said,
'It was almost dawn.'

'Good Lord!' cried Roy. 'You're mighty calm about it, I
will say. And you thought you would palm another man's
property off on me, did you?'

Martha came all the way out, and realized that Roy was
offensive.

The blood coursed hotly up her face. Brow, ears, neck,
were scarlet. She was not prepared to purchase immunity
from Roy's attentions at the price of insult. A double insult.
He had insulted her relationship with Luke and he had
insulted her relationship with himself.

She wanted to say so many things at once that she could
say none of them explicitly. Words would not come to her
either to justify herself, or clear Luke, or stigmatise the
filthiness of Roy's misapprehension. She broke into half-a-
dozen sentences and broke off from them all.

'O, damn *mistake*!' cried Roy, interrupting her roughly.
'I don't want to know what you mean by *mistake*. *You*'ve
made a mistake, it seems to me. I can understand that kind
of mistake –'

'Roy, on my honour –'

'Was that man telling the truth, or was he not?'

'O, go and ask him!' she cried.

'That's exactly what I mean to do.' He flung a glance back

over his shoulder to the wet road. With his motor-cycle he
would quickly overtake Stoddart.

'I can't stand here and argue,' Martha cried. 'Aunt
Josephine's needing me. She's sick.' She made to shut the
door against him.

'Was that man telling the truth?' persisted Roy.

She gave him a queer look. He could not have read it even
had he been at leisure to make the attempt.

'Of course it was the truth,' she said; and shut the door.

Aunt Josephine was miserably sick. For several hours
Martha's attention was held.

'Weel, weel, ye canna mak a better o't,' Aunt Josephine
would say in her moments of comparative ease. 'There's folk
waur nor me.' And with a smile, 'Ye jist tak a howffie an' a
kowkie an' ye're a' richt again.'

It was late in the evening, however, before she was right
again; or near it; and when at last she dozed, Martha sat
staring at the fire, without moving, for a long time.

The several hours respite had nerved her for the inevitable
tussle with herself. She thought of her fingers, gone dead on
a winter morning, and of how she had sometines plunged
them in water too hot for them, to restore the circulation.
Her mind, like dead fingers, had been plunged in water too
hot for it; and for a time she was conscious only of pain. Late
at night a fierce clarity came in her thoughts. She saw all that
had chanced in the last two years sort itself out in patterns.
The patterns shifted; no two were quite alike, yet all were
recognizably the same; and it seemed to her that she was
looking in succession at the events of her life through the
eyes of all the different actors in them.

She despised Roy very heartily now: and herself still more
for her dealings with him. Under his veneer of politeness he
was common: shoddy stuff. She writhed, remembering his
accusation; and having forfeited her self-respect, was all the
more desperate to justify herself in his eyes. To be counted
wanton – ! But reason mocked. He would never understand.
Though she talked with the tongues of men and of angels, he
would never understand the quality of her love for Luke.

But if she could give him new perception? – If she bared
her soul and forced him to look, surely he would see. 'I

could make a bigger man of him,' she thought. She thought a good many foolish things in the course of that night; and perhaps a few that were not foolish: but certainly her resolution to give spiritual insight to Rory Foubister's son had not quite so altruistic a motive as she tried to believe. 'I have wronged him. I've wronged womanhood. I've made light of love. I have to show him now what it's really like.' But in her heart she knew that it was justification for herself that she craved.

And what was love really like? Not so sheerly spiritual after all. She recalled the frenzy of her June desire. That was what had driven her to the wood. In intent she had been just what Roy supposed. Shame sucked her under. So! – There was a God after all, implacable, not to be gulled, punishing even the fiercely smothered desires of the heart. She had been no better than that Warrender creature she had hated so tumultuously. Like her, she had fished for Luke.

She sat up in bed then, remembering her agony over Luke's part in the Warrender affair. Waste! She had blamed him for giving to Lucy Warrender just what he had given to herself – friendship of the mind. She laughed at the recollection of her own torture. She should have been tortured that he had liked her too: dishonour in that as much as in the other – or as little. Half the agony in life came from blinded motives, an insufficient understanding of what one truly thought. Men's creeds are conditioned by their desires. Martha's ideas of right and wrong were altering under pressure of the discovery that she had condemned Luke for giving to Miss Warrender what, given to herself, had been the richest nurture of her spiritual life: what, in fine, she had wanted. Of course he had laughed at her remonstrance! She had been an intolerable fool – a prig in the name of the Spirit.

And she began to consider how best to initiate Roy into the spiritual mysteries. *All things are lawful*. Her mind sagged. Roy would not believe that. Suddenly and fiercely she saw that she did not believe it herself. Luke had had no right to all he had had of her. He had wiled her on, taking all she could give: as he had taken the contents of Lucy

Warrender's brain; raped her of what he wanted in her and
flung the rest aside; deflowered her, using colour and
contour and perfume for his delight, and refusing to see that
he had plucked the blossom whole to have them. Was it any
mitigation for him to say, *I did not want the flower*, since
the flower was taken? He had no right to her essence if he
did not want herself. Fiercely she resented his claim in her;
fiercely she repudiated her own proud passion of giving. She
hated Luke.

And what madness there was in the world's morality! She
had given herself utterly – all save the one thing that the
world condemns a woman for giving. Was she any whit less
guilty – if it were true that there was guilt in love – than the
woman who gave her flesh? – Or Luke less guilty in taking
her soul than though he had taken her body? – A consideration that left her only the more desperate to prove to Roy
the innocence of their kiss.

The woman who rose in the sombre and windless dawn of
Sunday felt many years older than the girl who heard Aunt
Josephine give thanks on Saturday that she had lived to see
that hour.

In the afternoon she walked to Cairns, through half-an-
inch of slush, to post the letter she had written. The writing
had taken her most of the morning.

On Tuesday evening Roy's answer was awaiting her.
When she walked in from school and saw the letter where
Aunt Josephine had propped it against the china shepherd-
boy on the mantel-piece, a deadly cold ran through her
body. Her stomach turned as at the smell of a nauseous
draught she had to swallow. She knew, even before she
touched the letter, that she had been a fool to suppose that
Roy would understand. She had profaned her Holy of
Holies; and without avail.

The letter confirmed her suspicion. Roy wrote in anger.
He had overtaken Stoddart on the Saturday, given him a lift
in the side car, and heard his story. In words Stoddart said
little beyond the truth; in insinuation much. Roy's anger
did the rest. The myth of Martha's young-girl innocence
was disposed of with finality. Well, his flesh was carrion,
but luckily he had not cut his pound. He was committed to

nothing; and if his riderless girl had been ridden before he found her, he could at least tell her so: and did it.

He had made a double discovery that Saturday regarding the girl. Another man's belongings, yes: but also with belongings of her own that he had not bargained for. She had a temper, had she! At his accusation she was like a wild thing trapped. He had not even guessed that she was wild until he saw her trapped. It came upon him with a nasty shock. He wanted neither experience nor much capacity for it in the woman of his choice.

The confession of her spiritual passion for Luke that had reached him on the Monday morning found him in no sweet mood, nor anxious in any way for the quickening of his own spiritual perceptions.

He replied at once.

Through every line of the letter Martha could hear again the distortion of his voice as he had said, 'And you thought you'd palm another man's property off on me, did you?'

Dismayed she thought, 'I've never had language like this used to me in my life before.' She burned to plead her integrity anew. This slur was not to be borne! But with a self-control that was heroic through the effort upon herself that it exacted, she put the letter in the fire and refrained from answering.

'You're some tired, my lady,' said Aunt Josephine, watching her as she leaned against the mantelpiece and saw the sheets of paper curl and glow and blacken in the flame. 'Ye're some sair ca'ed. It's a gey tyauve up yon brae in the deid o' winter.'

Martha came back with difficulty to the moment.

'Yes,' she said. 'And the roads are so soft. Slush. I'll need to get my boots off.'

'It's nae a terrible grand fire,' said Miss Josephine, glancing at the white charred remains of the letter. 'Gie't a kittlie up.'

Martha changed her shoes and made the supper; and Aunt Josephine told her about the *April eerand* that Rory had sent auld Willie Patterson (but he was young Willie then) and how Willie would tell the tale against himself. 'A terrible funny story,' she said. 'He leuch five minutes or

ever he got begun to tell't. But mebbe he added a bittie on
til't aince he did get begun.'

By Wednesday Roy's fury was over, and he was ready to
consider (though not to confess) that he might have made a
fool of himself by his hasty judgment. Oh, Martha was in
the wrong, of course. Still, a peccadillo. He hated perturbation of the spirit and was very willing to be on cordial terms
with all the world, provided the terms were his own. He
decided to be magnanimous and forgive Martha. All would
again be comfortable.

In the afternoon he went to meet her. It had not occurred
to him that his letter of Monday morning had reached her
only the evening before. She would have had time to forget
the terms of his diatribe, which, in any case, he had not
supposed to be offensive. He knew that she had been
transferred to Peterkirk and on bad days took train from
Beltie. He therefore went walking on the Crannochie road,
and fell in with her.

Martha was still smarting under the language he had
used. She had not yet had four-and-twenty hours in which
to get accustomed to it. When he addressed her as though
nothing had changed between them, she was astounded,
then contemptuous. As he continued she began to
understand that she was not believed, but was forgiven. She
felt she could afford to laugh at his magnanimity; and
laughed.

Here was something she had never imagined, that she
should be pardoned for not having transgressed the
common moral law; and should find it amusing.

'Life's funny,' she thought, and laughed still louder.

Roy's magnanimity did not stretch to being laughed at.

He turned in the road and left her.

SIXTEEN

The Ironside Brand

Geordie had stopped half-way up the brae to put sharps in the horse's shoes. The wind had shifted due north, with a bite to it: a wind as hard as the ridges of slush in the road had suddenly become beneath its influence. The frost had set in keen and quick; the *neips*, when Geordie was piling them in the cart, were sodden wet; now they glistered, catching the saffron light.

The sharps in place, Geordie glanced up and saw a young man come smartly down the road. He had seen him only once before but recognized him as Miss Josephine's friend from Africa; and passed the time of day. Roy, who had just parted indignantly from Geordie's daughter, gave him back his greeting.

'Hiv ye hurtit yersel that ye're hirplin' that gait?' Geordie said, with the intimate concern of a man whom all things human must concern. Roy's walk, though rapid, was limping.

'Oh, it's nothing,' he answered in haste. 'A fall on the ice.' And as one pressed for time and thrusting trifles aside, added, 'I must be getting on.'

'Ay, ay, it'll be a terrible slipper,' Geordie answered. Roy had already gone on his way. 'Ca' awa' there then,' cried Geordie to the horse; and they climbed the hill to the crossroad.

At the corner, seated on a stone, was Andy Macpherson.

Andy took his pleasures queerly, if it was for his pleasure he was seated on an icy-coated stone, surveying an empty world. A black wind had wallopped the clouds to tatters and driven in a frost that sharpened with every breath. Footmarks, cart ruts, the imprint of tyres, all the casual traffic of days of slush, were caught and patterned in a relief of shining steel; and already, blown up from nowhere, shaken amazingly from branches and sifted from the empty sky, eddies of powder fluttered in the ruts and indentations, icy against the cheek in the sudden worrying winds. Not much comfort in Andy's choice of a seat for his half-holiday; nor much apparently to watch for but a hardening of the whole temper of the land. Yet there he sat, arms folded on his bulging chest, with the air of a man who took his ease and relished it.

'Ay, ay, Andy, ye're gey weel pleased wi' the weather, man,' said Geordie, stopping his horse and beating his arms to get up the heat.

'Grand,' said Andy.

He was in no need of getting the heat up and had a saner use for his arms than pummelling his own chest with them. Pummelling another man's chest was the better occupation; and Andy had just felled his man with all the pleasure in the world.

His man was Roy Foubister.

Andy had heard that Matty was taking Roy; and had no objection to the arrangement. He was not in love with her. Oh, once – yes: perhaps two or three times, by way of incident in a busy career. Andy knew a great deal about girls. He had made excellent use of his evenings though his earliest attempt at kissing had failed. His earliest attempt was made on Martha, years before, as they walked home up the brae after a Church *swarry*. If, as Aunt Josephine declared, he 'had a gey ill e'e aifter her' then, he quickly cast the eye elsewhere: but out of sheer *divilment*, if for no sweeter cause, he hankered still for a kiss from the only girl who had refused him.

'I'll get ye yet, ye b—!' he had sworn to himself on the April Sunday when Martha spurned him from her company. the b— was too sure a runner for him. She ran on mountains. She was unapproachable. And Andy did not put himself about to chase her. A bit of fun – that was all he wanted. A struggle and a shriek and the subsequent boasting. An American tourist of lips – that was Andy. Meeting, on his half-holiday, the lad who had had her kisses (and Andy would have found much difficulty in believing that

Roy had known Martha for nearly seven weeks and had not yet kissed her: even though three of the weeks he had spent on a Christmas visit elsewhere), meeting the lad, Andy snorted joyfully and dashed in to have his fun.

The distance between failure and achievement is infinite; but the distance between a kiss that touches flesh and a kiss that smacks the empty air may be only the fraction of an inch. One can argue away the fraction of an inch. Sheer *divilment*. Andy enjoyed himself immensely in assuring Roy that his girl had been kissed before; and bashed Roy's head less to remind him that he was not the only man in the world than just for the joy of bashing.

Roy picked himself up and thought bitterly: 'Is this the lout that she allowed to kiss her?' He was not likely to try forgiving Martha a second time.

Seated on his stone, Andy let Geordie into the joke. Geordie's wits, *i' the length o' the lang*, made this of it – that Matty was courted by the motorcyclist and that Andy had hoped to get her.

'Andy,' he said, 'ye're a gomeril.'

Andy grinned at the soft impeachment.

Fine he knew that he would never have got Martha; nor would he have known what to do with her if he had.

'She's nae for the likes o' you, Andy. She'll be upsides doon wi' her mither's fowk – her mither'll be grand suited. A richt bonny lassie her mither was,' said Geordie, his mind running baack on his own *coortin'*. 'Matty's a fine lass, ay is she, but she hisna the looks o' her mither, nor yet her speerits – singin' the best ye saw, an' aye ready for a crack, an' a pair o' cheeks,' said Geordie, 'like a weel-skilpit backside.'

Chuckling he hoisted himself on top of the glistering turnips and rode home in his triumphal car. He had got back to a comprehensible level with his daughter lost so long amid the lights and ardours of learning. Courting needed no brains. Geordie could understand that employment. But to think that he had not known! That was what came of biding at her aunt's. How he would tease her, once he got her home again!

In the course of the evening Geordie, ruminating by the

fire, let out a bellow of laughter. 'A fa' on the ice!' quoth he. 'A fa' on the ice!'

Admirable joke: but neither of his listeners seemed disposed to rejoice with him. Madge gave him a cold stare and left the room; and Emmeline continued to grumble over her own ailments.

'I've got ane o' that ill-natur'd kind o' backs,' she said. 'Girnin'.'

Madge gone, Geordie shared the joke; but Emmmeline refused to be impressed.

'Yon Andy Macpherson,' she scoffed. 'He's nae near neebor to the truth, yon ane. O ay, I'se warren ye'd gotten a legammachy fae him. "We'll believe ye the day ye're deid, Andy," I says till him.'

She paid heed nevertheless to the news; but being out-of-sorts was cantankerous; and angry that Geordie should have heard before her – and from that *sklype* of an Andy Macpherson too – treated the subject with contempt.

The following day, after supper, Geordie walked to Crannochie.

'Ye'll need to come hame, I'm thinkin', lassie,' he said to Martha. 'Yer mither's terrible bad. She's got a sair inside.' He enlarged on Emmeline's symptoms.

'You'll have to send Madge to sleep here then,' said Martha. 'I can't leave Aunt Josephine alone all night.'

'Weel,' Geordie hesitated. He had news to bring out and found it none too easy. 'She's awa',' he said at last.

'She's – But what – ?'

'Jist awa'. Tired o' us, like.'

He explained that Madge had left the house before daylight that morning, carrying her property in a bundle. They had found a note to say that she was going to lodge with the woman who kept her brother Jim.

'And did she know that mother was ill?' asked Martha bitterly. 'Was she ill last night?'

'O ay, she's been gey queer for a day or twa. She cudna bit 'a' kent.'

'And she goes away just when she might have been a little use. O, she would. *She* won't trouble herself for anyone.'

She was furious against Madge.

'Well, I can't leave Aunt Josephine alone,' she said. 'You'd better go along to Drochety and see if Clem'll sleep here for tonight.'

'Why disna she get an 'umman?' Geordie asked; and turning to Miss Leggatt he bellowed, 'Ye sud get an 'umman. Tak ye the gweed o' yer siller, Josephine. Ye wunna hae a poochie in yer last robe.'

'Oh, it's not only the money,' said Martha impatiently. 'Will you go to Clem?'

'Ay, ay, I wull that.'

Martha remembered the circumstances in which she had refused Clem's offer to sleep in the cottage. And now she was asking her!

'Well, did you see her?' she said.

'O ay, I got her,' Geordie answered. 'Dirdin' on wi' her mou' a' kail an' her heels a' sharn. She's a roch ane, yon.'

Martha assented absently and forgot to say that if Clemmie was rough she was also good.

'Don't wait for me,' she said to her father. 'I've some things to do. I'll follow.'

'Oh, I'll wait aboot,' Geordie said.

Martha wanted to be alone. She was in no mood for a conversation. But Geordie wanted the conversation. A walk in the dark with his daughter – here was an excellent chance for intimacies. He was impatient to begin that process of teasing from which he anticipated such enjoyment.

Martha, though her father failed to see it, looked little like a maid new-courted. She had gone down through another circle of her Inferno. She had lost her self-respect; and her suffering was bitten on her countenance.

When he had her out in the comfortable privacy of night, Geordie punched her very gently in the ribs with his elbow and whispered:

'It's to be hopit yer young man wunna be oot needin' ye the nicht.'

Martha drew aside from the elbow. Gentle or not, she wanted no liberties taken with her person.

'I don't know what you mean,' she said, using the same words as she had used to Stoddart and to Roy.

Geordie tried again.

'Yer lad'll be in a gey takin' fan he gets ye awa'.'

'I don't know what you mean,' Martha repeated. 'I haven't a lad, or a young man either.'

There was such cold fury in her tone that Geordie held his tongue.

Emmeline was less reticent with regard both to Madge and to Martha's courting.

In the intervals of her own pangs and groans she made diligent enquiry into the story of the courtship.

Martha took refuge in an exaggerated gaiety and cried: 'You don't mean to say you've been hearing *that*? Oh, it's just a joke. An idea of Aunt Josephine's. She hoped to marry his father, you know, and she seems to think it'll make all square now if he marries me. That's all that's in it.'

She said it laughing. Her mother was not in her counsels and she had no intention that she should be. She knew that she was less than just to Aunt Josephine, but she had to find cover somewhere.

'Weel,' said Emmeline, 'an' why sudna he? Ye're nae sae weel to be seen as lots, I'm bound to say that, but I'se warren ye cud get him if ye wanted to.'

'I've no doubt I could, but you see I don't want to. He's not my kind.'

'Oh, he's nae your kind, is he?'

'No,' said Martha, still laughing. 'He's a dandy. Fond of his pleasures. He's much more Madge's style than mine.'

It was the bitterest thing she could find to say.

'Oh, Madge,' said Emmeline. Her tone was grim.

'What's she away for?' Martha said.

'Fa wad ken? A tantrum. An' mebbe mair. She's been ettlin' aifter a shift this whilie back. "I'll be a lodger," she says. "Ye can be a lodger here," I says, "an' pey yer wey as weel here as ony road." "I'm nae treated like a lodger," she says. Feart to fyle her han's, that's fat she was. But I didna think she wad up an' awa' like that. I'm thinkin' there's mair in't nor a tantrum. She hasna been behavin' hersel. I've jaloosed it this gey while. Bit jaloosin's nae provin'. She's been ower mony for me ilka road I've tried her. She's close. She peys nae mair heed to ye nor the win' blawin' by ye. Bit she'll fin' oot or she's muckle aulder that there's some things gey ill to hide.'

'What?' Martha asked. She asked in all innocence, not having understood her mother's hints.

'A bairn wunna hide,' said Emmeline tartly, 'an' that's fat she'll see or lang, or I'll bile ma heid an' shak' the banes.'

Martha was staring at her mother in consternation.

'A bairn,' she stammered. How could Madge have a bairn? 'She's only a bairn herself.'

'A gey bit bairn. She's seventeen. If she's sense eneuch to catch a lad she's sense eneuch to haud him aff. That's you an' yer beds in a girse park.'

Martha swung away in disgust. What travesty of her tranquil nights! Her anger against Madge had turned to a furious cold contempt. If her mother were right, she was thankful at least that the girl had gone away. It would have been horrible, having the child born there. She had had enough of illegitimate bairns. She hated them. Madge herself was one, and Jim, and all that long succession of children who had trooped through her life. Dussie was one, she remembered with a queer quick stab, and so was that youngster who lay in the corner of the kitchen and sucked his finger with a loud smacking relish: the youngster at whose arrival she had been so wrathful, whom she had proclaimed so passionately she would never tend. Well, she would have to tend him now, she supposed. Did one ever order one's life as one desired?

'He's ill-trickit,' said Emmeline, following Martha's glance. 'Tak his finger ooten his mou'. He'll hae it sookit ooten comprehension.'

Martha pulled the finger from the child's mouth and thrust it, a little roughly, under the coverlet.

As soon as she turned away the baby, pulling the blanket up with one hand to screen his action, began sucking as vigorously as before.

'Ye rascal 'at ye are!' cried Emmeline, clapping her hands loudly from the bed.

A glint from two black eyes. A roguish grin upon the baby's face. The coverlet pulled higher.

'He's a droll craiturie,' cried Emmeline. 'Wad ye think they'd hae sae muckle sense?'

Martha did not want to think about them at all and made
no answer.

It took short time to prove Emmeline's suspicion true.
The very next day, on her way from Beltie to Aunt Josephine's, Martha fell in with a Crannochie woman going
home from her marketing. The woman gave her the news
with a relish. Madge, carrying her bundle in the half-light,
had slipped on the ice and fallen headlong. 'She got a gey
cloor,' the woman said. She had scrambled to her feet again
and gone to the house of the woman who kept her brother
Jim. That night her child was born, too soon. 'An ablach,
they say.' The woman's avidity over detail disgusted
Martha. The whole business disgusted her. Her own passion
gave her no measure by which she might weigh Madge. The
brae to Crannochie was undesirably long; and her
companion insisted on coming in to see Miss Leggatt: she
wanted a more appreciative audience for her tale.

She got it. Clem had looked in; and both she and Miss
Josephine had long ears and ready tongues.

'The wratch o' a man, he deserves to be shot,' said Miss
Josephine.

'Shot!' cried Clem indignantly. 'The dirty deevil,
sheetin's ower gweed for him. Roas'n alive, that's mair like
the thing. Shut tae the door, Matty. Ye wad think ye was
born in a cairt-shed faur there wasna a door.'

Martha had left the door open on purpose, as a hint to the
visitor to be gone.

She left at last, saying to Martha, 'Yer mither kens, Matty.
Francie Hepburn fell in wi' Geordie on the cairt-road, an'
some o' the neebors'll likely hae gi'en her a look-in as weel.'

'Oh yes,' thought Martha bitterly. 'They'll all tell us.'

Having attended to Aunt Josephine's wants, she went
home.

Geordie and Emmeline were talking together, but ceased
as she entered.

'That's a gey begeck we've gotten,' said Geordie, breaking
the silence. He spoke heavily, a sorry and bewildered man.

'Ach!' cried Emmeline impatiently, 'you had aye a saft
side to Madge. Onybody wi' their twa een in their heid cud a'
seen the road she was like to tak. Wi' her palaverin' an' her

pooderin' an' her this an' her that. She had a' her orders, had
Madge. An' a stink o' scent 'at wad knock ye doon. Foozlin'
her face an' bamboozlin' her face wi' her pastes an' her
pooders. Eneuch to pit faces ooten fashion. I wadna be seen
ga'in' the length o' masel wi' a face like yon. I wadna ging to
the midden sic a sicht.'

'Weel, weel,' said Geordie, 'face or nae face, the bairn's
here. Ye wad mebbe need to gie a lookie in, Matty, an' see 'at
she's weel dane by.'

'She'll be weel eneuch dane by,' said Emmeline. 'It's nae
nane o' our business, her marchin' aff like that an' a'.'

'It wad be bit kindly like.'

Martha was busying herself with the baby in a corner, so
that she would not have to answer her father. Visit Madge!
How could she do it? Her mind revolted from the very
thought.

Geordie opened his lips twice again during the evening.
The first time he said,

'Fa' wad a' thocht it? A grand sonsy lass she was – great
stumperts o' legs she had on her.'

And the second time:

'The frost's loupit. Terrible coorse roads we'll hae the
morn.'

He said no more of visiting Madge.

Martha knew she ought to go. She felt that they were
responsible for Madge, even though she had left them; and
had they had no news of her she would have gone: but they
heard that she was well and well looked after; and Martha's
hands were very full. On Saturday, through the filthy roads
that the thaw had brought, she went back to Crannochie and
found Aunt Josephine worse. Between her two invalids and
her long school day, she had little time for visiting.
Emmeline luckily had improved: Martha did not require to
sleep at home; but invalids have privileges and Emmeline
exercised hers – she did not waste her strength on
housework.

On the following Saturday, early in the afternoon, Martha
was walking down from Crannochie to Wester Cairns. She
had taken, not the road through the wood, but an opener
path that skirted the fields and ran past the Macphersons'

cottage. By some rough stone steps this path crossed a low
dyke into the field beyond; and Peter Macpherson, Andy's
brother, with a couple of other young fellows, was idling
beside the dyke. They were talking and snichering together
as Martha approached, and, obstructing her path, made no
offer to move. 'Are they talking about me?' she wondered;
and edged her way behind on to the steps. One of the youths
was whistling, and hardly had Martha passed when the other
two took up the tune and gave it words. The words came
clearly down the wind to Martha.

'Tak the floonces fae yer goon,
Mak a frockie tae yer loon,
For ye're like to need it soon,
Bonny lassie, O!'

The scarlet rushed to her face as she walked on. Though
their snicher might have been for her, their song at least was
not pursuing her; but it set her thinking of Madge. 'I'll go
tonight,' she thought.

Mrs. Davie was the name of the woman to whom Madge
had gone. Martha had only a vague idea of where she lived,
and was obliged to ask. The passer-by to whom she applied
was a stranger to her, but answered her query with, 'O ay,
Miss Ironside, it's the fourth door, roon' the corner there.'
Martha thought, 'You know me, and you know why I've
come.' She held her head high and knocked.

'She's nae here,' said the woman.

'Not – ? Oh, I thought . . . Where is she, then?'

'Weel – ' Mrs. Davie hesitated. 'But come in-by,' she said,
holding the door wide.

Martha went in.

The kitchen was light and hot. The gridle was on the fire
and a good smell rose from it and filled the room.

'I was just makin' a crumpet,' said Mrs. Davie. She
hurried across to the fire, seized her knife, slid it beneath the
nearest crumpet and lithely slapped the smoking delicacy
over.

'Sit doon,' she cried over her shoulder to Martha. 'I canna
lat them burn.'

Martha sat and waited. When the batch of crumpets was
turned, Mrs. Davie began her story, but interrupted herself

almost immediately to lift the first of the batch and offer it to Martha.

'Het aff'n the girdle, Miss Ironside. Jist you snap it up.'

She laid it on a towel and pushed it towards the girl, who thought, 'I suppose I must,' and lifted it. It broke in her hand, a tiny portion remaining in her fingers while the larger part fell back on to the towel.

'They're that free,' said Mrs. Davie. '"Ye're a grand hand at the crumpets, Lizzie," ma man aye tells me.'

'But Madge?' Martha was thinking impatiently. She said nothing and waited.

Mrs. Davie put a second batch on to the girdle and resumed her tale.

Madge had walked away that very morning, bairn and all, just as she had walked away from the Ironsides'. She had been seen at the railway station and had told someone that she was joining her sweetheart.

'She had siller,' said Mrs. Davie, 'fatever wey she cam by it. She peyed me, an' she was buyin' a ticket as fine's ye like.'

'But with an eight-days' old baby,' Martha said. She was appalled. 'I should have come sooner,' her brain was saying, 'I should have come sooner.' The words ran like a refrain through and through her head; and aloud she added, 'Do you suppose – was she really going to him? I mean, was he expecting her?'

'Fa wad ken? She had nae letter a' the time she was within my doors, nor posted nane. I wadna say but that she's aff aifter him a' on her ain. They men's a scurvy set.' Mrs. Davie greased her girdle for another batch of crumpets and said, raising her voice above the sizzling of the hot fat, 'But ye ken that ower weel yersel, Miss Ironside.'

The thought glanced in Martha's brain that this woman also had heard of Roy; but she was too sincerely concerned over Madge to let it trouble her. She remembered her mother's saying some time before that Madge's fine lad had gone back to Glasgow whence he came. Had Madge gone seeking him in Glasgow? And with no letter sent or received. He could not even have known about the child. Martha felt herself groping in a dark oppresive place.

'Perhaps she'll come back here,' she ventured.

'O ay, she may.'

'Or – do you think she'd write to Jim? – if she – gets to Glasgow, I mean. If she does, if she writes, or comes back, do you think – could you – would you let us know?' Martha's words came out in spurts. She wanted air. She was oppressed by the ugliness of life. 'If you could send a message,' she said. 'You see, I'm so busy, I haven't much time.'

'O ay,' said Mrs. Davie genially. 'I'se warren ye've lots to dae. Yer ain loonie'll be wearin' up. Gettin' on for a year auld, is he?'

'Who?' said Martha. – 'Oh, you mean the child my mother keeps.' And she wished that outsiders would leave their family affairs alone.

'Weel, he's yours, isna he?' Mrs. Davie asked it cheerily.

'Mine?' said Martha.

She was astonished.

'Is't nae true then?' Mrs. Davie asked.

'True!' Martha began to laugh. 'I never had a child in my life,' she cried; and instantly thought, 'Of all the ridiculous things to have said!'

She stopped laughing.

Her astonishment was turning to dismay.

'An' sae it's nae your bairn ava'?' said Mrs. Davie. 'Weel, weel, fat'll fowk nae say? They've got a haud o' some story aboot a lad ye used to tryst wi' up in the woodie. "She bides oot a' nicht," Leebie Longmore says to me. "A bonny-like cairry-on." An' it's nae your bairn?' – And observing that Martha had left her crumpet lying with the little portion broken from its side, she added, pushing the towel towards her:

'But tak it up. Ye'll easy manage it. A crumpet's an idle eat. A knap-at-the-win'.'

She would have been just as hospitable had Martha owned to the child.

Martha's dismay had turned to sickness. She remembered the snicher and the ribald song of Peter Macpherson and his companions. And the woman who had called her by her name when she asked the way that evening. Filthy place the world was! She pulled herself together and said:

'You'll let me know if there's any news,' and rose to go.

'Ay, ay, I'll fairly lat ye ken,' said Mrs. Davie; and added, 'But dinna be sae upset at an idle word. I says to Leebie, "I dinna ken Miss Ironside," I says, "to speak to, like, but a nicer quaeter lassie ye wadna wish to meet. Ye've ta'en the story up wrang," I says.'

Martha walked out without reply.

She had to pass through the village, in front of the lighted shops. The women were doing their Saturday shopping. They stood in *bourrachs* about the doorways. She felt the curious eyes, guessed the purport of the whispering. She supposed herself to be in every mouth and her heart sickened within her; but she recollected the motto of Marischal College, that Luke had quoted: 'Quhat say they? Lat them say.' Pride came to her aid. She walked truculently past the women; reported at home what she had heard concerning Madge, shut her lips upon what she had heard concerning herself, and returned to Crannochie.

The weather had cleared. On the Sunday, Emmeline walked to the field end and held some lively discourse with Bell Macpherson, mother of Andy and Peter. She had just returned from her expedition when Martha came home.

She opened fire at once.

Martha perceived that her mother had heard the scandal. She hardened herself to hear what would come. Emmeline's indignation, however, was all for the scandal-mongers: she had championed her daughter with gusto and let her daughter know it.

'"It's a sair peety," says she,' – Emmeline reported at length the conversation between herself and Bell – '"that Matty didna get him aifter a'."' "Fa didna Matty get?" I speirs. "Weel, weel, that's fat ye've nae need to speir, I'se warren," says she. "A'body kens that." "Dear me," I says, "ye're farrer ben nor me, than, the lot o' ye." "Nyod, noo, Mistress Ironside," she says, "ye needna be sae blate aboot it. A'body kens that Matty near got the laddie." – "Fatna laddie are ye meanin'?" – "The laddie Foubister," she says. "Fa' else? Him an' Matty was terrible chief awhile. But he up an' awa' fan he heard the wey she's misconducted hersel. An' wad ye wonder?" "Misconducted hersel?" I says, rale

gypit-like. "O ay, she didna behave hersel richt." "Behave?"
I says. An' than she up an' gied me i' the face wi' the bairn.
"Deil tak ye," I said, "an' may the Lord forgie ye the evil o'
yer blabbin' tongue! Fat'n a wey cud it be Matty's bairn?
Matty was aye at her school." "O," she says, "ye're sayin't.
But we werena to ken. Her sae muckle awa' fae hame an' a'."
"Nursin' her aunt," I says. "Ay, ay," she says, "the auld
body was beddit up at a likely time, wasna she? Matty was
grand suited to be awa' fae hame an' nae tales tell't. Nine
month fae midsummer," says she sleekit-like. "Midsummer?" I says.'

'Oh!' cried Martha, 'I've heard it all already. You needn't
tell me it again.'

She wanted to brush her mother past the one incident of
the story that was not conjecture.

Emmeline was for leaving nothing out.

'Oh, ye've heard it?' she said. '"An' fat had midsummer to
do wi't," I says. "I'll be at the reet an' the rise o't," I says.'

Martha rose abruptly and began tidying away the papers
and dusters and dirty garments that littered the room. She
kept her back to her mother. Emmeline fought her battle
o'er again, too absorbed in her indignation to pay much heed
to her daughter. She tongued Bell Macpherson a second
time.

'"It's a sair haud-doon for a girl," she says. "A haud-
doon," I says. "It's you that wad need to be hauden doon," I
says. "It's yer lugs nailed to the gallows that you wad need.
Ye wad gar a deid dog tak the kink-hoast. But I'll pit the
Deil's trot on the lot o' ye if I hear ye at yer lees again. I'll ram
yer lees doon the ugly throats o' ye." "Lees," she says.
"Weel, weel, there's some lees gey like the truth." "It's
mebbe the truth," I says, "but it's gey like a lee. Yer wits is
hairy-moulded if ye suppose I cudna see a thing like that
aboot ma ain lassie an' her back an' fore ilka week an' whiles
twa-three times a week a' the time. An' her as flat's a
bannock for a' to see. Sic a say-awa'," I says, "aboot naething. They're an ill-thochted crew, the fowk hereaboots – the
best at ransackin' ither fowk's affairs 'at ever I heard tell o'.
As happy's a blake amon' traicle fan they're cairdin' honest
fowk."'

Martha remained silent.

Emmeline, surveying the landscape that had been presented to her view, came back in course of time to Stoddart Semple's tale. Cross-examined, Martha admitted its basis of truth.

'An' fa micht you be meetin' in the deid o' nicht?' demanded Emmeline. Her indignation swirled to a new channel.

Martha remained silent.

'I'll be bound it was yon lang-leggit doctor chap, Dussie's man. It's fat I've aye said, ye canna trust a skin. A jolly fat chap, noo – a' on the surface – a body kens faur they are wi' them. But wi' a thin man ye never ken faur ye are.'

Martha did not know where she was with Luke. She did not know where she was with herself; and she longed to be again what she had been – possessed only of herself, unbroken. She saw that Luke had broken her integrity, and by not loving her had put a larger wholeness beyond her reach. 'He had no right,' she cried savagely to herself. Emmeline's accusation against Luke stirred all the smouldering resentment in her own mind: she did not trouble to refute the charge on his behalf.

'But that Dussie,' Emmeline continued, 'she was aye a besom. She was aye amon' the loons.'

Martha knew the singleness of Dussie's eye, but neither did she defend Dussie.

She heard her mother out, sullen, murky-eyed, saying nothing. Her flame had gone to smoke.

'Oh, ye're in an' the door steekit, are ye?' said Emmeline. Having failed to draw any answer she was left to her own conjecture over her daughter's affairs; which did not prevent her from continuing her indignant denunciation of the scandal-mongers.

'Fat ither wad ye expeck fae a hoose like yon?' Bell Macpherson was reported to have said. 'Steerin' wi' weans an' nae ane amon' them 'at's honest come by. That's yer Ironsides for ye!'

Even her Aunt Sally's story was revived to swell the evidence against Martha. To be an Ironside was apparently sufficient to brand her.

'Gin onybody said the likes o' that to me,' declared
Geordie, ruminating over his wife's report upon the current
gossip, 'I'd be aweirs o' takin' the graip to them.'

No one however said it to him; and there was no assault.

'Ach!' said Emmeline. 'If ye're to start believin' that lot,
ye micht as weel eat a' ye see.'

'Bit fa wad a' startit it?' said Geordie.

'Deil kens,' his wife replied. 'An' the Deil has nae
business to ken.'

Her Aunt Sally came often to Martha's mind in the weeks
that followed. Madge had not been heard of. She stayed, a
dull rankling spot of offence, in Martha's consciousnesss.
She remembered that her aunt had been working among
outcasts in Glasgow. If Madge were there, an outcast too – .
Martha did not allow herself to formulate definite thoughts
on the subject, shelving as far as she could her sense of
responsibility towards Madge; but as the weeks passed her
secret uneasiness grew.

She was not alone in harbouring a secret uneasiness. Aunt
Josephine too was troubled. Roy had given over his visits;
and Martha was unapproachable on the theme. Aunt Josephine teased, and hinted, and openly marvelled, and finally
held her tongue; and Martha held hers. If Clemmie spoke,
or Stoddart Semple, Aunt Josephine had more wit than to
believe their idle havers.

On an evening in February Martha was walking home.
She was late and the weather was heavy. Dark fell from a
brown sky and had not far to fall. As she came nearer she
saw that the light was shed from the lamps of a motorcycle
and that the cyclist was bending over his machine. She
knew him at once for Roy and stopped. He visited, she was
aware, at a house in the vicinity of Slack; doubtless it was
there he had been. Her instinct was to turn before she came
within the radius of the light, go back and through the
wood: but despising her own dread of meeting him, she
went on; and glancing up he saw her.

He was embarrassed but polite. Martha was amused to
see how polite: but there was not the semblance of intimacy
between them.

'I'm judged and found wanting,' she thought amusedly.

'I'm just a common slut, I suppose – not even worth his anger. We're like chance acquaintances. We're polite to each other.' But in spite of her amusement she was piqued by his indifference and remembered hotly the letter she had sent him. The futility of her confession mocked her; but putting restraint upon herself she said aloud, 'Will you come and see Aunt Josephine before you go away? She's wondering that you haven't come' – and could not resist adding, 'You can come on a school-day, you know, when I'm not there.'

He ignored the remark; and came the next Saturday. 'Just to spite me, I suppose,' said Martha to herself.

He came, and Aunt Josephine was jubilant; but learning that he had come to say farewell, and was about to sail again for Africa, looked from her niece to her visitor and back to her niece with a puzzled concern.

Neither niece nor visitor took heed. They continued to be polite to each other. Roy was very entertaining and kept Miss Josephine delighted by his talk. Martha sat silent and wished she had never had occasion to look beneath his pleasant veneer. They parted at the door, still politely.

'We're done with each other,' she thought. 'We're strangers. He's come to see his father's old friend and I'm just her grand-niece.'

Roy too was thinking, 'We're done with each other.' They parted with relief and supposed they would not meet again. In this they were wrong. He was back in Europe not so very long afterwards, fighting in France; and on his first leave came straight to Martha. Aunt Josephine was dead by then and Martha still teaching in Peterkirk. He wanted to marry her then and there, but she gave him a steady and smiling refusal.

She was smiling now as she shut the door upon Roy and returned to face Aunt Josephine, but the smile was not steady.

'Well, that's our visitor gone,' she said as lightly as she could.

'Ay, ay,' said the old lady, 'but I'se warren he'll be back or he gings awa'.'

'Oh no! Why should he? He has said goodbye.'

Aunt Josephine remained puzzled and in distress.

Geordie also had his secret anxiety. He was bothered about Matty's lad. He knew well enough what folk had said about his daughter; he knew well enough that it was false: but plainly it had driven away the young man who was courting her; and plainly she was not happy. Geordie sought a remedy in vain. He had no great opinion of a youth who allowed the clack of tongues to prejudice him against his sweetheart. Still, the lass was fretting. Geordie was sorely exercised. He tried more than once to open the subject with the girl, but the most delicate insinuation was enough to waken the nastiest furies that inhabited Martha's mind. She snubbed him brutally.

One evening in March he met his daughter at the corner of the field. It was gloaming, and in the dusk he gathered courage to say, as they crossed the field together:

'I'm main stupid, lassie, I ken that fine. I canna un'erstan' a lot o' things, but I can see fine that ye're frettin'. I thocht it was aboot yon lad o' yours, but it seems I was wrang. Weel, we'll nae say nae mair aboot that. But I canna bide to see ye fret, Matty ma lass, an' nae dae naething to pleasure ye. I'm nae askin' fat ails ye, I'm nae bit askin' to be lat help ye gin I can.'

To his surprise, and perhaps to her own, Martha answered him.

'Father, do you know anything about your sister Sally? Where she is, I mean? Is she still in Glasgow?'

'Sally?' said Geordie, stopping on the path. He required time to adjust himself to this sudden change of theme.

Martha began to explain why she wanted news of Sally. If she was fretting, she said, it was over Madge.

'Ay, ay.' Geordie approved. His knowledge of Sally's whereabouts, however, was vague. She had come home but the once. She never wrote. She might be still working for the Salvation Army in Glasgow; or she might not.

'I could find out,' said Martha.

'O ay, ye cud try a letterie.'

Martha was silent. She had other intentions. She wanted to go herself to Glasgow and seek her aunt. By letter she could not effectively secure her co-operation in what must seem at best a hopeless search for Madge. Common-sense suggested that it would be wise to discover first, if she could by letter, whether her aunt was still in Glasgow; but Martha thrust the suggestion under. She wanted the hardest way.

She was suffering from a festered conscience: not that she held herself responsible in any way for Madge's fault or flight; but she had dishonoured her own nature in her dealings with Roy; and obscurely she felt that there was evil in the disruption her self had undergone in her dealings with Luke. He had neither claimed her nor let her alone. She had been tampered with; defaced; and she felt it in her like the degradation of disease. She tried but could not reason it out with herself in how far the breaking of her integrity had involved the breaking of the laws that governed her being. All she could be sure of was that she felt unclean; and she hankered after purgation – some expiation, arduous, impossible, that would restore her soul. To pursue a half-apocryphal Aunt Sally on behalf of a Madge she had hated offered at least the consolation of activity. Emmeline demurred but yielded. Easter was approaching; and when her holiday began Martha set out alone one morning in pursuit of her wild geese.

As far as her aunt was concerned the chase was easy. Sally was still in the Salvation Army and still in Glasgow. A brusque woman, harsh-featured, big-boned, she had no need of her kin and did not think of writing; but there was honesty in her ugly face and Martha felt at home. She blurted out her tale, but Sally interrupting dragged her niece to the light and scrutinized her closely.

'Thank the Lord He's made you with a big mouth, Matty,' she said; and forthwith prepared the supper. Not till the meal was over did she say, 'Now let's hear your story all over again.'

'I suppose it's impossible that you'd ever come across her,' Martha said when she had told Madge's story.

'Just about it,' said Sally cheerfully. 'Still, there's no knowing. There's queerer things happen than we've the right to expect.' And she began to tell her niece the queer things that happen.

'I've had a venturesome life,' said Sally.

A footnote to her life might have run: For *venturesome* read *betrayed, persecuted, forsaken, hampered and undaunted*: but the general public finds footnotes uncomfortable reading and leaves them alone.

'She's come through the hards, yer Aunt Sally,' Geordie had said to Martha. Sally had thriven on the hards. She had her brother's hearty capacity for life – a big eater and a big endurer, with power to exist spiritually for a long season on one joke or one idea.

Martha returned home the following evening. She felt happier than for long. 'Because,' she told herself, 'I've done something about Madge.' She did not realize how much the lightening of her heart was due simply to the hurry and excitement of her journey, and to her contact with the vigorous personality of her aunt. The very rushing of the train had brought her exhilaration.

SEVENTEEN

Martha Flies in a Rage

Aunt Josephine grew steadily weaker.

'She's gey far awa' wi't, I'm thinkin',' said Geordie; and though Geordie had said that already more than once, this time, in the shimmering June evening that made all the earth look new, it seemed truer than it had ever been.

Even Emmeline dragged her unwieldy bulk up the hill and sat *pechin'* beside her aunt.

'I wunna see her again,' she said to Martha across Aunt Josephine's bed and body.

Talked over thus, Aunt Josephine waxed indignant. There was a subacid flavour in the tone in which she answered Emmeline's 'Ye're gey sair made, I'm thinkin', aunt' with a ready 'O ay, auld age disna come its lane'; and when Mary Annie, frail now herself and useless, crept in about and said in a small and pitiful voice, 'I'm richt sorry to hear that ye're sae far yer road,' – 'Weel, than, I wasna ga'in ony road the day, Mary Annie,' responded Miss Josephine tartly.

She brooked no public mention of her disease, talked (out of a mouth twisted and drawn with pain) as though every tomorrow would see her on her feet and active, and met every reminder of death with an obstinate flare of the little life that was left in her.

'If I jist had a guff o' the earth I'd be gran' – that wad seen hae me weel again,' she said to Emmeline; disconcerting Mrs. Ironside, who had arrived in pious frame for a death-bed meditation. 'She'll be the death o' me yet, yer aunt,' she grumbled afterwards to Martha. 'Garrin' a body aye believe she's deein' an' nae deein' after an' a'.'

'I wad jist like to howk a holie i' the earth an' get a waucht o' it – the smell o't aye gaed aboot ma hairt an' me the lassie at

the fairm,' Aunt Josephine continued; and Emmeline,
collecting herself, answered, 'O ay, ye were aye fond o' yer
bit gairden.'

The old lady dragged herself laboriously up on her pillow,
whence she could just see her patch of ground.

'There's a gey bicker o' weeds,' she answered Emmeline,
letting herself fall again in the bed. 'I tell Matty whiles to rug
them oot, but she's some hard ca'ed – she hasna time.
They'll be a' the langer an' she'll get the better haud o' them
fan she has time.'

And as though there were tonic properties in the weeds,
she turned to Emmeline with a brisker air and demanded her
news.

Nothing loath, Emmeline fell to gossip.

Martha slipped away from the gossiping and into the
weedy garden. The air was limpid, the hills a frail smoke-
blue. She looked at them dully and told herself that they
were beautiful; but their beauty did not move her. Her old
vivid sense of the life of earth and sky had gone. She was no
more of their company; and as she stood there, listless and
sorry, she caught the words upon her lips and repeated them
aloud:

 'Strange that the spirit's infelicity
 Should rob the world of beauty –'

the opening of Luke's first sonnet, that had shaken her so
fiercely years before; the sonnet he had begun and left
unfinished, as he had begun and left unfinished so much
besides; as he had begun, and left unfinished, the evocation
of a new woman from the aloof and alien dreamer that had
been Martha Ironside. No dreamer now! But what instead?
And she smiled, a bitter mirth. 'I'm an uncompleted work of
art. My creator has flung me aside.' But stung suddenly by
the admission the thought implied, 'Good Lord!' she
exclaimed. 'Am I such a slave as that? Dependent on a man
to complete me! I thought I couldn't be anything without
him – I can be my own creator.'

And for a moment she slipped outside herself and
regarded the thing she was with a smiling inquisitive deta-
chment; but the point of vision was too novel and uncomfortable and she quickly returned to the safer ground of

self-scorn. In a fever of fury she turned back from the hills and began to tug at Aunt Josephine's weeds – tangles of dead-nettle, fistfuls of groundsel, mats of chickweed; but when her fury had spent itself she rose in a sort of disgust and left the garden.

She paced the road outside and wished she had not thought of Luke. It disturbed her peace. She had shunned the thought of him, living in holes and corners of her being where he was not. The past was too painful to be courted. It shamed her and she did not know where. It puzzled her and she could not resolve its contradictions. So she had run away from it, and hidden herself in the present. She did not want to see Luke. She was glad that this year she could not go to Liverpool: Aunt Josephine's tenure of life was from day to day. And Luke and Dussie could not come north for their holiday, as once they had talked of doing. In April Dussie had given birth to another son, who lived and throve. They named him Ironside and called him Ronnie; and Dussie was aching to show him off: but the journey was too long for a three months' baby. Martha wrote that she was sorry and in secret was glad. She did not want to see Luke's son.

The summer wore on. August was harsh, hard on the frail. One day the sisters were summoned. They came, Aunt Margot older and larger, Aunt Leebie older and smaller, Aunt Jean older and more majestic; but before they arrived Aunt Josephine had got the turn again and talked of bonnets instead of grave-clothes.

'She's a thrawn auld buckie, ye wunna rug her aff,' said Uncle Sandy Corbett when he heard the report on Aunt Josephine.

Aunt Leebie remained for some weeks at Crannochie, dottling in and out, getting into Martha's way, and providing Aunt Josephine with a mirror of frailty in which she never thought of looking for her own reflection.

'Ye're gettin' terrible crined, Leebie,' she said. 'Ye're rale auld like. Yer face is pickit.'

When school began again Martha was glad enough to have Leebie there. She had never imagined another session beginning with Aunt Josephine still alive. Yet there she was!

September came in sweet and mellow, and Aunt Josephine sat up in bed.

'The sunshine gars a body cantle up,' said she.

A few days later, stumbling painfully and exultantly between the district nurse and Martha, she reached her armchair. Soon she was sitting up most of the day. One afternoon Martha, coming home from school, found her dragging a timid and unstable Leebie across the floor. Leebie, ostensibly the supporter, looked by far the feebler of the two.

'I'm hippit wi' sittin' sae lang,' said Aunt Josephine, collapsing on a chair. 'But I'll be as fleet's a five-year auld aince I get ma legs to wark.'

She got her legs to work, and Leebie departed.

'I'm nae needed ony mair,' she told Jean. 'Forbye she's that restless – a body canna get sitten doon.'

And Aunt Josephine, smiling triumphantly to Martha, was saying:

'We're best by wersels. She had her fingers inen a'thing.'

So another winter began.

To Martha it seemed that she stood outside life. The world went by her, colourless shapes on a flat pale background. Nothing had solidity or warmth. She felt numb, as though she could never be passionately alive again.

'I suppose one gets like this as one grows older,' she said to herself, remembering that she was twenty-four and a half. 'One stops feeling acutely.'

It did not seem to be true, however, of Aunt Josephine, who had just celebrated her seventy-ninth birthday with every token of exquisite enjoyment: nor yet, Martha was forced to admit, of her father, whom she discovered time after time on her hasty visits home taking with a relish the hobgoblin liveliness of little Robin, Emmeline's latest addition to the household. Not much evidence of numbness there! Geordie kittled the loonie with appetite.

He was now some twenty months old, being three months older than the gossips would have had him, though his size might have justified their belief that Emmeline had lied anent his age. 'An ablach,' Emmeline had called him when she brought him home, 'a sharger.' 'A deil's limb,' she called him now; but with pride; delighting, as Geordie did, in his quick and tricksey nature. 'There's mair nor the speen pit in in that ane,' she would declare. Martha's early resentment against the child's presence had worn down to indifference. She seldom gave him a thought: but one day coming home before supper-time and finding Emmeline out, she had set to work tidying the slovenly kitchen.

Emmeline had increased in flabbiness of temper as of body. She indulged seldom now in the clean sharp rages that drove her to scour and scrub. 'It's a thocht to me to begin,' she would say: or, waiting for the kettle to boil, 'I wad need to be scrapin' the brook affen ma kettle – it's barkit. It'll never bile': or, impatiently to Geordie, 'Fat needs ye tak the loonie oot in a' that muck? In ye come the pair o' ye an' scatter it a' aboot, an' than I get a' the jollification o' the dirt.' But the dirt remained.

Habituated to the dirt, Martha as a rule ignored it: but on this particular evening she was having supper at home and had no mind to eat among filth. She had been busy for several minutes before she became aware that she was watched: Robin was in the room; though she had not seen him where he stood, motionless as a caryatid, under the shelf that projected from the window ledge. His head and elbows were pressed against the shelf and his two big eyes stared out unwinking.

Martha was embarrassed by his scrutiny into a closer attention. Queer grave little imp! – bowed forward as though some massive weight were resting on his uplifted arms. And though she stared back at him he neither moved nor spoke. She resumed her work; but the caryatid had fascinated her and she looked again and again. An engaging little face, she decided. And this was the child they had mothered upon her! – Hers! Suddenly she thought, 'I wish he were!' The swiftness and power of the desire astonished her. She wanted to crush the child against her body, cover him with passionate kisses. Her fastidiousness revolted: a dirty waif . . . Then she clutched him fiercely, pressing him in a savage grip. It was the child's turn to be astonished. He fought and screamed, battling with his fists against her face; and wrenching himself free just as Emmeline and Geordie entered together, he ran to Geordie and sobbed out his terror in his arms.

'Fat's a' the tae-dae aboot?' said Emmeline. 'He disna aften greet. He's a biddable bairn. Fat wad a' angered him, wad ye think?'

'Oh, nothing, said Martha, arranging spoons on the supper table.

The meal began.

Martha made only a pretence at eating. Robin sat on Geordie's knee. Sometimes he looked rapidly round at Martha, but if she were looking at him hid his head instantly against Geordie's waistcoat; and once when Martha spoke to him he screamed. Martha sat and fiddled with her bread and was absurdly angry and quite incomprehensibly upset.

After supper a couple of neighbours dropped in. There was tobacco smoke and a clatter of tongues. Emmeline, luxurious in an armchair and the sweet savour of gossip, called out to Martha to put the bairn to his bed; but when Martha approached him the child beat her off with his hands, crying.

Martha was furious. She made a wild grab and caught his arm. Robin screamed the louder.

'Michty me, sic a skirlin',' cried Emmeline looking round. 'He's ta'en an ill-will at ye, Matty. Ye've surely bad-used him.'

'I'm sure I never did, said Martha, flaring. She was indignant that outsiders should see her defeated by the child.

Emmeline began to argue the point with alacrity.

Geordie's voice interposed, cool and equable.

'Fat needs ye pit the lassie's birse up? Canna ye lat her be? She's gotten the teethache.' Martha flashed a curious glance at her father. 'It's a sair bide, the teethache,' went on Geordie, settling stolidly down to the first imaginative falsehood of his life. 'I've had it masel.'

The company discussed teeth. Emmeline hoisted herself out of her chair and began undressing Robin. Martha under cover of her apocryphal ailment slipped out and returned to Crannochie.

'Hap ye yer mou' weel up,' Geordie cried after her; and added to the company, 'It's the cauld that does't,' but

immediately after was overcome by the glorious absurdity of
discussing solemnly a thing that had no existence. Laughter
rumbled within him. Within him also was a blurred perception of those loyalties that force a man to do violence to his
appetites; and heroically he repressed the surging tide. But
not to have his laugh out was a continence as foreign to
Geordie's habit of body as any other continence. It was a
physical distress.

The placid talk went on.

Geordie could restrain himself no longer. He broke into a
prolonged stentorian bellow, that considerably startled the
auditors, who seeing no cause for mirth demanded leave to
share the joke. Now was the deceitful man caught: for
Geordie was in evil case unless forthwith he could invent a
glorious lie, a lie with heat and *smeddum* enough to justify
that uproar of laughter.

Shuffle as he might he could invent nothing. His wits
went out on him.

'She hadna the teethache ava,' said Emmeline contemptuously. 'That's fat he's lauchin' at. I dinna see onything extra
funny aboot that.'

Geordie rubbed his neck and admitted defeat. Still, the
lass had got away.

The lass came back the following week and found
Geordie and Robin taking their game with gusto. Geordie
was prodding the bairn to the accompaniment of an old
rhyme:
> 'The craw's ta'en, the craw's ta'en,
>   The craw's ta'en wee pussie, O!
> The auld cat, she sat an' grat
>   On Robbie's thackit hoosie, O!'

and the bairn shouted with glee as Geordie's clumsy fingers
ruffled his hair. Martha watching was shaken by a passion of
jealousy. She sat smouldering at the supper-table,
crumbling her bread and leaving it uneaten on the plate.

'So he won't look at me, will he?' she thought angrily.

She began to intrigue for his affections as she had
intrigued for candles years before. She took to coming home
more frequently than she had hitherto considered necessary. Perhaps Aunt Josephine was a little lonelier in conse-

quence, but no one asked her and she said nothing. On her
first two visits Martha ignored the boy. She kept herself well
in his presence, but neither looked at him, mentioned him
nor spoke to him. On the third occasion, Emmeline being in
a snooze, she sat down on a stool by the fireside and began
telling the fire a story. It was a jolly story, with hens
clucking, dogs barking and pussy-cats scampering one after
the other. When she had come to the end of it she began
again at the beginning and told it all over again to the fire.
There was no sound in the room behind her and she did not
dare to turn and look for Robin. At the end of the second
recital Emmeline awoke and Martha began immediately to
talk to her.

Her next visit was on a Sunday afternoon. Emmeline was
sleeping on the bed. Martha again took her stool and sat by
the fire and again told the story of the hens and dogs and
cats. Towards the end of the story she heard a very quiet
movement behind but did not turn her head. Then Robin
came into view, dragging his own little stool, which he set in
line with hers, sitting on it in the same attitude as Martha.
When the story was done, "Gain,' he said; and when
Martha made capering motions with her hands to indicate
the scampering, Robin made capering motions too.

Martha's heart bounded. She had the same impulse as
before to snatch the child and press him to her; but she
contained herself and did not even look aside. At that
moment Geordie put his head round the door.

'Come oot-by a meenutie, Matty,' said he.

Martha was exasperated. Just when the bairn was coming
to! And what could her father want that was of any
importance? She rose impatiently and went outside. A light
rain was beginning to fall.

Geordie was holding a baker's bag.

'Ye're nae eatin' naething, Matty ma lass,' he said. 'Ye
used to be terrible fond o' a saft biscuit.' And he thrust the
baker's bag into her hand, saying, 'Fu' sorra's better'n
teem,' and made away round the corner of the house.

Martha stood staring at the paper bag. Waves of resentment surged over her. What right had he to interfere? And
what did it matter to him, or to anyone, what she ate, or

what she did? With a churlish movement she flung the bag
from her and watched it fall against a broken pail that had
lain there time out of mind. She watched until the rain
soaked through the thin paper, that clung transparent
against the bumpy rounds of the soft biscuits. Then she went
back to the kitchen.

'And my story's spoilt and all,' she thought.

Robin was bouncing up and down on her stool. He keeked
round at her with a roguish grin and instantly turned back
his head again, hunching his shoulders as though for cover.
She made a feint of catching him, but he slipped from the
stool and hid. When she made to seek him, he beat her off.

Martha gulped, and went through to the bedroom. She
was both angry and sorry. 'If I hadn't thrown it where he'd
see it,' she said to herself: but she was too proud, and too
resentful still, to go outside and pick the baker's bag from
the ground. By and by she heard Geordie come in; and in a
while, knowing that it was tea-time and that her father did
not like waiting for his tea, she pushed open the kitchen
door.

Inside the door she paused. She wanted to laugh, but her
lip quivered as though she was going to cry. Geordie had the
child between his knees. His hand was fumbling in his jacket
pocket, and Martha saw him pull some tousled paper out and
fling it on the fire. It was the sodden baker's bag. Then he
broke the fragments from the rejected biscuits and began
putting them in his mouth. The child clamoured for a share,
and got it. Martha shut the door as softly as she could and
hastened back to the bedroom. Shame and vexation blinded
her. She squeezed her eyes hard to keep back the tears, but
they came scorching. When at last she heard Emmeline rise,
she put on her outdoor things and called in at the kitchen
door, 'I'm off. I'm not waiting for tea,' and went.

On her next visit she sat again on her stool and told the fire
a story. Robin came almost at once and ranged his stool
alongside. At the end of the tale, "Gain,' he commanded;
and "Gain' at the second conclusion; but in the middle of the
third recital he grew tired. 'Ga'in to Mama,' he said, setting
off to find Emmeline in the shed. 'Tell 'tory to 'at,' and he
pointed Martha imperiously to the fire. Martha continued

her tale for a sentence or two and then sat gazing into the flames; but the child, turning at the door, ran back and shook her arm, 'Nae tellin' 'tory,' he remonstrated. 'Tell 'tory to 'at.' Martha took up the tale again, thinking he might linger within hearing: but he joined Emmeline in the shed and did not return.

The following day she met Emmeline trailing through the field for a bout of gossip at Bell Macpherson's. The child was trailing after her, some distance behind, and making no very expert job of his progress. Martha walked past him without speaking. She gave no overt invitation; but hardly a minute after she had entered the house she saw Robin had followed her. Without comment she sat down on her stool. Robin sat on his; and the routine began.

In the story there was an old woman who prodded her pig to see if he was fat. Martha prodded the chair beside her: Robin prodded the chair beside her. Then somehow, Martha hardly knew how, she was prodding Robin and Robin her. They prodded each other ecstatically, shouting with laugh-ter. In another minute they were rolling tumbled together on Emmeline's grubby floor.

Martha was ridiculously happy. Geordie came in, *dubbit* and weary, and stretched himself by the fire. She was so happy that her resentment evaporated. She was no longer put to shame by the recollection of her father nibbling at the soft biscuits she had flung away. Suddenly she loved him for it. A passion of ruth laid hold of her – tender, amused, affectionate, profoundly moving. She wanted to tell him she was sorry, but the words would not come. So she poked him instead, a little, hesitant poke on the knee, as though inviting him to share the game. It suited Geordie better than an apology. He poked back, at Robin and at Martha alternately. They were all breathless and merry. It was a gracious interlude.

Emmeline burst upon them, hasty and flustered from too long a diet of chatter.

'Sittin' there wi' yer mou's open,' she grumbled, 'like a lot o' gorbals waitin' to be fed. Ye micht a' had the supper set, Matty. I didna fash masel fan I kent ye were in.'

Martha jumped from the floor and caught Robin under

one arm. She had been too happy to remember supper. She balanced the bairn by his middle across an arm and with the other hand began placing cups and plates upon the table.

'Oh, nae sae forcey there,' cried Emmeline. 'Ye'll be brakin' something.' And as she spoke a cup crashed to the ground. 'There ye are, ye see.'

'Hard words break no bones,
Happy words break the cups,'

chanted Martha to a nondescript tune. She caught Emmeline suddenly with her disengaged arm and whirled her round on the floor.

'Gweed sake, lassie, ye're fey whiles,' panted her mother.

'I know,' said Martha. But it was so long since she had been fey! She gathered up the fragments and flung them on the ashes; then catching Robin, made to fling him after them.

'Throw him away! Throw him away!' she cried.

'Dae't again, dae't again!' breathed Robin at every feint. He was bounding so with laughter that she could hardly hold him securely.

'That wad be a geylies sicht,' said Geordie behind their backs to his wife, 'for them as thocht he was her ain.'

'Thocht!' snorted Emmeline. 'Naebody ever thocht it – it was jist a speak.' She added, 'Fa wad believe fat yon Stoddart Semple says – a face like a diseased pancake.'

'That's the bit about Luke,' thought Martha, who had heard the dialogue through Robin's laughter. And she wondered what her mother really believed about Luke. Though apparently it did not matter much: the nine days' talk was over. Folk had forgotten her affair already; though she supposed they would be quite ready to revive it if they had opportunity. 'But I'll never give them the opportunity,' she thought savagely. She might have remembered that they had revived her Aunt Sally's story when the opportunity had certainly not been given by Sally. But remembering Sally all she thought was, 'I'm sure they may say what they like if I can be as independent of their tongues as she was.'

'I don't believe mother thinks about Luke at all,' she thought; and with a sigh she wished she were less sure of what Aunt Josephine thought about Roy.

Aunt Josephine was openly distressed about Roy.

For awhile she had watched the post, sure that he would write to Martha. Martha evaded her hints and ignored her teasing. One day exasperated she cried,

'Why do you suppose Roy should write to me? He doesn't want to write to me and I don't want to hear from him. – Oh, I know you thought we were to marry each other, or some such thing, but you're quite wrong. I wouldn't marry him if he came back tomorrow. And what's more he won't come back.'

Aunt Josephine listened and was unconvinced; but as the posts went by and no letter came, a new conviction took hold on her: Roy had deserted the niece as Rory had deserted the aunt.

Martha repudiated the suggestion with disdain. She laughed in Aunt Josephine's face at the idea. Aunt Josephine was the more settled in her conviction. Martha was annoyed and warded off the theme.

Being friended now by Robin, she filled her visits home, never very lengthy, exclusively with him; and hardly lifted a hand to redeem the house from its bondage to Emmeline. One Saturday, however, Emmeline being from home, Robin climbed upon her in such a welter of filth that she cried out in disgust: and looking round the room seemed to see it in a flash of revelation. Her stomach rose. Her blood was up. She felt a raging anger against her mother, a passion of divine intolerance against dirt and disorder. She was possessed of a devil. A tearing energy possessed her and would not let her be. It drove her down a steep place violently. She cried to the boy, 'Come on, Bobbin, we're going to have a grand game!' and had off her frock and was wrapped in a wincey apron in the twinkling of an eye.

She chased the boy, about with a broom. 'Here's a muckle big c'umb,' he cried, running in front of her brush. She swept grimly but with a violence of vitality that allowed her energy for play. The 'muckle big crumb' had his fill of delight. She sent the window roaring wide to the chill air, and pitched a wilderness of rubbish out. The chairs went reeling. She dived savagely beneath the bed. Choked with the dust she shook herself like a terrier. Robin gurgled and shook himself too. Then she got on her knees with a pail of water and scrubbed. 'Flood's coming, Bobbin. On you go!' And the loonie, driven back, made forays on the wet and was driven back again. It was a game for the gods. How they must glory, now and then, in clearing up the mess that mortals leave behind them!

Martha scrubbed and sang. Like her mother she had to be angry to be intolerant of dirt. She was angry now to singing-point. Martha seldom sang, was not in her normal moods a song-bird, and her indulgence over the scrubbing was proof enough that her blood was up. The song she chose was not, strictly speaking, appropriate. It was *Ye Banks and Braes*. But her repertory of songs was limited and it served as well as another.

Martha scrubbed and droned her tune; but her heart went to a larger music than her lips. How clean this scrubbing made one feel! She could scrub to all eternity. A jolly kind of heaven, an eternity of this vehement physical action, that cleared the head and set the body glowing! Wholesome and strong – a cosmic harmony. . . .

'Sae ye're makin' a ceremony o't,' said Emmeline's voice behind her.

'Not on that patch, Bobbin,' Martha cried; and sprang up to face her mother. Bright defiance was in her countenance.

'No, we're making a game of it,' she said.

'A bonny-like thing, a body's goods an' chattels meetin' them at the mou' o' the place, an' the yaird packit an' a'.'

'Oh, *that*,' said Martha. 'What's outside's useless, the lot of it. It's not coming back here. We're making a bonfire of that.'

'Ye can mak a kirk or a mill o't for a' I care,' said Emmeline; and she picked her way across the floor and plumped upon a seat. 'I canna get lived for a sair heid,' she grumbled, plaintively, as though in exoneration of the state of her dwelling. 'Yon Bell Macpherson – she's a tongue that wad deave a dog.'

Martha got on her knees again and wiped the floor. She saw that Emmeline was secretly relieved and would make no commotion.

'Your turn to be scrubbed next, Bobbin,' she said.

They made a game of that too.

'Weel, weel,' said Emmeline, watching. 'Ye're daein' dirdums. Ye've fair been eident.' She kicked her dirty boots off her feet and let them tumble on the floor, where the mud in contact with the damp ran in little spreading streaks. 'An' there's me fylin' the fleer,' she cried; and tossed the boots on to the coal-scuttle. The dirty streaks spread through the damp.

Martha having washed Robin was looking with distaste at his filthy clothing. She rose from her knees and rummaged in all the drawers and boxes.

'Ye'll jist hae to shak' his shirt an' pit it on again,' said Emmeline. 'There's nae anither ane clean.'

Martha turned back from her fruitless search.

'He's going to have some new clothes as soon as ever I've time to make them,' she proclaimed.

'Ye're michty concerned wi' him a' at aince,' said her mother.

'Am I? Well, yes, I am. And I'm going to be concerned with him. He's going to be mine.'

'Weel,' said Emmeline, 'ye micht dae a lot waur nor gie the bairn a shog alang.'

'Once I get home again,' Martha answered, 'he'll maybe get two or three shogs along.' She had had her eye on Robin's table manners and was determined they should improve.

'O ay, we'll a' be gettin' that, I'se warren,' said Emmeline. 'Ye've been that ta'en up wi' yer aunt. But it canna be for muckle langer noo.'

'No,' said Martha. And she wondered what she would find it like to be at home again.

EIGHTEEN

Death of Aunt Josephine

Aunt Josephine grew steadily weaker.

The flaring of her life in September that had sent Aunt Leebie home, died out with the month. By mid-October she was bedded up again, and for good. She was helpless now and could do nothing for herself. It was impossible to leave her alone, and Martha engaged a woman from Beltie to stay with her while she was at school. Aunt Josephine appealed against the sentence, but Martha was obdurate. She marched straight out of the house and found her woman, made her terms and engaged her before she showed face again in Crannochie. She had had no idea she could be so masterful. Something of the security of her handling of Robin seemed to have passed into her relations with other folk. Her old diffidence was gone. The current of her life was running strong and sure; but underground; deeper as yet than her own knowledge.

In the early autumn she was too excited over Robin to give Aunt Josephine much but the *ootlins* of her mind; but one Saturday she bethought herself and took Robin to visit the old lady. He had new clothes now and was very important and in high glee over his excursion. Aunt Josephine was as pleased as the bairn.

'Eh, the littlin,' she said.

And her very tones rejoiced. A kind of song, Martha thought. After that she fetched Robin every Saturday; and every Saturday Aunt Josephine was just as pleased. Her life was shot through with pain now and riddled with sickness.

'Whan we canna dae naething else, we can aye thole,' she would say; and as soon as the pain released her she *cantled* up and told Martha interminable stories from the past; but always when the tales were of Rory Foubister she sighed, looking at Martha with a rueful countenance. Martha read her thought; and at first it annoyed her; till she began to perceive that the old woman suffered. Her grief was deep and tender; the more that it was not for herself. A second time she had seen the promise unfulfilled. Her *Nunc dimittis* was a betrayal.

'Foubister flesh an' blood's nae to lippen till,' she said one evening, sorrowfully, by firelight.

'If only she would understand,' thought Martha. 'She hurts herself.' And she slipped to the floor beside Miss Leggatt's bed and laid one arm gently across the old lady's body.

'But auntie,' she said, 'you mustn't make yourself unhappy over what isn't true. I didn't love Roy. I wouldn't have married him though he had stayed till Doomsday. I don't want to marry him.'

'O ay. O ay,' was all Miss Josephine's rejoinder. She herself had made the same protestations when Rory went away.

Martha sighed a little, and remained where she was on the floor, touching with her strong firm fingers the cold and wrinkled skin of Miss Leggatt's hand. Impossible to disabuse Aunt Josephine. But did she want to disabuse Aunt Josephine? She sat a long time quietly on the floor, leaning against Miss Leggatt, and it seemed to her that the heavens were opened and the spirit of God descended and brooded on the frail and wasted frame of the old woman. She had taken upon herself what she conceived to be the young girl's sorrow and was carrying it. Martha understood that her mistake altered nothing of the grandeur of her action. The strong serenity of life that dwelt in the old woman seemed to possess and inhabit the girl, purchased for her – was it idle to suppose? – by the love and suffering she had divined.

That night she wept into her pillow noiseless and flooding tears, tears without salt in them, that washed the last bitterness from her heart; and in the morning rose and went about her work marvelling at the redemptive vitality of an old woman's misapprehension.

She knew now that her heart-break was of no one's causing, but in the nature of things; that the shame that had

torn her was as wrong as her resentment against Luke; and
the shattering of her selfhood not evil, but the condition of
growth. She had given love and had received only adoration:
and love is so much bigger a thing than adoration – more
complex and terrible. At its absolute moments it holds
resolved within itself all impulses and inconsistencies, the
lust of the flesh, the lust of the eyes, the pride of life, the
spirit's agonizing. Martha seemed to herself that morning to
touch one of its absolute moments. She had no more fear of
what love might do to her.

In the watches of that winter she was closer in spirit to
Aunt Josephine than at any time since she was a little child.
Together they enjoyed Robin and laughed at Clemmie's
upcomes and antics; and upbraided Jeannie Mortimer
(though not to her face) for her treatment of her aged
mother.

'Lattin' her ging aboot a ticket like yon,' said Aunt
Josephine indignantly. 'Jist an objeck. A rickle o' banes. An'
her claes! – patched an' yea-patched. Ye cudna tell the
maisterpiece. Forbye some bits as thin's ye cud pick bird's
meat through them. A tink's mair weel-to-be-seen than
yon.'

'She's not much better to look at herself,' said Martha.
Jeannie's pride of person had been slowly going down before
the advancing tides of her religion.

'Na,' Aunt Josephine agreed. 'It's a gey whilie sin' she
was in-by, bit the hin'most time she cam' I jist sat an' beheld
her. "That's gey-like coats ye've gotten, Jeannie. If ye dinna
sell them ye'll come aff by the loss." "They're gweed eneuch
to pray in, Miss Leggatt." Weel, weel! She's an awfu' wife
wi' her tongue fan she speaks to common fowk like you an'
me, fatever like she be fan she's speakin' to the Lord.'

In November Mary Annie took to her bed. It was not easy
to visit her: Jeannie brooked no interference. For the
intrepid few who entered she prayed in loud and offensive
terms: but on a Sunday she left her mother alone locked in
the cottage, and tramped to town to meet her brethren and
sisters in righteousness.

'See if ye cudna get in,' suggested Aunt Josephine to
Martha.

'Oh, if there's a way in I'll find it,' said she. They giggled together like two conspirators. 'There's an upstairs window open,' said Martha after reconnoitring. 'I'll have a shot at it.'

Aunt Josephine was like a lassie again at the idea. Many was the time she had clambered in at windows. 'I was a wild limmer,' she said, 'aye at some prank or ither. – But dinna fleg the auld body,' she added.

Martha got on the roof from the branches of a tree and squeezed her thin body through the window. In the kitchen Mary Annie looked at her with bleared and uncomprehending eyes. After what seemed a long time she began to understand who Martha was and what she wanted. 'Miss Josephine's terrible kind,' she said. Then clutching Martha's arm, in an importunate whisper and pointing with a claw-like finger at the dresser, 'Tak it doon,' she said. 'Tak it doon. I wad richt like a haud o'it for a meenutie. Tak it doon.'

Martha tried the japanned tea-caddy, but it was not that. She tried the blue kiln-cracked sauce-boat, and the greedy glitter in Mary Annie's eyes told her she was right.

In the sauce-boat was a wedding-ring.

Mary Annie grabbed it from her and began rubbing it gently with her hand. Martha noticed that her wedding finger was bare.

'I tint it,' she said. 'I tint it mair nor aince, an' it cudna be gotten. She thinks I dinna ken that she's gotten't, bit I ken fine. She disna want me to ken case be I tine't again. I'm an auld dane craitur, ma finger's awa' to naething – it aye slippit aff.'

She had put the ring in its place and was twisting it round and round, touching it with light caressing fingers. There was love in the movement.

'Dinna bide,' she said after a minute to Martha. 'Dinna bide. She micht come hame. Hae.' And she pulled the ring off and held it out. 'Pit it back again. Pit it jist faur it wis afore.'

Pity and indignation rushed upon Martha.

'Why should you put it back?' she asked. 'She's no right to keep it from you. It's yours. You keep it. She needn't know.'

'I micht tine't again,' said Mrs. Mortimer. 'I'm a peer dane body, I canna anger Jeannie. She's that gweed – she's ower gweed for the likes o' me.'

Martha put the ring in the sauce-boat and the sauce-boat on the dresser, exactly as she found it; and went away by the upstairs window.

A few days later, having risen early in the morning to give Aunt Josephine a hot-water bottle, she heard a harsh powerful chanting through the still air. She knew at once that it was Jeannie Mortimer. Jeannie was an inconvenient riser. She rose at five in winter, at any hour in summer – 'makin' wark to hersel,' Miss Josephine declared. 'Hain yer licht, Jeannie,' she had said to her once. 'Ye'll be gettin' up the nicht afore or lang.'

Miss Josephine too had heard the singing. Jeannie's psalms and spiritual songs rent the morning air frequently. 'She's coorse,' said Miss Leggatt, 'raryin' aboot the hoose at this time i' the mornin' an' keepin' her mither fae her sleep. Peer auld stock, I'm hairt-sorry for her. Ging ower, Matty, an' speir if there's onything she wad like.'

Martha demurred. At that hour in the morning, to penetrate the arcana of the Babylon inhabited by Jeannie! But perceiving that Aunt Josephine was set on it ('Though she does pray for yer soul,' said Miss Leggatt, 'it wunna dae ye nae ill.') she humoured her and went.

The raucous singing dropped suddenly as she approached, and she knew that she had been seen. Through the deathly silence that followed she stood uncertain in the raw grey air. At last she tried the door. It gave and she pushed it open. A gabble reached her ear, and looking in she saw Jeannie on her knees in the middle of the floor, unsupported by any furniture, gesticulating to the Almighty. At the eddy of chill air she raised her voice, spluttering and screaming her frenzied ejaculations. Martha closed the door and waited. The thin knob of greyish hair, the great boots sticking out behind, the clumsy evolutions of her powerful frame, the clutching skinny hands, the strident voice – all seemed the crude material for some grinning modern caricature of death.

As the prayer continued, Martha walked past Jeannie and spoke to Mrs Mortimer.

'She's terrible kind, is Miss Josephine, terrible kind,' said the old done voice – 'extinct,' Martha thought – ' Naething, naething. Jeannie there – she's ower gweed for the likes o' me. She's prayed for me. There was a while she wadna dae't – I wisna gweed eneuch for her.'

Her habitual expression was unchanged, but the horrible graven stare of anxiety had become a mask. She was secure in Jeannie's prayers.

Late that night Mary Annie died. Aunt Josephine was great-hearted, and talked of her own end. She bade Martha take the feather-stitched nightgown from its drawer and hold it up for her to see. It was flecked with mould. 'Ye'll need to air it,' she said. 'I cudna lie quaet in ony but that.'

'But it's so narrow,' Martha was thinking; and she was heart-sick, looking down upon the old woman's body swollen and monstrous with disease.

'Ye canna pit that on her,' said Clemmie, coming in aboot as she shook it in the sun and wind.

'I have to say I will, or she'll be miserable.'

'Ach,' said Clemmie, 'slit it up the back an' stap it in ahin. She'll never be a penny the wiser an' her deid.'

Alive still, Miss Leggatt regarded the nightgown with a jealous eye; though once she had seen it comfortably airing by the fire, her talk was but little on the grave. There was too much else to be interested in.

The back-end of the year was open, kindly to unwell folk. A dead November, heavy-skied; but the year went out in sunshine, after weeks of warm uncertain winds. Aunt Josephine had seen another new year, and she liked it. She sat a little higher up in bed. 'I've diddled you all yet,' said the wrinkles round her mouth. She had the same complacent serenity over her doing as when she set out so long ago for Birleybeg and left Martha dinnerless and forlorn. There was no question at all as to the absolute rightness of her continuing to live. The world was hers and the fulness thereof, and she had no intention of giving it up.

And such mornings January brought! A sky of silver-point, the east like mellowed ivory. Floating in saffron, the morning star was there and gone. No breath of wind: but gusty, blowing from one tree to another, the song of the blackbirds.

Later a powdery sunlight filled the room, irradiating the feathery *caddis* from the blankets that had drifted into corners. The *steer* of life floated in from the road. Hens cackled, dogs barked, women scolded, crying on their bairns in sharp resonant voices that carried far through the empty winter air. Peter Mennie stamped along the road with the post-bag, his greeting still in the air when already the echoes of his voice clanged up from Drochety. The *littlins* bickered past from school, chasing cats and hens, flinging stones, calling names after an occasional stranger or carrying on for his benefit a loud and important conversation mainly fictitious. And the bigger the loons, with stolen *spunks* that had all but burned holes in their *pooches* through the day, fired the whins along the roadside. Prometheus with a vulture indeed! – They tortured the wrong side of his body, those undiscriminating gods. A good old-fashioned *skilping* would have served the nickum better. What had he to do with anything as sophisticated as a liver?

The crackle of the flame reached Aunt Josephine's ear, the pungent odour of the burning delighted her nostril. Sometimes the flame would roar up, towering into view beyond the dyke; but for the most part the laddies were cautious and struck no matches till they were round the bend and out of sight of the clachan. But there were other fires to see as the year wore on – all the cleansing and renewing fires of an out-of-door winter, fires of refuse, whin fires, heather fires. All up and down the valley they were visible, long trails of smoke blowing the one way, smudged brown thinning to blue, lit with the sun; or soft and inconspicuous like morning mists. At night an eye of fire would wink – elemental, evil, uncanny, on the homely land.

And in the dusk Drochety's two pair of horse clumped home, young Drochety himself on the offhand beast of the first pair, whistling like a mavis and always first to *louse*; the hired man with the second pair, dour and silent.

There were crows too, vivid black eddies of them, and sometimes a ploughshare of wild ducks flew overhead. And when the wind rose and blew from the south, the smell of the new-turned earth went about Aunt Josephine's heart.

As though anyone, thirled to pain and days and nights of sickness notwithstanding, could possibly want to leave a world like that!

That January Martha loved the earth as she had never loved it before. Her pilgrimages in the growing and waning light, to and from school, were exquisite initiations. On the homeward way she loitered, steeping herself in the life of earth and air. Once, at the head of the brae, she saw the brown ploughed field stretch out, empty and dark against a golden afterglow; but turning to look back on it she saw a plough left in the furrow, catching the glow and gleaming. It seemed to focus for her the life of the soil. And once she had a far-off glimpse of Geordie, in a steep field some distance from the road. She watched the horses straining up the furrow, back and neck one rigid line. She watched them turn. Then horses and plough and man were swallowed up in the darkness at the far end of the field, against the upturned earth and the blur of wood. Only when the team swung round and their white foreheads and noses glimmered through the brown could she distinguish where they were. It was surely impossible that Geordie could see longer to cut the furrow; but his eyes had been bent so long upon the darkness of the earth that he seemed to share its life, know his way with it by touch. Martha brooded, her eyes on the slow sombre darkening; then lifted them and saw the arch of sky. When she looked again her father and his team were blotted out, one with the earth.

She thought, 'I've come from him.' She too was at one with the earth. 'I'd like to follow a plough,' she thought: and she laughed, 'What boots I'd have! – and what legs I'd have! and what a back!' and shook herself and hastened home.

In middle February snow began to fall – few and irresolute flakes.

'The snaw's comin' doon as if it didna care gin it cam' doon or no,' said Geordie. 'There'll be a terrible storm.'

Next day each bough and telegraph wire and paling post was piled with snow, light, fluffed, that seemed to float in air rather than lie upon substantial surfaces. Then the wind rose; for two days there was *blin' drift*; and the wind went as it came, leaving the roads choked and the sky blown bare. Frost followed. Martha's hands were chapped and *tangles* hung from the cottage eaves. Aunt Josephine shivered and shrank within herself. Her face grew smaller, disproportionate above the bloated horror of her body; her hands shrivelled and were deadly cold to the touch.

'She's geal cauld,' said the woman who noticed her when Martha came in glowing and breathless from her long tussle through the storm.

'She may go at any minute now,' the doctor said.

The sisters were again summoned.

They came: Aunt Margot and Uncle Webster in the Ford over roads that were *byous coorse*. Uncle Webster sat in the kitchen and talked in a loud assertive voice of the hazards of the journey – the block, the digging out, the skidding upon icy braes. *Ben the hoose* Aunt Margot stood with Jean and Leebie, and gazed melancholy on Josephine's grim and yellow face.

'She's nae takin' nae notice,' said Leebie. 'She's oot amon't a' thegither.' Josephine, as though to repudiate the libel, looked up and became aware of her sisters.

'Ye're come to see me dee,' she said. 'Sit ye doon. – Na, na. Sit faur I can see ye. An' Matty – faur's Matty? Bid Matty come an' see me dee.'

Leebie called Matty through.

Martha found her aunts in a row upon the sofa; and at Aunt Josephine's peremptory command sat herself down beside them.

'I'm jist hingin' on by the brears o' the e'e,' Aunt Josephine said.

A silence fell upon the room. The aunts breathed hard. Once Leebie sniftered; and once snow slurred upon the roof and thudded *reeshling* to the ground. 'Fresh,' Martha thought, 'what roads there'll be.' Aunt Josephine seemed to doze. No one spoke or stirred; but Leebie sniftered for the second time.

Aunt Josephine looked sharply up. She had always hated a snifter. Her eye fell upon the row of sisters – an ironic antagonistic eye.

'Fat are ye sittin' there glowerin' at me for like a puckle

craws a' in a raw?' she demanded; and fixing her eye upon her youngest sister, 'Leebie,' she said in a reproachful voice, 'are ye nae ga'in to dee afore me yet?'

'She fair sorted me, glowerin' like yon,' said Leebie afterwards.

Aunt Margot too thought it well to shelter from the glower. She had done her duty by Josephine (though she had not seen her die) and departed with Uncle Webster in the Ford.

Aunt Jean and Aunt Leebie slept in the kitchen bed. 'It's a sort of eternal recurrence,' thought Martha as she lay down on the sofa in Aunt Josephine's room. 'We do the same things again and again.' She was to waken Aunt Jean at two in the morning and take her place in bed for the remainder of the night: but a little after twelve she came to the kitchen, hurriedly, and shook Leebie, who was nearest the door. 'She's going, I think. You'd better come.'

Leebie got out of bed and began to pull on some clothes, but pausing for a moment to meditate on mortality, from very weariness fell asleep at the bedside. Waking again with a start, she envisaged in horror her unfaithfulness; but deciding, with the optimism of the sleeper, that her nap could have lasted only a matter of seconds, she resolved to say nothing of the delay to Jean; and rousing her with a stern serenity she made her way across the passage to fulfil her sober task.

Thus it came about that when Leebie thrust her head fearfully round the door-cheek, she was met by the extraordinary apparition of Aunt Josephine sitting up in bed and clutching an egg-cup to her bosom with one claw-like hand, while she supped the contents of the egg with vigour: having cantled up during Martha's absence from the room, and decided on her return that she would enjoy a little nourishment. Thus also it came about that Leebie, withdrawing her head hastily from the doorway, met the further apparition of Mrs. Corbett ghastly in candle-gleam and white nightgown and fallen puckered mouth without its garnishing of teeth, and clutching her by the arm whispered vehemently, 'Faith, Jean, she wunna dee.'

After two days Mrs. Corbett departed. She was uneasy.

The routine of Muckle Arlo required her, and Josephine apparently did not.

Leebie remained and dottled in and out as before.

On the fourth day the doctor thought her gone: but she *warstled* through and spoke in weak uncertain syllables.

'She can't last the night,' he said.

'If onything happens, than, doctor,' said Leebie, whose habit of mind was dependent, 'we'll jist send for you.'

He shook his head. 'There's nothing I can do,' he said, 'nor yet anyone else. I'll come back first thing in the morning,' he said, 'and bring the death certificate with me. Her fight's done.'

It had been a magnificent fight, he reflected. She had the quality of life in her that the antagonists in ballad and in saga must have had – dour, obstinate, invulnerable; withstanding the repeated hack and shock of battle.

In the morning Aunt Josephine was drinking tea.

'Weel, doctor,' she said genially, 'I'm aye livin', an' livin' like.'

'Ay, ay, and so you are,' he answered her, marvelling when the epic would end. He carried the death certificate away again in his pocket. He carried it for five days, because Josephine Leggatt, seventy-nine years of age, and grievously afflicted with cancer, would not die.

In the end she died swiftly and unexpectedly, having rallied a little just before and spoken in a loud and firm voice.

The following week, on the second day of March, Martha went home to Wester Cairns. Aunt Josephine had left her her house and what money she possessed: which was more than she had allowed folk to suppose. Martha might have made her abode at Crannochie and ordered her life and surroundings at her pleasure. She was tempted sometimes so to do. A few months before she would hardly have hesitated; but now there was Robin. He wiled her back. Afterwards, perhaps, when he was older . . . and her mind rioted across the future. She meant to educate Robin. He was now two years and two months old, and already his mind was alert and his speech engaging. Another game for the gods was ahead of her.

So she went home.

NINETEEN

The Pillars of Hercules

'You must thraw her neck for me,' said Martha, crossing from the hen-house with a plump Rhode Island Red under her arm.

'Fairly that,' Geordie answered; and having despatched the business added, 'Ye'll need to larn to dae't yersel.'

'I can manage the cockerels,' said Martha, laughing, 'but I haven't strength of grip for that big fat duchess.'

'Ay, ay, she's a fair size. A bit o' the packin' o' that and a new tattie wad wark awa' fine.'

'Just you wait till Sunday then, and you shall have it.'

Geordie stood with an admirer's eye upon the fat breast of the fowl, holding her out from him until her spasms of involuntary twitching were over. Martha watched, breathing the clean sweet air of a July morning. When she raised her head she saw the wet fields and the soft gleam of the river. 'How fresh it is,' she said.

'Ay, ay,' answered her father, still holding the hen. 'It's a grand thing to get leave to live.'

Martha took the hen, which had stopped twitching, plucked it and hung it in the shed. On Sunday Luke and Dussie were coming to dinner, with their fifteen-month-old son, her name-child Ronnie. It was three years since they had parted. Now they were coming to spend their holiday in the cottage at Crannochie that had been Aunt Josephine's. Later Martha was to let it and use the money for Robin's education.

'Them that disna like hen can just tak want,' Emmeline declared triumphantly, setting the ashet on the table with an air that proclaimed her utter incredulity in anyone's not liking hen. 'We'll gar Matty divide. She's grand at dividin'.' And she pushed the ashet towards her daughter, deranging Martha's carefully appointed table.

'She's some sair birstled, mither,' said Geordie with an eye on the dish.

'I thocht ye likit it like that.'

'O ay, ay. I div that. But there's mair nor me to be considered.'

'We like it bristled too,' cried Dussie smiling.

'Birstled, lassie,' said Geordie, coming out with a great roar of laughter at the mispronunciation. 'Ay, ay, I mind fine. You were aye the ane for the birstled bits oot o' the pots.'

'An' mony's the skilpin' ye didna get for't,' said Emmeline.

'I know. Marty got half my skilpings and scoldings, I think.'

'Weel, weel,' said Geordie benignly, 'she's been skilpit the richt gait ony road – she can mak grand packin' till a hen. We'll hae a bittie mair o't, lassie, jist to help awa' wi't, like.' And he held out his plate for a second helping of oatmeal stuffing.

He helped away with it to such good purpose that at the end of the meal he pushed his chair back, *pechin'*. 'I'm fair stappit fu'.'

'Ye'll need to sit an' swage a while, than,' said Emmeline.

'We'll ging oot to the doors, than.' They sat in the July afternoon, idly, till Dussie said, drowsily, her baby asleep in her arms, 'This is perfect. I couldn't move for toffee. But Luke's aching for a walk. Do go with him, Marty.'

Watching Martha, and feeling (though she did not reason it out) her gay strong assurance, the poise of her whole nature, Dussie had been thinking, cheerfully, 'She's got over it. Of course she would.'

Luke too had been watching Martha. He knew life better now and was less sure of his theories; but until he saw her again he had continued to think of her as of spirit. Now he understood that he was wrong. She too had understood that this was no demi-god but a man; and there fell between them a constraint that neither knew how to break.

Watching her, Luke thought, *A sword of Spain, the ice-brook's temper*; and suddenly the lightning that had blinded him for a moment when he held Dussie weeping in his arms, lit up his universe from end to end. He knew now that passion had gone to the making of this new Martha and for the first time he realized that it might be for him. The blood thudded in his temples. His thoughts were in confusion. A thousand meanings were in the air and he dared grasp at none. The brightness of the blade turned him back.

He began to tell her of his work in Liverpool. For both of them the afternoon was inconclusive. Life was stranger than they had supposed. Of the two Martha was the happier: she had acquiesced in her destiny and so delivered herself from the insecurity of the adventurer. *Sail not beyond the Pillars of Hercules.*

As they neared the house a gentle rain was falling. It sent the idlers in. The kitchen was filled with their clatter, till Emmeline cried, 'Haud the lang tongues o' ye or I see if ma kettle's bilin',' and made the tea.

And they all drew in about their chairs and ate.

Glossary

Ablach, tiny undersized creature
anent, over against, concerning
antrin, one here and there
aweirs o', inclined to
barkit, covered as with bark, peeled
begeck, set-back
ben the hoose, inside, further into the house or next room
besom, hussy
birse, vb., to force, press upwards; *n.*, *to have one's birse up*, one's temper roused
birstled, cooked till hard and crisp
blake, cockroach, beetle
blate, shy, diffident
blaud, dirty, soil
blin' drift, drifting snow
bog-jaaveled, completely at a loss
bourrach, small group, swarm
bow-hoched, bow-legged
brear, first small blade appearing above the ground; *brears o' the e'e*, eyelashes
broch, halo
brook, soot
buckie, limpet
bung; *ta'en the bung*, taken offence
byous, beyond the ordinary
caddis, dust, fluff
ca'ed, driven
canalye, Fr. *canaille*
cantle up, perk up
chappit, (thumb), hacked
chau'mer, chamber, bothy
cloor, blow
clorted, covered with mud
clyte, fall

collieshangie, disputatious gathering
coorse, bad
connach, ruin
contermashious, contradictory, obstinate
creish, fat
crined, shrunk, shrivelled
curran, a number
dambrod, chess-board
dander, to have one's dander up, temper roused
deave, deafen, torment with insistence
dicht wipe
dingin' on, raining or snowing hard
dird, strike a blow
dirdums, daein' dirdums, doing great things
dirl, tingle, vibrate
doit, small copper coin
dowie, spiritless
drookit, soaked, drowned
drummlie, physically upset
dubbit, covered with mud
dubs, mud
dwam, faint, swoon
e'e, e'en, eye, eyes
eident, diligent
ettlin', desirous after
f=wh
  fa, who; *fan*, when; *fat*, what; *faur*, where
fairin', present from the fair
fash yersel, put yourself to trouble
ferlies, wonders
fey, beside oneself
ficher, fumble nervously

211

flan, gust
foo, how
forfoch'en, exhausted, fought done
fleg, fright, frighten
flist, storm of temper
fou', drunk
ful, proud
fyle, soil, dirty
gait, way
gar, make
geal-cauld, ice-cold
geet, child
gey, used as an intensive
geylies, considerable
gin, if
girn, fret
girse, grass
gomeril, fool
gorbals, nestlings
graip, fork (for land work)
greet, weep
guff, smell
gumption, sense, vigour, initiative
gype, stupid person
gyte, ga'en gyte, gone out of one's
    mind
halarackit, high-spirited, rowdy
    without offensiveness
hantle, a good deal
hain, save, spare
hairst, harvest.
heelster-gowdie, upside down
hippit, stiff in the hips
hirple, limp
hotter, boil vigorously
howff, draught
howk, dig
hurdies, hips
ill-fashioned, inquisitive
ingan, onion
jaloose, guess, suspect
kink-hoast, whooping-cough
kowk, retch
lave, rest
legammachy, long story without
    much in it
leuch, laughed
limmer, hussy
lippen, trust

loon, boy, young man
louse, loose, unharness
lowe, blaze
lug, ear
mavis, song thrush
mowse, right (with sense of Latin
    fas), *nae mowse, nefas*, uncanny
neips, turnips
nieve, fist
nimsch, fragment
nowt, cattle
nyatter, nag
ootlin, outsider, outcast
or, before
oxter, arm-pit, *vb.*, to put the arm
    round
pech, sigh
penurious, particular, ill to please
pooches, pockets
preens, pins, fir-needles
puddock, frog
pyockie, poke, bag
raivelled, confused
rary, go about noisily, clamour
reeshle, rustle
rickle, a structure put loosely
    together, loose heap
rive, tear asunder
roarie-bummlers, (noisy blunderers)
    storm clouds
rug, pull
sair, sore
scalin', dispersing
scunnered, disgusted
scutter awa', do things slowly and
    not very thoroughly
shaltie, pony
sharger, runt
sharn, dung
sheen, shoes
shog, push
skellochin', shrieking
skirp, splatter
sklype, clumsy worthless person
smeddum, vigour of intellect
sonsy, of generous proportions
soo, sow
sotter, untidy mess
sowens, a kind of fine-meal porridge.

spangin', walking vigorously
speir, ask
spunk, match
stap, stuff
steekit, shut
stew, dust
sumph, heavy lout
swack, free, not stiff
swage, loosen, make easy
sweir, lazy
'angle, icicle, seaweed
teem, empty
teen, temper, mood

thole, endure
thraw, to wring; *thrawn*, obstinate
thrums, scraps of thread
tine, loose; *tint*, lost
trauchle, n. , trouble, heavy toil
tyauve, struggle
whammlin', jogging
warstle, wrestle
waucht, draught
wersch, without savour, insipid
whin, gorse, furze bush
yird, vb., to give a blow

The Canons are books without boundaries.
Some are classics already, the rest will be soon.

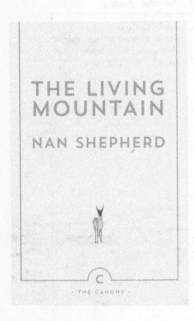

'A blazingly brilliant writer, a true original'
Robert Macfarlane

CANON❙GATE